Praise for the *Teardrop* saga

'If you loved the *Fallen* series, you are going to fall head over heels for this epic new saga' *Sugarscape*

'An emotional tale with a mystical twist. Just. Read. It.' *Bliss*

'Full of romance, dark magic and danger' *Booktrust*

'*Teardrop* is one of those books that will keep you up until the early hours reading. I just couldn't get enough! It was riveting, fast paced, enjoyable and exciting. I definitely recommend it!' *uncorkedthoughts.blogspot*

'Fans will dive in eagerly' *Booklist*

'Epic' *Teen Now*

Also by Lauren Kate:

TEARDROP
LAST DAY OF LOVE: A TEARDROP STORY
(ebook short story)

The FALLEN series:
FALLEN
TORMENT
PASSION
RAPTURE
FALLEN IN LOVE

THE BETRAYAL OF NATALIE HARGROVE

Waterfall

LAUREN KATE

CORGI BOOKS

WATERFALL
A CORGI BOOK: 978 0 552 56752 7

First published in Great Britain by Doubleday,
an imprint of Random House Children's Publishers UK
A Penguin Random House Company

Penguin
Random House
UK

Doubleday edition published 2014
Corgi edition published 2015

1 3 5 7 9 10 8 6 4 2

Text copyright © Lauren Kate, 2014
Jacket photography copyright © Elena Kalis, 2014
Lettering copyright © Patrick Knowles, 2014

Penguin Random House is committed to a sustainable future for
our business, our readers and our planet. This book is made from
Forest Stewardship Council® certified paper.
Set in Simoncini Garamond

MIX
Paper from
responsible sources
FSC
www.fsc.org   FSC® C016897

Corgi Books are published by Random House Children's Publishers UK
61–63 Uxbridge Road, London W5 5SA

www.**randomhousechildrens**.co.uk
www.**totallyrandombooks**.co.uk
www.**randomhouse**.co.uk

Addresses for companies within The Random House Group Limited can be found at:
www.randomhouse.co.uk/offices.htm

THE RANDOM HOUSE GROUP Limited Reg. No. 954009

A CIP catalogue record for this book is available from the British Library.

Printed and bound in Great Britain by CPI Group (UK) Ltd, Croydon, CR0 4YY

For Venice

It's satisfying to think
that the weight of the ocean
and the weight of meaning
could be in some way connected.

—JOE WENDEROTH,
"THE WEIGHT OF WHAT IS THROWN"

1

THE THIRD TEAR

The sky wept. Sorrow flooded the earth.

Starling opened her mouth to catch the raindrops falling through the hole in her cordon. The Seedbearer's transparent sanctuary was pitched over the bonfire like a camper's cozy tent. It sealed out the deluge, except for the small opening at the top meant to vent the fire's smoke and admit a sample of the rain.

Starling smacked her lips, probing the rain for something else. She closed her eyes and rolled the rain over her tongue like a sommelier sampling wine. She could not yet taste Atlantean spires interrupting sky. She could not taste the edges of Atlas, the Evil One.

This was good but confusing. Tears shed by the Tearline girl were meant to bring Atlantis back. Preventing those tears' fall had been the Seedbearers' single objective.

They had failed.

And what had happened? The flood was here, but where was its ruler? Eureka had brought the horse but not its rider. Had the Tearline swerved? Had something gone wrong in the right way?

Starling hunched over the fire and studied her nautical charts. Teardrops streamed down the cordon walls in sheets, accentuating the warmth and brightness of the citronella-scented space inside. If Starling had been someone else, she might have curled up with a mug of cocoa and a novel, let the rain lull her into another world.

If Starling had been someone else, old age would have killed her millennia ago.

It was midnight in the Kisatchie National Forest in central Louisiana. Starling had been waiting for the others since midday. She knew they would come, though they had not discussed this location. The girl had wept so suddenly. Her flood dispersed the Seedbearers along this vile new marsh, and there had been no time to plan their regrouping. But here was where it would happen.

Yesterday, before Eureka cried, this site had sat a hundred and fifty miles from the Gulf. Now it was a shard of disappearing coastline. The bayou—its banks, dirt roads, dance halls, twisting live oak trees, antebellum mansions, and pickup trucks—lay entombed in a sea of selfish tears.

And somewhere out there swam Ander, in love with the girl who'd done this. Resentment brewed inside Starling when she thought of the boy's betrayal.

Beyond the flame's glow, against the sideways rain, a shape emerged from the forest. Critias wore his cordon like a slicker, indiscernible to any but Seedbearer eyes. Starling thought he looked smaller. She knew what he was thinking:

What went wrong? Where is Atlas? Why are we still alive?

When he reached the edge of Starling's cordon, Critias paused. Both of them braced for the rough blast that would signal their cordons joining.

The moment of their union struck like lightning. Starling crossed her arms to withstand the gale; Critias squeezed his hands before the fire. She had coordinated what her taste buds told her with her charts. "Most of Manhattan, all of the Gulf—"

"Wait for the others." Critias nodded into the darkness. "They are here."

Chora staggered toward them from the east, Albion from the west, the storm glancing off their cordons. They approached Starling's cordon and stiffened, girding themselves for the unpleasant entry. When Starling's cordon had absorbed them, Chora looked away and Starling knew her cousin didn't want to risk feeling nostalgic or pathetic. She didn't want to risk feeling. It was how she had lived for thousands of years, never looking or feeling older than mortal middle-aged.

"Starling is listing the fallen lands," Critias said.

"It doesn't matter." Albion sat down. His silver hair was soaked, his neat gray suit now mud-stained and torn.

"A million deaths don't matter?" Critias asked. "Didn't you see her tears' destruction on your journey here? You have always said we were the protectors of the Waking World."

"What matters now is Atlas!"

Starling looked away, embarrassed by Albion's outburst, though she shared his vexation. For thousands of years the Seedbearers had struggled to prevent the rise of an enemy they had never met in the flesh. Long had they suffered the projections of his terrible mind.

Imprisoned in the sunken realm of the Sleeping World,

Atlas and his kingdom neither aged nor died. If Atlantis rose, its residents would be restored to life exactly as they had been when their island sank. Atlas would be a strapping man of twenty years, at the zenith of his youthful power. The Rising would make time begin again for him.

He would be free to pursue the Filling.

But until Atlantis rose, the only things stirring in the Sleeping World were dreaming, scheming, sickened minds. Over time Atlas's mind had made many dark voyages into the Waking World. Whenever a girl met the conditions of the Tearline, Atlas's mind worked to be near her, to draw tears from her eyes that would restore his reign. Right now he was inside the girl's friend Brooks.

The Seedbearers were the only ones who recognized Atlas each time he possessed the body of a person close to the Tearline girl. Atlas had never succeeded—partly because the Seedbearers had murdered thirty-six Tearline girls before Atlas could provoke them into weeping. Still, each one of his visits brought his unique evil into the Waking World.

"We are all remembering the same dark things," Albion said. "If Atlas's mind has been this destructive inside other bodies, waging wars and murdering innocents, imagine his mind and body joined, awake, and in our world. Imagine if he succeeds in the Filling."

"So then," Chloe said, "where is he? What is he waiting for?"

"I don't know." Albion tightened his fist over the fire until the smell of burning flesh alerted him to move it. "We were all there. We saw her cry!"

Starling thought back to that morning. When Eureka's tears fell, her sorrow had seemed bottomless, as if it would never end. It had seemed that each tear shed would multiply the damage to the world tenfold—

"Wait," she said. "Once the conditions of her prophecy were met, three tears needed to fall."

"The girl was a blubbering mess." Albion dismissed her. No one took Starling seriously. "Obviously, the three required tears were shed."

"And then some." Chora looked up at the rain.

Critias scratched the silver stubble on his chin. "Are we sure?"

There was a pause, and a burst of thunder. Rain spat through the cordon's hole.

"One tear to shatter the Waking World's skin." Critias softly sang the line from the Chronicles, passed down by their forefather Leander. "That's the tear that would have started the flood."

"A second to seep through Earth's roots within." Starling could taste the spreading of the seafloor. She knew the second tear had been shed.

But what about the third, the most essential tear?

"A third to awaken the Sleeping World and let old kingdoms rebegin," four Seedbearers said in unison. That was the tear that mattered. That was the tear that would bring Atlas back.

Starling glanced at the others. "Did the third tear fall to Earth or didn't it?"

"Something must have caught it," Albion muttered. "Her thunderstone, her hands—"

"Ander." Critias cut him off.

Albion's voice was high with nerves. "Even if he did think to catch it, he wouldn't know what to do with it."

"He is with her now, not us," Chora said. "If the third tear was shed and captured, the boy controls its destiny. Ander doesn't know the Tearline is tied to a lunar cycle. He won't be prepared for Atlas, who will stop at nothing to get the third tear before the next full moon—"

"Starling," Albion said sharply. "Where has the wind taken Ander and Eureka?"

Starling drew in her tongue, chewed and swallowed, belched softly. "She is shielded by the stone. I can barely taste her, but I believe Ander travels east."

"It is obvious where he has gone," Chora said, "and whom he has gone looking for. Outside of the four of us, only one knows the answers Ander and Eureka seek."

Albion glowered into the fire. When he exhaled, the blaze doubled in size.

"Forgive me." He took a measured inhale to tame the fire. "When I think of Solon . . ." He bared his teeth, stifled something nasty. "I am fine."

Starling had not heard the name of the lost Seedbearer spoken in many years.

7

"But Solon is lost," she said. "Albion searched and could not find him—"

"Perhaps Ander will look harder," Critias said.

Albion grasped Critias by the neck, lifted him off his feet, and held him over the fire. "Do you think I have not been looking for Solon since the moment he fled? I would age another century in exchange for finding him."

Critias kicked air. Albion freed him. They straightened their clothes.

"Calm, Albion," Chora said. "Do not succumb to old rivalries. Ander and Eureka must come up for air sometime. Starling will discern their location."

"The question is," Critias said, "will Atlas discern their location first? In the body of Brooks, he will have ways to draw her out."

Lightning flashed around the cordon. Water lapped the Seedbearers' ankles.

"We must find some way to take advantage." Albion glared into the fire. "Nothing is as powerful as her tears. Ander cannot be the one in possession of such power. He is not like us."

"We must focus on what we know," Chora said. "We know Ander has told Eureka that if one Seedbearer dies, all Seedbearers die."

Starling nodded; this was the truth.

"We know he is protecting her from us using our artemisia, which would exterminate all of us if any of us were to inhale it." Chora strummed her lips with her fingers. "Eureka won't use the artemisia. She loves Ander too much to kill him."

"Today she loves him," Critias said. "Name one thing more mercurial than a teenage girl's emotions."

"She loves him." Starling puckered her lips. "They are in love. I taste it on the wind around this rain."

"Good," Chora said.

"How can love be good?" Starling was surprised.

"One must love to have one's heart broken. Heartbreak causes tears."

"One more tear hits Earth and Atlantis rises," Starling said.

"But what if we gained possession of Eureka's tears before Atlas could reach her?" Chora let the question seep into the others.

A smile filtered onto Albion's face. "Atlas would need us to complete the rise."

"He would find us very valuable," Chora said.

Starling flicked a slug of mud from a pleat on her dress. "You are suggesting we align ourselves with *Atlas*?"

"I believe Chora is suggesting that we blackmail the Evil One." Critias laughed.

"Call it what you like," Chora said. "It's a plan. We track Ander, take possession of any tears; perhaps we generate more. Then we use them to seduce Atlas, who will have us to thank for the great gift of his freedom."

Thunder rattled the earth. Black smoke twisted up out of the cordon's vent.

"You're insane," Critias said.

"She's a genius," Albion said.

"I'm afraid," Starling said.

"Fear is for losers." Chora sat on her haunches and stoked the fire with a wet stick. "How much time until the full moon?"

"Ten nights," Starling said.

"Time enough"—Albion smirked into the distance—"for everything to change in the last word."

2

LANDFALL

The silver surface of the ocean danced above Eureka's head. Her legs fluttered toward it—the urge to pass from water into air was irresistible—but she stopped herself.

This wasn't the warm Vermilion Bay back home. Eureka was treading inside a transparent sphere in a dark, chaotic ocean on the other side of the world. The sphere and the voyage Eureka had made in it were possible because of the thunderstone pendant she wore around her neck. Eureka had inherited the thunderstone when her mother, Diana, died, but she'd only recently discovered its magic: when she wore the necklace underwater, a balloon-shaped sphere bloomed around her.

The reason the thunderstone shield encased her now bewildered Eureka. She had done the one thing she was not supposed to do. She had cried.

She'd grown up knowing tears were forbidden, a betrayal to Diana, who had slapped Eureka the last time she'd cried, eight years before, when she was nine and her parents split up.

Never, ever cry again.

But Diana had never told her why.

Then she died, sending Eureka on a quest for answers. She discovered that her unshed tears were connected to a world trapped beneath the ocean. If that Sleeping World rose, it would destroy the Waking World, her world, which she was learning to love.

She couldn't help what happened next. She had stepped into her backyard to find her four-year-old twin siblings, William and Claire, beaten and gagged by monsters that called themselves Seedbearers. She had watched Dad's second wife, Rhoda, die trying to save the twins. She had lost her oldest friend, Brooks, to a force too dark to fathom.

The tears came. Eureka wept.

It was a deluge. The storm clouds in the sky and the bayou behind her house joined with her sorrow and exploded. Everything and everyone had been swept up in a wild, new salty sea. Miraculously, the thunderstone shield had also saved the lives of the people she cared about most.

Eureka looked at them now, pitching unsteadily beside her. William and Claire in their matching Superman pajamas. Her once-dashing father, Trenton, with his lightning-struck heart yearning for the wife who'd fallen from the sky like a raindrop made of blood and bone. Eureka's friend Cat, whom she'd never seen look so afraid. And the boy who with one magic kiss the night before had gone from crush to confidant—Ander.

Eureka's shield had saved them from drowning, but Ander was the one who'd guided them across the ocean, toward what he promised was sanctuary. Ander was a Seedbearer, but he didn't want to be. He had turned away from his cruel family, toward Eureka, vowing to help her. As a Seedbearer, his breath, called a Zephyr, was mightier than the strongest wind. It had carried them across the Atlantic at an impossible speed.

Eureka had no idea how long the journey had taken, or how far they had come. At this depth, the ocean was unchangingly dark and cold, and Cat's cell phone, the only one that had made it into the shield, had died a while ago. All Eureka had to measure time were the white creases at the corners of Cat's mouth, the rumbling of Dad's stomach, and Claire's crouching squat dance, which meant she really had to pee.

Ander propelled the shield closer to the surface with a crawl stroke. Eureka was eager to break free of the shield and terrified of what she'd find on the other side. The world had changed. Her tears had changed it. Under the ocean, they were safe. Above it, they could drown.

Eureka held still as Ander brushed a strand of hair from her forehead.

"Almost there," he said.

They had already discussed how they would make landfall. Ander explained the ocean surges would be treacherous, so their exit from the shield had to be calculated. He had stolen a special anchor from the Seedbearers that would grip a rock and steady them—but then they had to pass through the limits of the shield.

Claire was the key. Where everyone else's touch met stone-like resistance, Claire's hands passed through the shield's edges like a wildfire through fog. She bobbed on her heels, swirling her hands against its surface, finger-painting an invisible escape. Her wrists passed in and out of the shield the way ghosts reached through doors.

Without Claire's power, the shield would pop like a bubble when it crested the surface and touched air. Everyone inside it would be scattered like ashes across the sea.

So once Ander found a suitable rock, Claire would become their pioneer. Her hands would pass through the shield and hook the anchor on the stone. Until the others were ashore, Claire's arms would remain partway in and partway out of the shield, keeping it open for their passage, keeping it from shattering on the wind.

"Don't worry, William," Claire told her brother, who was older by nine minutes. "I'm magic."

"I know." William sat cross-legged in Cat's lap on the translucent floor of the shield, picking pills off his pajamas. Beneath them, the sea built hills and valleys of debris. Black

14

strands of algae slapped like shaggy beards against the shield. Branches of coral jostled its sides.

Cat hugged William's shoulders. Eureka's friend was smart and audacious—together they had hitchhiked to New Orleans, Cat wearing only a bikini top and cutoffs, singing raunchy Navy songs her dad had taught her. Eureka could tell Cat thought the plan with Claire was a bad idea.

"She's just a kid," Cat said.

"There." Ander pointed to a broad, barnacle-covered slab of stone ten feet overhead. "That one."

White foam sparkled beneath its crevices. The stone's surface was above water.

Eureka's arm joined Ander's in propelling the shield higher. The water changed from black to dark gray. When they were as close as they could get without breaking the surface, Eureka clasped her thunderstone and sent a prayer Diana's way that they make it out safely.

Though only Eureka could erect the shield they traveled in, Ander could maintain it for a while. He would be the last to leave.

He studied Eureka. She glanced down, wondering what she looked like to him. The intensity of his gaze had made her nervous when she first encountered him on the road outside New Iberia. Then last night he told her he'd been watching her for years, since both of them were very young. He'd betrayed everything he was raised to believe about her. He said he loved her.

15

"When we get above the ocean," he said, "we will see terrible things. You must prepare yourself."

Eureka nodded. She had felt the weight of her tears as they left her eyes. She knew her flood was more horrible than any nightmare. She was responsible for whatever lurked above, and she planned on redeeming herself.

Ander unzipped his backpack and withdrew what looked like an eight-inch silver stake with a wedding-band-sized ring at the top. He flicked a switch to release four curved flukes from the stake's base, transforming it into an anchor. When he pulled on the ring, a fine chain of silver links spurted from the top.

Eureka touched the strange anchor, amazed by its lightness. It weighed less than half a pound.

"Pretty." William touched the anchor's sparkling flukes, which were forked at the edges and had a scalelike hammered texture that made them look like little mermaid tails.

"It is made of orichalcum," Ander said, "an ancient substance mined in Atlantis, stronger than anything in the Waking World. When my ancestor Leander left Atlantis, he had five pieces of orichalcum with him. My family has held on to them for millennia." He patted his backpack and managed a mysterious, sexy smile. "Until now."

"What are the other toys?" Claire stood on her toes and stuffed a hand into Ander's backpack.

He hoisted her in his arms and smiled as he zipped his bag

up. He placed the anchor in her hands. "This is very precious. Once the anchor grips the rock, you must hold on to the chain as tightly as you can."

The links of orichalcum jangled in Claire's hands. "I'll hold tight."

"Claire—" Eureka's fingers brushed her sister's hair, needing to convey that this wasn't a game. She thought about what Diana would have said. "I think you're very brave."

Claire smiled. "Brave and magic?"

Eureka willed away the strange new urge to cry. "Brave and magic."

Ander lifted Claire over his head. She planted her feet on his shoulders and plunged one fist up, then another, just as he'd instructed. Her fingers passed through the thunderstone shield and she flung the anchor toward the rock. Eureka watched it sail upward and disappear. Then the chain grew taut and the shield shook like a cobweb hit by a sprinkler. But it did not let in water, and it did not break.

Ander tugged the chain. "Perfect."

He pulled, drawing more chain inside the shield, lifting them closer to the surface. When they were only inches below the crashing waves, Ander shouted, "Go!"

Eureka grabbed the chain's smooth, cold links. She reached past Claire and began to climb.

Her agility surprised her. Adrenaline flowed through her arms like a river. When she crossed the shield's border, the surface of the ocean was just above her. Eureka entered her storm.

It was deafening. It was everything. It was a voyage into her broken heart. Every sadness, every ounce of anger she had ever felt manifested in that rain. It stung her body like bullets from a thousand futile wars. She gritted her teeth and tasted salt.

Wind slashed from the east. Eureka's fingers slipped, then clung to the cold chain as she reached for the rock.

"Hold on, Claire!" she tried to shout to her sister, but her mouth filled with salt water. She buried her chin against her chest and pressed upward, onward, urgent with a determination she'd never known before.

"Is this all you can do?" she shouted, gurgling through her torrential pain.

The air smelled like it had been electrocuted. Eureka couldn't see beyond the deluge, but she sensed that there was only flood to see. How could Claire hold on in all this thrashing water? Eureka envisioned the dispersal of the last people she loved across the ocean, fish nibbling their eyes. Her throat constricted. She slipped essential inches down the chain. She was up to her chest in ocean.

Somehow, her fingers found the top of the stone and gripped. She thought of Brooks, her best friend since the womb, her childhood next-door neighbor, the boy who'd challenged her to be a more interesting person for the past seventeen years. Where was he? The last she'd seen of him was a splash into the ocean. He'd dove in after the twins had fallen from his boat. He hadn't been himself. He'd been . . . Eureka couldn't stomach what he'd been. She missed him, the old Brooks. She could almost hear his bayou drawl in her good ear, lifting her up: *Just like climbing a pecan tree, Cuttlefish.*

Eureka imagined the cold, slick rock was a welcoming twilit branch. She spat salt. She screamed and climbed.

She dug her elbows into the rock. She flung one knee onto its side. She felt behind her to make sure the purple bag containing *The Book of Love*—the other part of her inheritance from Diana—was still there. It was.

She'd gotten a portion of the book translated by an old woman named Madame Blavatsky. Madame B had acted like Eureka's sorrow was full of hope and promise. Maybe that's what magic was—looking into darkness and seeing a light most people missed.

Madame Blavatsky was dead now, murdered by Ander's Seedbearer aunts and uncles, but when Eureka tucked the book under her elbow she felt the mystic spurring her on to make things right.

The rain fell so intensely it was difficult to move. Claire clung to the chain, keeping the shield permeable for the rest of them. Eureka thrust herself over the rock.

Mountains stretched before her, ringed by a pearly mist. Her knees slid on the rock as she turned and plunged her arm into the churning sea. She felt for William's hand. Ander was supposed to lift him to her.

Small fingers traced, then grasped Eureka's hand. Her brother's grip was surprisingly robust. She pulled until she could reach under his arms and heave him above the surface. William squinted, trying to focus his eyes in the storm. Eureka moved over him, needing to protect him from her tears' brutality, knowing there was no escape.

Cat came next. She practically launched herself from the water and into Eureka's arms. She slid onto the stone and whooped, hugging William, hugging Eureka.

"The Cat endures!"

Pulling Dad up was like an exhumation. He moved slowly, as if drawing himself up required a strength he had never hoped to possess, though Eureka had cheered him across the finish line of three marathons and watched him bench-press his weight in the sweltering garage at home.

Finally, Claire rose in Ander's arms above the surface of the waves. They held the orichalcum chain. Wind lashed their bodies. The shield glimmered around them—right up until Claire's toes slipped past its bounds. Then it split into mist and vanished. Eureka and Cat pulled Ander and Claire over the ledge and onto the rock.

Rain pinged off Eureka's thunderstone, stabbing the underside of her chin. Water sprayed up from the ocean and down from the sky. The rock they stood on was narrow, slippery, and dropped steeply into the ocean, but at least they had all made it to land. Now they needed shelter.

"Where are we?" William shouted.

"I think this is the moon," Claire said.

"It doesn't rain on the moon," William said.

"Head for higher ground," Ander called as he unhooked the anchor from the rock, pressed the switch to retract its flukes, and slipped it back inside his backpack. He pointed inland, where the dark promise of a mountain sloped up. Cat and Dad each took a twin. Eureka watched the backs of her family as they slipped and slid along the rocks. The sight of them stumbling and helping each other up, traveling toward a shelter they didn't know existed made her loathe herself. She'd gotten them—and the rest of the world—into this.

"Are you sure this is the way?" she shouted at Ander even as she noted that the rock they'd landed on jutted out above the sea like a small peninsula. Every other way was white water. It stretched forever, no horizon.

For a moment she let her gaze float on the ocean. She listened to the ringing in her left ear, deaf since the car accident that had killed Diana. This was her depression pose: staring straight ahead without seeing anything, listening to the lonely and unending ring. After Diana died, Eureka had spent months like this. Brooks used to be the only one who let her go into these sad trances, gently needling her when she was through: *You're a nightclub act without the nightclub.*

Eureka wiped rain from her face. She couldn't afford the luxury of sadness anymore. Ander had said she could stop the flood. She would do it or die trying. She wondered how much time she had.

"How long has it been raining?"

"Only a day. Yesterday morning, we were home in your backyard."

Only a day ago, she'd had no idea what her tears could do. Her eyes focused on the ocean, made wild by a single day's rain. She leaned down and squinted at something bobbing on its surface.

It was a human head.

Eureka had known she would face terrible things above the ocean. Still, seeing what her tears had done, this demolished life. . . . She wasn't ready. But then—

The head moved, from one side to the other. A tan arm stretched out of the water. Someone was *swimming*. The head pivoted toward Eureka, took another breath, and disappeared. Then it appeared again, a body moving fast behind it, riding the waves.

Eureka recognized that arm, those shoulders, that dark, wet head of hair. She'd watched Brooks swim to the breakers since they were little kids.

Reason vanished; amazement prevailed. She cupped her hands around her mouth, but before the sound of Brooks's name escaped her lips, Ander leaned in next to her.

22

"We need to go."

She turned to him, brimming with the same unbridled excitement she used to experience when she crossed a finish line first. She pointed at the water—

Brooks was gone.

"No," she whispered. *Come back.*

Stupid. She'd wanted to see her friend so badly her mind had painted him in the waves.

"I thought I saw him," she whispered. "I know it's impossible, but he was right there." She pointed weakly. She knew how she sounded.

Ander's eyes followed hers to the dark place in the waves where Brooks had been. "Let him go, Eureka."

When she flinched his voice softened. "We should hurry. My family will be looking for us."

"We crossed an ocean. How would they find us here?"

"My aunt Starling can taste us in the wind. We must make it to Solon's cave before they track us."

"But—" She searched the water for her friend.

"Brooks is gone. Do you understand?"

"I understand it's more convenient for you if I let him go," Eureka said. She started toward the rainy outlines of Cat and her family.

Ander caught up and blocked her path. "Your weakness for him is inconvenient to more people than me. People will die. The world—"

23

"People are going to die if I miss my best friend?"

She yearned to go back in time, to be in her room with her bare feet against the bedpost. She wanted to smell the fig-scented candle on her desk that she lit after going for a run. She wanted to be texting Brooks about the weird stains on their Latin teacher's tie, stressing over some petty comment Maya Cayce made. She had never realized how happy she was before, how rich and indulgent her depression had been.

"You're in love with him," Ander said.

She edged past him. Brooks was her friend. Ander had no reason to be jealous.

"Eureka—"

"You said we should hurry."

"I know this is hard."

That made her stop. *Hard* was how people who didn't know Eureka used to refer to Diana's death. It made her want to strike the word from existence. Hard was a biochemistry exam. Hard was keeping a great piece of gossip to yourself. Hard was running a marathon.

Letting go of someone you loved wasn't hard. There was no word for what it was, because even if you didn't *let* them go they were still gone. Eureka hung her head and felt raindrops slide off the tip of her nose. Ander must never have suffered so great a loss. If he had, he wouldn't have said that.

"You don't understand."

She'd meant it as a way to let him off the hook, but as soon

24

as it came out, Eureka heard how harsh it sounded. She felt like no words existed anymore; they were all so insufficient and mean.

Ander spun toward the water and let out an exasperated sigh. Eureka saw the Zephyr visibly leave Ander's lips and smash into the sea. It spat up a gaping wave that curled above Eureka.

It looked like the wave that had killed Diana.

She caught Ander's eyes and saw guilt widen them. He inhaled sharply, as if to take it back. When he realized that he couldn't, he lunged for her.

Their fingertips touched for an instant. Then the wave slid over them and swelled toward land. Eureka was flung backward, spiraling away from Ander into the battering sea.

Water shot up her nose, crashed against her skull, bashed her neck from side to side. She tasted blood and salt. She didn't recognize the waterlogged moan coming from her mouth. She fell out of the wave as the water dropped out from under her. For a moment she was running on a path of sky. She couldn't see anything. She expected to die. She screamed for her family, for Cat, for Ander.

When she landed on the rock the only thing that told her she was still, ridiculously, alive was the echo of her voice against the cold, incessant rain.

3

THE LOST SEEDBEARER

In the central chamber of his subterranean grotto Solon took a sip of tar-thick Turkish coffee and frowned.

"It's cold."

His assistant Filiz reached for the ceramic mug. Her mother had cast it specially for Solon on her wheel, had baked it in her kiln two caves to the east. The mug was an inch thick, designed to hold heat longer in Solon's porous travertine cave, which sat in the constant clutches of a bone-deep chill.

Filiz was sixteen, with wavy untamed hair she dyed a fiery shade of orange and eyes the color of a coconut husk. She wore a tight, electric-blue T-shirt, black tapered jeans, and a choker studded with short silver spikes.

"It was hot when I brewed it an hour ago." Filiz had

been working for the eccentric recluse for two years and had learned to navigate his moods. "The fire's still going. I'll make more—"

"Never mind!" Solon flung his head back and poured the coffee down his throat. He gagged melodramatically and wiped his mouth with a pale arm. "Your coffee is only slightly worse when it's cold, like being transferred from Alcatraz to Siberia."

Behind Solon, Basil snickered. Solon's second assistant was nineteen, tall and swarthy, with slick black hair combed into a ponytail and an impish twinkle in his eyes. Basil wasn't like the other boys in their community. He listened to old country music, not electronica. He idolized the graffiti artist Banksy and had painted several of the nearby rock formations with colorfully distorted superheroes. He thought he had done the graffiti anonymously, but Filiz knew he was the artist. He liked to show off his English by speaking in proverbs, but he never translated them right. Solon had taken to calling him "the Poet."

"You can lead a horse to water, but your coffee tastes like poop," the Poet said, chuckling into Filiz's glare.

The Poet and Filiz looked older than their boss, whose pale and sculpted face was as smooth as a child's. Solon appeared to be about fifteen, but he was far older than that. He had searing blue eyes and shorn blond hair dyed with black and brown leopard-print spots. He stood over a silver robot that lay on a long wooden table.

The robot's name was Ovid. He was five foot eleven, with enviable human proportions, a handsome face, and the blank stare of a Greek statue. Filiz had never seen anything like him and had no idea where he had come from. He was composed completely of orichalcum, a metal neither the Poet nor Filiz had heard of before, but which Solon insisted was priceless and rare.

Ovid was broken. Solon spent long days trying to resurrect him but would not tell Filiz why. Solon was full of secrets that straddled the border between magic and lies. He was the kind of crazy that made life interesting, and dangerous.

In the seventy-five years since he'd arrived at the remote Turkish community, Solon had rarely left the vast warren of narrow passageways that led to the cave he called the Bitter Cloud. He had a workshop on the grotto's lower level. From there, a spiral staircase led to the living quarters—his salon—then up another flight to a small veranda. It offered a scenic view, overlooking a field of cone-shaped rocks that formed the rooftops of Solon's neighbors' caves.

The most magical feature in the Bitter Cloud was Solon's waterfall. Tumbling fifty feet from top to bottom, the waterfall spanned two towering stories and comprised the back wall of the cave. Its salty water was dove white and always roaring, a sound Filiz heard even after she left work. At the waterfall's summit, a fuchsia orchid clung perilously to the stony peak, trembling against the current. And at the waterfall's base, a deep blue pool of water bordered Solon's workshop. The Poet had told Filiz a long flume connected the pool to the ocean hundreds of kilometers away. Filiz longed to take a dip in the pool but knew better than to ask permission. So much inside the Bitter Cloud was forbidden.

Turkish rugs hung over small alcoves in the salon, sectioning off two bedrooms and a kitchen. Candles flickered on stalagmite candelabra, constructing ropy hills of wax with their drippings. Skulls lined the walls in elaborate zigzag designs. Solon had positioned each skull carefully in his Gallery of Grins, choosing them for size, shape, color, and imagined personality.

Solon was also the artist of a vast floor mosaic depicting the marriage of Death and Love. Most nights, after giving up anew on Ovid, he sifted through a heap of jagged stones in search of the right shade of translucent blue for Cupid's wedding veil or the proper flash of red for Death's blood-dripping fangs.

Filiz specialized in finding these russet stones on local creek banks. Every time she brought Solon an acceptable stone, he allowed Filiz a few moments to wander through the secret butterfly hall behind his bedroom. A hot spring burbled through it, so the hallway was a natural steam room. Millions of species of winged insects roamed the humid chamber and made Filiz feel like she was inside a Jackson Pollock painting.

"You know where they have real coffee?" Solon asked as he dug through a dented metal toolbox.

"Germany," Filiz and the Poet said, and rolled their eyes.

29

Solon compared everything with Germany. It was where he'd been old and in love.

Solon, like all Seedbearers, was haunted by an ancient curse: love drained life from him, aging him rapidly. Knowing this had not prevented him from falling desperately in love with an exquisite German girl named Byblis seventy-six years earlier. Nothing could have prevented that, Solon had told Filiz many times; it was his destiny. He'd aged ten years leaning in for their first kiss.

Byblis was a Tearline girl, and she had died for it. Her death had regressed Solon as rapidly as her love had aged him. Without Byblis, he returned to eternal boyhood by shutting off his emotions more completely than any Seedbearer ever had. Filiz had caught him admiring his reflection in the pool at the bottom of his grotto. Youthful beauty radiated from Solon's face, but it was pore-deep, with no suggestion of soul.

Solon thrust his hand inside Ovid's skull and probed the ridges of the robot's orichalcum brain. "I don't recall if I've ever switched these two circuits here—"

"You tried that last week," the Poet reminded him. "Great minds think alike."

"No, you're wrong." Solon clenched a pair of pliers between his teeth. "Those were different wires," he said, and switched them.

The robot's head popped off its shoulders and hurtled into the dark wilderness on the far side of the room. For a moment Solon and his assistants listened to a stalactite drip water onto the robot's always-open eyes.

Then the wind-chime doorbell sounded. Its flat link pulleys and the triangular sprockets connecting them jerked back and forth across the ceiling of the cave.

"Don't let them back here," Solon said. "Find out what they want, then send them far away."

Filiz didn't make it to the door. She heard the telltale buzzing, then Solon's curse. The gossipwitches had let themselves in.

There were three of them today: one looked sixty, the next a hundred, the third no more than seventeen. They wore floor-length caftans of amethyst-colored orchid petals that rustled as they filed down Solon's spiral staircase. Their lips and eyelids had been painted to match their gowns. Their ears were pierced from lobe to tip with stacks of the thinnest silver hoops. They went barefoot and had long, beautiful toes. Their tongues were subtly forked. A cloud of bees swarmed above each witch's shoulders, continuously encircling their heads—the backs of which no one ever saw.

Two dozen gossipwitches lived in the mountains around Solon's cave. They traveled in multiples of three. They always entered a room walking forward in single file, but for some reason, they left by flying backward. Each one possessed spellbinding beauty, but the youngest was exceptional. Her name was Esme, though only another gossipwitch was allowed to call a gossipwitch by name. She wore a gleaming crystal teardrop on a chain around her neck.

Esme smiled seductively. "I hope we haven't interrupted anything important."

Solon watched the candlelight playing off the young witch's necklace. He was taller than most of the gossipwitches, but Esme had several inches on him. "I gave you three damselflies yesterday. That buys me at least a day without your persecution."

The witches glanced at one another, sculpted eyebrows raised. Their bees swarmed in busy circles.

"We are not here presently to collect," the oldest of them said. The lines on her face were mesmerizing, pretty, like a sand dune shaped by a strong wind.

"We bring news," Esme said. "The girl will arrive shortly."

"But it isn't even raining—"

"How would a hermetic fart-hammer like you know?" the middle witch spat.

A spray of seawater shot out of the waterfall's pool, drenching the Poet but glancing off of Solon's Seedbearer skin.

"How long will it take you to prepare her?" Esme asked.

"I've never met the girl." Solon shrugged. "Even if she's not as stupid as I suspect, these things take time."

"Solon." Esme fingered the charm on her necklace. "We want to go home."

"That's crystal clear," Solon said. "But the journey to the Sleeping World is not possible at this juncture." He paused. "Do you know how many tears were shed?"

"We know that Atlas and the Filling are near." Esme's forked tongue hissed.

What was the Filling? Filiz saw Solon shudder.

"When we glazed your home, you promised to make it worth our while," the oldest witch reminded Solon. "All these years we have kept you out of view from your family. . . ."

"And I pay you for that protection! Three damselflies only yesterday."

Filiz had heard Solon grumble about being indebted to these beasts. He hated obliging their incessant requests for winged creatures from his butterfly hall. But he didn't have a choice. The witches' glaze rendered the air around Solon's cave imperceptible to the senses. Without it, the other Seedbearers would detect his location on the wind. They would hunt down the brother who betrayed them by falling in love with a Tearline girl.

What did the witches do with the fluttering dragonflies and damselflies, the regal monarchs and occasional blue morpho butterflies that Solon bestowed on them in small glass jars? Judging from the gossipwitches' hungry eyes when they snatched the jars and slipped them in the long pockets of their caftans, Filiz imagined it was something terrible.

"Solon." Esme had a way of speaking that made it sound like she was both a galaxy away and inside Filiz's brain. "We won't wait forever."

"Do you think these visits speed the process? Leave me to my work."

Instinctively, everyone looked at the pathetic spectacle the headless Ovid made, wires protruding from its neck.

"It won't be long now, Solon," Esme whispered, drawing something from the pocket of her caftan. She placed a small tin on the floor. "We brought you some honey, honey. Farewell."

The witches smirked as they arched their arms behind their heads, lifted their feet off the ground, and flew backward, up the waterfall and out of the damp, dark cave.

"Do you believe them?" Filiz asked Solon as she and the Poet laid the robot's head next to its body. "About the girl being on her way? You knew the last Tearline girl. We have only heard the stories, but you—"

"Never mention Byblis," Solon said, and turned away.

"Solon," Filiz pressed, "do you believe the witches?"

"I believe nothing." Solon set about reattaching Ovid's head.

Filiz sighed and watched Solon pretend to forget that she existed. Then she crept upstairs to the entrance of the cave. On her way to work the sky had been a strange silvery color that reminded her of a wild foal she used to see frequently in the mountains. There had been a chill in the air that made her walk quickly, rubbing her arms. She'd felt nervous and alone.

Now, as she stepped outside the cave, a great shadow fell over her. An immense storm cloud dominated the sky, like a giant black egg about to crack. Filiz felt her hair begin to frizz, and then—

A raindrop fell onto the back of her hand. She studied it. She tasted it.

Salty.

It was true. All her life, her elders had warned her of this day. Her ancestors had lived in these mountain caves since the great floodwaters receded millennia ago. Her people possessed a murky collective memory of Atlantis—and a deep-rooted fear that another flood would one day come. Was it actually going to happen, now, before Filiz had climbed the Eiffel Tower or learned to drive a stick shift or fallen in anything resembling love?

Her shoe smashed her reflection in a puddle, and she wished she were smashing the girl who'd made this rain.

"What's your problem, frizzball?" The middle gossipwitch's voice was unmistakable. Her forked tongue flicked as the gossipwitches hovered in the air over Filiz.

Filiz had never understood how the wingless witches flew. The three of them were suspended in the rain, arms slack at their sides, making no visible effort to stay aloft. Filiz watched droplets of salty water settle like diamonds on Esme's lustrous black hair.

Feliz ran her hand through her own hair, then regretted it. She didn't want the witches to think she cared about how she looked. "This rain will kill us, won't it? Poison our wells, destroy our crops—"

"How would we know, child?" the oldest witch asked.

"What will we drink?" Filiz asked. "Is it true what they

say, that you have an infinite supply of freshwater? I have heard it called—"

"Our Glimmering is not for drinking, and it is certainly not for you," Esme said.

"Are the girl's tears as powerful as they are said to be?" Filiz asked. "And . . . what did you mean when you mentioned Atlas and his Filling?"

The witches' beautiful bright caftans contrasted with the giant cloud above them. They looked at one another with amethyst-lined eyes.

"She thinks we know everything," the oldest witch said. "I wonder why. . . ."

"Because," Filiz said nervously, "you're prophets."

"It is Solon's task to ready her," the eldest said. "Take up your fear of mortality with him. If he can't prepare the girl, your boss will owe us his cave, his possessions, all of those pretty little butterflies—"

"Solon will owe us his life." Esme's eyes darkened, and in a suddenly terrifying voice she said: "He will even owe us his death."

The witches' laughter echoed over the mountains as they floated backward and disappeared into the strengthening rain.

4

NEW BLOOD

Rain nailed Eureka to the precipice. She'd landed on the wrist broken in the accident that killed Diana. It was already swelling. The agony was familiar; she knew she'd broken it again. She struggled to her knees as the remnants of the wave flowed back over her.

A shadow fell across her body. The rain seemed to taper.

Ander was above her. One of his hands clasped the back of her head; the other caressed her cheek. His heat made it hard for Eureka to catch her breath. His chest touched hers. She felt his heartbeat. His eyes were so powerfully blue, she imagined them throwing turquoise light on her skin, making her look like sunken treasure. Their lips were centimeters apart.

"Are you hurt?"

"Yes," she whispered, "but that's nothing new."

With Ander's body against hers, no rain fell on Eureka. Heavy drops of water gathered in the air above them, and she realized his cordon covered her. She reached up and touched it. It felt smooth and light, a little spongy. It had a there-yet-not-there quality, like the scent of night-blooming jasmine when you rounded a corner in spring. Raindrops slid down the cordon's sides. Eureka looked into Ander's eyes and listened to the rain, falling everywhere on earth but on them. Ander was the shelter; she was the storm.

"Where are the others?" she asked.

Images of the twins swept out to sea filled Eureka's mind. She jumped to her feet and stood outside Ander's cordon. Rain streamed down her face and dripped from her sleeves onto her shoes.

"Dad!" she called. "Cat!" She couldn't see them. The sky looked like the deep end of a pool that kept growing deeper.

It had been only one exquisite moment, taking refuge in Ander's arms, but it frightened Eureka. She could not let desire distract her from the work she had to do.

"Eureka!" William's voice sounded far away.

She scrambled toward it. The wave had flooded the final portion of their path from rock to land, so Eureka had to jump back into the water and wade ten feet against the current to reach the shore. Ander was at her side. The water was up to their ribs, not high enough to reach her thunderstone. Their hands found each other underwater, holding tight until they could pull each other out.

Strange slopes of pale gray rock stretched before Eureka. In the distance, taller rocks formed an odd skyline of narrow cones, like God had thrown giant swells of stone on a potter's wheel. A burst of blue appeared among the rocks—William, in his soaked Superman pajamas, waved his arm.

Eureka closed the distance between them. William stuck his thumb in his mouth. Blood stained his forehead and his hands. She grabbed his shoulders, studied his body for wounds, then held him against her chest.

He laid his head on her shoulder and hooked his forefinger on her collarbone like he always had.

"Dad's hurt," William said.

Eureka scanned the rocks, icy water up to her ankles. "Where?"

William pointed at a boulder rising like an island from a puddle. With her brother in her arms and Ander beside her, Eureka sloshed around the side of the rock. She saw the back of Cat's black jeans and her lacy crocheted sweater. The patent-leather stilettos Cat had saved six months of babysitting money to buy were wedged in the mud. Eureka crouched close to the ground.

"What happened?" she asked.

Cat spun around. Mud caked her face and clothes. Rain

dripped from her unraveling braids. "You're okay," she breathed, then stepped to the side to reveal two bodies behind her. "Your dad—"

Dad lay on his side at the base of the boulder. He cradled Claire so closely they looked like a single being. His eyes were tightly closed. Hers were tightly open.

"He was trying to protect her," Cat said.

As Eureka rushed toward them her mind scrolled back to the thousands of times Dad had protected her: In his old blue Lincoln, his right arm flinging across Eureka in the passenger seat whenever he hit the brakes hard. Walking the New Iberia cotton fields, his shoulder shielding Eureka from a tractor's dusty wake. When they had lowered Diana's empty coffin into the ground and Eureka wanted to follow it, Dad had shook with the effort of holding her back.

Gently she lifted his arm off Claire.

"The wave picked them up and threw them on the rock and . . ." Cat swallowed and couldn't go on.

Claire slithered free, then changed her mind and tried to crawl back to Dad's arms. When Cat held her, Claire flailed her fists and wailed, "I miss Squat!"

Squat was their Labradoodle. The twins mostly used him as a beanbag. He'd once swum against the current through the bayou to catch up to Eureka and Brooks in a canoe. When he'd arrived on shore and shaken out his fur, he'd been the color of weak chocolate milk. God only knew what had become of him in the storm. Eureka felt guilty that Squat hadn't crossed her mind since her flood began. She studied Claire, the raw fear in her eyes, and recognized at once what her sister dared not say: she missed her mother.

"I know you do," Eureka said.

She checked Dad's pulse; it was still pulsing, but his hands were white as bone. A deep bruise discolored the left side of his face. Ignoring the stabbing pain in her wrist, Eureka traced her father's temple. The bruise spread behind his ear, along his neck, to his left shoulder, which had been deeply sliced. She smelled the blood. It pooled in the sandy crevices between the rock's grooves, flowing like a river from its source. She leaned closer and saw the bone of his shoulder blade, the pink tissue near his spine.

She closed her eyes briefly and remembered the two recent times she'd awoken in a hospital, once after the car accident that took Diana from her, and once after she'd swallowed those dumb pills because life without her mother was impossible. Both times Dad had been there. His blue eyes had watered as hers opened. There was nothing she could do to make him stop loving her.

One summer in Kisatchie, they'd taken a long bike ride. Eureka had sped ahead, joyful to be out of Dad's view, until she wiped out while rounding a sharp bend. At eight years old the pain of skinned elbows and knees had been blinding, and when her vision cleared, Dad was there, picking pebbles from her wounds, using his T-shirt as a compress to stanch the blood.

Now she unbuttoned her own wet shirt, stripping down to the tank top she wore beneath it, and wrapped the cloth as tightly as she could around his shoulder. "Dad? Can you hear me?"

"Is Daddy going to die like Mommy?" Claire wailed, which made William wail.

Cat wiped the blood from William's face with her cardigan. She gave Eureka a bewildered WTF-do-we-do look. Eureka was relieved to realize William wasn't physically wounded; no blood flowed from his skin.

"Dad's going to be okay," Eureka said to her siblings, to her father, to herself.

Dad didn't stir. There was so much blood soaking through Eureka's attempt at a tourniquet. Even as the rain washed swells away, more flowed.

"Eureka," Ander said behind her. "I was mad and my Zephyr—"

"It's not your fault," she said. None of them would have been here in the first place if Eureka hadn't cried. Dad would be home battering okra over his oil-spattered stovetop, singing "Ain't No Sunshine" to Rhoda, who wouldn't have been gone. "It's my fault."

She remembered something one of her therapists had said about blame, how it didn't matter whose fault anything was after it was done. What mattered was how you responded, how you recovered. Recovery was what Eureka had to focus on: her father's, the world's . . . Brooks's, too. But she didn't know how any of them could recover from a wound so deep.

A longing for Brooks swept over her like a sudden storm. He always knew what to say, what to do. Eureka was still struggling to accept that her oldest friend's body was now possessed by an ancient evil. Where was Brooks now? Was he as thirsty, cold, and afraid as Eureka was? Were those shades of feeling possible for someone welded to a monster?

She should have recognized the change in him sooner. She should have found some way to help. Maybe then she wouldn't have cried, because when she had Brooks to lean on, Eureka could get through things. Maybe none of this would have happened. But all of it had happened.

Dad breathed shallowly, eyes still tightly closed. For a few seconds he seemed to rest more easily, like he was detached from the pain—then the agony returned to his face.

"Help!" she shouted, missing Diana more than she could stand. Her mother would tell her to find her way out of this foxhole. "How do we find help? A doctor. A hospital. He always keeps his insurance card in his wallet in his pocket—"

"Eureka." Ander's tone told her, of course, that there would be no help, that she had cried it away.

Cat shivered. "My alarm clock is going to go off any second. And when we meet at your locker before Latin, and I tell you about my insane dream, I'm going to embellish to make this part a lot more fun."

Eureka scanned the barren mountains. "We're going to have to split up. Someone needs to stay here with Dad and the twins. The other two will look for help."

"Look where? Does anyone have any clue where we are?" Cat said.

"We're on the moon," Claire said.

"We need to find Solon," Ander said. "He'll know what to do."

"Are we close?" Eureka asked.

"I tried to steer us toward a city called Kusadasi on the western coast of Turkey. But this doesn't look like any of the pictures I researched. The coastline is . . ."

"What?" Eureka asked.

Ander looked away. "It's different now."

"You mean the city you were trying to get us to is underwater," Eureka said.

"Have you even met this Solon guy?" Cat asked. She was trolling the landscape for large swaths of seaweed, bundling them under one arm.

"No," Ander said, "but—"

"What if he sucks as bad as the rest of your horrible family?"

"He's not like them," Ander said. "He can't be."

"Not like we'll ever know," Cat said, "because we have no idea how to find him."

"I think I can." Ander ran his fingers through his hair quickly, a nervous habit.

Cat swiped rain from her cheeks and sat down with her mound of seaweed in her lap. She knotted strands of it together, until it almost resembled a blanket. For Dad. Eureka felt stupid she hadn't thought to do the same.

"He *thinks* he can?" Cat muttered to her blanket.

Ander lowered his face to Cat's. "Do you have any idea what it's like to reject everything you've been raised to believe? The one true thing in my world is what I feel for Eureka."

"If I never see my family again—" Cat said.

"That's not going to happen." Eureka tried to mediate. "Who's coming with me to find help?"

Cat stared down at the seaweed. Eureka realized she was crying.

Dad's wound was serious, but at least he was here with Eureka and the twins. Cat didn't even know where her father was. Eureka's tears had dissolved Cat's family. She had no idea what had become of any of them. All she had was Eureka.

"Cat—" Eureka reached for her friend.

"Do you know what the last thing I told Barney was?" Cat said. "I told him to eat two turds and die. Those can't be the last words I ever say to my brother." She cupped her face in her hands. "My mom and I were supposed to take this opera class where they teach you how to sing falsetto. My dad promised to cartwheel me down the aisle at my wedding. . . ." She stared at Eureka's father, semiconscious in the mud, and seemed to be seeing her own father. "You have to fix this, Eureka. And not like when you duct taped your mom's rearview mirror back on. I mean, really fix, like, everything."

"I know," Eureka said. "I'll find help. You'll call your family. You'll tell Barney what he already knows, that you love him."

"Right." Cat sniffed. "I'll stay here. You two go." She laid her blanket of seaweed over Dad, then sat down miserably on a rock. She drew the twins into her lap, tried to cover their heads with her cardigan. This was a girl who refused to join summer camping trips if there was the slightest chance of drizzle.

"Let me help you." Eureka tried to stretch the cardigan over the twins and her friend. She felt a twist of heat behind her and spun around.

Under a crook of rock extending from the boulder, Ander had started a small fire using scraps of wood debris. It blazed at Dad's feet, mostly out of the rain.

"How did you do that?" she asked.

"Only takes a couple of breaths to dry out wood. The rest was easy." He lifted a corner of the seaweed blanket to reveal a pile of dry twigs and larger wood chips. "If you need more fuel before we're back," he said to Cat.

"You should stay with my dad," she told Ander. "Your cordon could protect him—"

He looked away. "My family can erect cordons bigger than football fields. I can't even shelter someone standing right beside me."

"But back there, in your arms after the wave—" Eureka said.

"That just happened without me trying, but when I try . . ." He shook his head. "I'm still learning my strength. They say it gets easier." He glanced over her shoulder, as if reminded of his family. "We should hurry."

"You don't even know where we are, where we're going—"

"I know two things," Ander said, "the wind and you. The wind is the way I got us across this ocean and you are the reason why. But I can only help you if you'll trust me."

Eureka remembered the day he'd found her running in the woods in the innocent rain. He'd dared her to get her thunderstone wet. She'd laughed because it sounded so absurd. You could get anything wet.

If it turns out I'm right, he'd said, *will you promise to trust me?*

Eureka liked trusting him. It gave her physical pleasure to trust him, to touch his fingertips and say the words aloud: "I trust you."

She looked behind her and saw lightning strike a distant wave. She wondered what happened at the point of impact. She turned and gazed at the mountains and wondered what lay on the other side.

She tightened her grip on the purple tote bag under her arm. Wherever she was going, *The Book of Love* was going, too. She leaned down to kiss her father. His eyelids tensed but didn't open. She hugged the twins.

"Stay here with Cat. Look after Dad. We won't be long."

Her eyes met Cat's. She felt awful for leaving.

"What?" Cat asked.

"If I hadn't been so angry and depressed," Eureka said, "if I'd been one of those happy people in the hall, do you think my tears would have done this?"

"If you'd been one of those happy people in the hall," Cat said, "you wouldn't be you. I need you to be you. Your dad needs you to be you. If Ander's right, and you're the only one who can stop this flood, the whole world needs you to be you."

Eureka swallowed. "Thanks."

Cat nodded toward the stony hills. "So go on with your bad self."

Ander's hand found its way into Eureka's. She squeezed and started walking inland, hoping Cat was right and wondering how much there was left of the world to save.

5

DEEP FREEZE

Eureka and Ander followed a swollen stream through a shallow valley and into a world of soft white stone. They crossed a forest of rocky cones flanked by table mountains. They held hands as cacti bordering the stream reached out with needles inches long and sharp enough to tear away the skin.

Eureka worried about the cacti weathering the salt in the rain. She imagined her favorite plants around the world—orchids in Hawaii, olive groves in Greece, orange trees in Key West, birds-of-paradise in California, and the comforting labyrinths of live oak branches back home on the bayou—their fibers parched and shriveled, disintegrating into salt. She squinted to make the cactus needles appear longer, thicker, sharper, and imagined them fighting back.

Her mud-obscured running shoes reminded Eureka of the photos her teammates used to post after cross-country practice in stormy weather. Brown and gray points of pride. She wondered whether anyone would enjoy a rainy run ever again. Had she robbed the rain of its beauty?

They came around a bend where the steel-blue bay was visible below. There was the rock where they'd made landfall and the tall triangular boulder behind which Cat and her family crouched in front of Ander's fire, hanging on. The boulder looked tiny. They had traveled farther than she had thought. It made her nervous to be so far away.

She looked beyond the boulder, at the ocean spreading around them in cloudy light. Slowly, a more regular geometry emerged. Man-made shapes sagged in the deluge. Rooftops. The ghost of the city that had been washed away.

She imagined people beneath those roofs, drowned in her pain. She had floated underneath her devastation in the thunderstone shield, but now Eureka saw it. She didn't know what to do. She wanted to disintegrate in the rain. She wanted to make everything right, right now.

"You know," Ander said, "you're going to make things better."

Eureka tried to let his support make her stronger, like a buttress on a cathedral, but she wondered from where Ander drew his faith in her. He seemed to truly believe that she could fix things, but was it simply because he liked her—or was there more to it? He kept saying Solon would answer all their questions . . . if they ever found him.

The path widened into two forked trails. An instinct she couldn't explain told her to go left. "Which way?" she asked Ander.

He pivoted right. "We go east. Or—north? We need to go up into the mountains so I can see more clearly where we are."

Ander had seemed so confident a moment before, when he was believing in her. "Do you have a map?" she asked.

He stopped walking and faced Eureka with such sad eyes that she took his hand. She marveled at the way it fit in hers, like no one else's ever had. He looked down and caressed her fingertips.

"I see," she said. "No map."

"The map is in my memory, drawn with lines muttered by my aunts and uncles when I was very young. I don't know why I memorized their words, maybe because talk of the lost Seedbearer sounded strange and romantic, and there was so little excitement in my life."

Eureka dropped his hand. She imagined Cat's reaction upon learning Ander had led them to the other side of the world based on an imaginary map. She didn't want to blame Ander. They were here now. They needed to support each other. But she couldn't help thinking about the way that Brooks, though he couldn't read a map even if you held a gun to his head, always wound up in the right place. He'd wound up in her imagination earlier, skimming dark water with his arms. What shore had he landed on when she'd blinked and made him disappear?

Ander chose the path's steep right fork. "Solon made plans before he escaped. He was headed for a cave in western Turkey, which he called the Bitter Cloud."

The path widened. Eureka sped into a jog. Her right wrist throbbed with every impact of her shoes against the earth, but running lent something familiar to the alien landscape. Her body found a gear she understood.

Ander kept up. When he glanced at her, an agreement flashed between them. They began to race. Eureka pumped her legs. Wind whistled at her back. The salt in the rain stung her eyes and the pain in her wrist was excruciating, but the faster she ran, the less she felt it.

She didn't think she could ever slow down. They were lost and she knew it, entering a tight passage only a few feet wide, bordered on either side by sharply sloping stone. It was like running through a very narrow hallway in the dark. Every step carried them deeper into goneness, but Eureka had to run until this burning was out of her system, until this fever had subsided. Sometime, later, they would catch their breath and figure out what to do.

"Eureka!"

Ander stopped ahead of her. She skidded into his back. Her cheekbone slammed into his shoulder blade. She felt his muscles stiffen, like he was trying to shield her from something. She stood on her toes to see past him.

A dead girl lay at the edge of the stream. She looked about twelve. Leaves clung to her hair. She was on her side, straddling a long, twisted log. Eureka stared at her white blouse, her pale pink pleated skirt stained with blood. Ebony bangs were matted to her cheeks. Her long ponytail was tied with a cheerful yellow ribbon.

Eureka thought about who she'd been when she herself was twelve years old—big hands and feet like a puppy's, perpetually tangled hair, a gap-toothed smile. She hadn't yet met Cat. The summer she was twelve, she'd had her first French kiss. It was twilight, and she and Brooks had been swimming under the dock at his boathouse. Feeling his lips softly on hers was the last thing she'd expected when she came up for air from a breaststroke. They'd treaded water after the kiss, laughing hysterically because they were both too embarrassed to do anything else. She had been so different then.

She felt a burning at the back of her throat. She wished she were back there, in that warm Cypremort water, far away. She wished she were anywhere but standing over this dead girl.

Then she wasn't standing over her. She was kneeling next to her. Sitting in the stream beside her. Lifting the girl's misshapen, broken arm off the log. Holding her cold hand.

"I hurt you," Eureka said, but what crossed her mind was *I envy you,* because the girl had left behind this world's problems and its pain.

She started to pray to the Virgin, because that was how she'd been raised, but Eureka felt disrespectful quickly. Odds were this girl hadn't been Catholic. Eureka could do nothing to help her soul get where it needed to go.

"I'm going to bury her."

"Eureka, I don't think . . . ," Ander started to say.

But Eureka had already pulled the girl's body from the log. She lay her flat against the bank and smoothed her skirt. Eureka's fingers dug through pebbles and reached mud. She felt the silty grit fill the space beneath her fingernails as she cast fistfuls aside. She thought of Diana, who'd never been buried.

This girl was dead because Diana had never told Eureka what her tears would do. Anger she'd never before felt for her mother seized Eureka.

"There won't be time to attend to every death," Ander said.

"We have to." Eureka kept digging.

"Think about your father," Ander said. "And my family, who will find you if we don't find the Bitter Cloud first. You can do more to honor this girl by moving on, finding Solon, learning what you must do to redeem yourself."

Eureka stopped digging. Her arms shook as she reached for the girl's yellow ribbon. She didn't know why she pulled on the bow. She felt it loosen as it slid from the girl's wet black hair. The wind wove the ribbon between Eureka's fingers and blew a sudden lightness into her chest.

She recognized the sensation distantly—it was an old friend, returned after a long prodigal journey: hope.

This girl was a bright flame that Eureka's tears had extinguished, but there were more flames out there burning. There had to be. She tied the yellow ribbon around the chain bearing her thunderstone. When she was lost and disheartened, she would remember this girl, the first tear-loss Eureka had seen, and it would spur her on to stop what she had started, to right her wrongs.

Eureka didn't realize she had tears in her eyes until she turned to Ander and saw his panicked expression.

He was at her side immediately. "No!"

He grabbed her broken wrist. The pain was blinding. A tear rolled down her cheek.

Out of nowhere she remembered the heirloom chandelier back home, which Eureka broke when she slammed the front door in a rage. Dad had spent hours repairing it and the chandelier had looked almost like new, but the next time Eureka closed the front door, carefully, so lightly, the chandelier had trembled, then shattered into shards. Was Eureka like that chandelier, now that she'd cried once? Would the lightest force suddenly shatter her?

"Please don't shed another tear," Ander pleaded.

Eureka wondered how anyone ever stopped crying. How did pain fade? Where did it go? Ander made it sound temporary, like a Lafayette snowfall. She touched the yellow ribbon.

She had already cried the tear that flooded the world. She'd assumed the damage was done. "What more can my tears do?"

"There is an ancient rubric predicting the power of each tear shed—"

"You didn't tell me that!" Eureka's breath came shallowly. "How many tears have I shed?"

She started to wipe her face, but Ander grabbed her hands. Her tears hung like grenades.

"Solon will explain—"

"Tell me!"

Ander took her hands. "I know you're scared, but you must stop crying." He reached around and cradled the back of her head in his palm. His chest swelled as he inhaled. "I will help you," he said. "Look up."

A narrow column of swirling air formed over Eureka's head. It twisted faster, until a few raindrops faded and slowed . . . and turned into snow. The column became thick with bright, feathery flakes that tumbled down and dusted Eureka's cheeks, her shoulders, her sneakers. Rain thundered against the rocks, splashing into the puddles all around them, but over her head the storm was an elegant blizzard. Eureka shivered, enthralled.

"Stay still," Ander whispered.

She felt goose bumps as hot tears cooled, then froze against her skin. She reached to touch one, but Ander's fingers covered hers. For a moment they held hands against her cheek.

He drew a spindle-shaped silver vial from his pocket. It looked like it had been crafted of the same orichalcum as the anchor. Carefully, he pulled the frozen tears from Eureka's face and dropped them into the vial, one by one.

"What is that?"

"A lachrymatory," he said. "Before the flood, when Atlantean soldiers went to war, their lovers made presents of their tears in vials like this." He placed the pointed silver lid atop the vial, slipped it into his pocket.

Eureka was jealous of anyone who could shed tears without deadly consequences. She would not cry again. She would make a lachrymatory in her mind where her frozen pain could live.

The snowflakes on her shoulders began to melt. Her wrist ached more deeply and miserably than before. The windy rain returned. Ander's hand brushed her cheek.

There now, she remembered him saying the first time they'd met, *no more tears.*

"How did you do that," she asked, "with the snow?"

"I borrowed a band of wind."

"Then why didn't you freeze my tears before I cried the first time? Why didn't someone stop me?"

Ander looked as haunted as Eureka had felt when she lost Diana. Outside of her own reflection, she had never seen anyone look so sad. It attracted her to him even more. She was desperate to touch him, to be touched—but Ander stiffened and turned away.

"I can move some things around to help, but I can't stop

you. There is nothing in the universe half as strong as what you feel."

Eureka faced the girl in her half-dug grave. Her dead eyes were open, blue. Rain gave them vicarious tears.

"Why didn't you tell me how dangerous my feelings were?"

"There's a difference between power and danger. Your feelings are more powerful than anything in the world. But you shouldn't be afraid of them. Love is bigger than fear."

A high giggle made both of them jump.

Three women wearing amethyst-colored caftans stepped out from behind scrubby trees on the other side of the stream. Their garments were woven out of orchid petals. One was very old, one was middle-aged, and one looked young and crazy enough to have roamed the halls of Evangeline with Cat and Eureka. Their hair was long and lush, ranging from silver to black. Their eyes scoured Eureka and Ander. Swarms of buzzing bees made clouds in the air around their heads.

The youngest wore a silver necklace with a charm at the end that gleamed so brightly, Eureka couldn't make out what it was. The girl smiled and fingered the chain.

"Oh, Eureka," she said. "We've been waiting for you."

6

ENEMIES CLOSER

The women were so strange they were familiar, like dreaming of a future déjà vu. But Eureka couldn't imagine where she would have seen anyone like them before. Then Madame Blavatsky's scratchy voice entered her mind, and she remembered sitting on the bayou behind her house at sunrise, listening to the sage old woman read from her translation of *The Book of Love*.

The muscles in Eureka's face tightened as she struggled to accept that she was experiencing something she had longed for as a child: characters from a book had come to life—and it was terrible. There was no way to flip ahead and reassure herself that this chapter would end happily. She knew no more than the hero of her story knew; she was the hero, and she was lost.

She squared her shoulders and lifted her chin.

The women arched their black eyebrows.

"Go on," the middle-aged one goaded. "Say it." Her tongue was forked like a snake's.

"Gossipwitches," Eureka said in a tone more dramatic than she had intended.

In *The Book of Love,* the gossipwitches were ageless sorceresses who lived in the cliffs overlooking the Atlantic Ocean. They were no one's confidants but knew everyone's secrets. They'd warned Selene that she and Leander might escape the island, but they would never escape Delphine's curse.

Doom decorates your hearts and will forevermore.

When Madame Blavatsky had translated that line, the word *forevermore* had clutched Eureka's heart. Selene was her ancestor; Leander was Ander's ancestor. Could the gossipwitches' ancient curse touch what Eureka and Ander felt for each other? Was there more to Eureka's ancestry than forbidden tears? Was love impossible, too?

"Gossipwitches!" the oldest woman hooted, and Eureka realized that all the witches' tongues were forked. The eldest one's black eyes were twinkly and enchanting, reminding Eureka of her grandmother Sugar's. It was easy to see how stunning the witch must have been in her youth. Eureka wondered how long ago that youth had been.

The old witch smacked her two companions' backs, sending raindrops flying from their orchid garments like fireworks. "The young are so attached to classifications!"

"I've heard stories about you," Ander said. "But I was taught that you belonged to the Sleeping World."

The young witch tilted her chin toward Ander, revealing the gleaming crystal charm in the perfect hollow of her neck. It was shaped like a teardrop. "And who are you, whose teachers are so boring?"

Ander cleared his throat. "I am a Seedbearer—"

"*Are* you?" She feigned intrigue, grabbing Ander's body with her greedy eyes and wrapping her gaze around him.

"Well, I was," Ander said.

"And what are you now?" The young witch narrowed her eyes.

He looked at Eureka. "I am a boy without a past."

"What's your name?" The mesmerizing murmur of the young witch's voice made Eureka dizzy.

"Ander. I was named after Leander."

"What are your names?" Eureka asked. If they were the aunts and cousins of Selene, as *The Book of Love* had said, then these women were Eureka's relatives and she shouldn't fear them.

The gossipwitches blinked as if they were queens and she had guessed their weight. Then they howled with exaggerated laughter. They bent over each other for support and stomped their pale feet in the mud.

The youngest one collected herself and dabbed the corners of her eyes with her petal sleeve. She leaned into Eureka's deaf ear:

"No one is ever what they seem. Especially you, Eureka."

Eureka pulled away and massaged her ear. She had heard the girl's voice with absolute clarity in the ear that heard so little else. She remembered hearing with her bad ear the lovely song of Madame Blavatsky's Abyssinian lovebird Polaris. That song had found her like a miracle. The gossipwitch's whisper landed like a telepathic punch, bruising something deep inside her.

"Your name means 'I have found it,' yet you've been lost your whole life." The eldest witch flicked her tongue into the cloud of bees, snatched one, twirled it on its stinger like a top, then released it back into the swarm.

"Never more than now." The middle witch's gaze circled their surroundings, then fell again on Eureka.

Slowly, they turned their heads to stare at the purple tote bag slung over Eureka's shoulder. Eureka palmed the damp canvas protectively. "We should get going."

The witches laughed.

"She thinks she's leaving!" the eldest witch cried.

"Reminds me of that song: *'She ain't goin' nowhere, she's just leavin','*" the middle witch sang.

"Come, Eureka," the young witch said. "You are lost, and we will lead you where you want to go."

"We're not lost," Ander said firmly.

"Of course you are." The eldest witch rolled her big dark eyes. "You think you can find the Bitter Cloud on your own?"

She leaned in close and grasped Eureka's broken wrist until Eureka yelped.

"Give her the salve," the old witch said impatiently.

From a deep pocket made of petals, the youngest witch withdrew a small glass bottle. A shimmery purple substance swirled inside. She tossed the bottle to Eureka, who scrambled to catch it.

"For your pain," she said. "Now come this way." She pointed across the muddy stream, toward a jagged mountain peak a hundred feet high.

Built into the cliff was a steep natural staircase leading up the mountain. Again, Eureka felt a puzzling impulse that this was the way to go. She glanced at Ander. He nodded subtly.

She unscrewed the cap from the bottle and gave the contents a sniff. The sweetly floral scent of jonquils entered her nose—followed by the throbbing sensation that her bone was shattering again.

"They'll want something in return," Ander whispered to Eureka.

"Let Solon worry about that." The witches laughed.

"Go ahead," the young witch said. "It will heal your bones. We'll wait."

Eureka splashed some of the purple liquid onto her palm. It was flecked with gold, like the nail polishes at her aunt Maureen's salon. She swirled a fingertip in the salve and rubbed it on a portion of her wrist.

Searing heat gripped her, and she felt immensely stupid for trusting the gossipwitches. But an instant later the heat subsided and a pleasant coolness washed over her, vanquishing the pain. The swelling shrank; the bruise faded where the salve had been, then disappeared. It was miraculous. Eureka spread more of the liquid over her wrist. She bore the heat, waiting for the cool relief and the pain it lifted like a layer of clothing. She closed her eyes and sighed. She tucked the bottle into her tote bag, eager to share the rest with Dad.

"Okay," she told the gossipwitches, "we'll follow you."

"No." The young witch shook her head and pointed to the staircase in the rock. "We'll follow *you*."

The path was steep and flooded. The clouds hung low, black as smoke from a house on fire. The witches guided Eureka and Ander through the lacework of delicate mountain peaks, always walking behind them, barking commands like "Left!" when the route forked unexpectedly, "Up!" when they were meant to scale a steep, slippery bluff, and "Duck!" when a half-dead snake slipped from a branch and cough-hissed at them as they passed. The middle witch yelled commands that Eureka didn't understand—"Ye!" and "Ha!" and "Roscoe Leroy!"

Every step took Eureka farther from her family and her friend. She imagined William and Claire peering at the mountain. She wondered how long before they gave up watching.

She entered a scattered forest of dying hazelnut trees. The leaves were turning brown and the shells of salt-crusted nuts crunched beneath Eureka's shoes. A spider's web dangled between two branches and swayed in the wind. Droplets clung to it like pearls a young nymph had abandoned in the woods.

"Eureka!"

She looked up and saw William and Claire cradled in the branches of a giant hazelnut tree. The twins hopped to the ground and splashed through the mud, running toward her. She didn't believe it was them, even when she had them in her arms. She closed her eyes and breathed in their scent, wanting to believe: it was ivory soap and starlight.

"How did you get here?"

The twins each took one of her hands. They wanted to show her something.

On the other side of the tree a long white object shimmered in the rain. Eureka approached it cautiously, but the twins laughed and pulled her harder. It was shaped like a hammock, but its fabric made it look more like a huge cocoon. Eureka studied it, amazed by what appeared to be a million iridescent moth wings woven together. The tiny, fragile pieces formed a massive bower that hovered in the air, floating on its own.

Inside the bower lay Eureka's father. A thin canopy of soft brown wings shielded his face from the rain. The sliced shoulder Eureka had bound in her shirt had been expertly redressed in a silky fuchsia gauze. A poultice of the same material was wrapped around the bruise on his forehead. He was awake. He reached for her hand and smiled.

"Good doctors on this side of town."

"How's the pain?" Eureka asked.

"A nice distraction." His eyes looked lucid but he spoke like he was dreaming.

She reached into her pocket, pressed the vial of salve into his hand. "This will help."

Beyond the moth-wing bower, three new gossipwitches huddled under another, sadder tree, murmuring to each other behind the backs of their hands. The witches who had led Ander and Eureka here flowed toward the others, kissing them on the cheeks and whispering as if they had years of news to catch up on.

"How many are there?" Eureka wondered.

Cat appeared at her side. "The freaky fairy godmothers showed up a few minutes after you left. I was like, 'Where are all my baby teeth you took?' Thanks for sending them down to help us."

"I didn't send them," Eureka said.

"One of them flicked her tongue in a hole in a tree," William said, "and a zillion bugs flew from it."

"The bugs made a big white diamond in the sky, then carried Dad up into the rain!" Claire added.

"These toddlers shit you not," Cat said.

"Dad can fly!" William said.

Cat reached for Eureka's thunderstone, studying its rain-reflective surface. "When they showed up on the beach, I knew they had something to do with you. It's like, somehow, you fit in more here than you ever did at Evangeline."

"And I thought I'd never find my clique," Eureka said dryly.

"I mean," Cat said, "you make sense where impossible things are possible. You're one of those impossible things." Cat held out an open hand to catch some rain. "Your powers are real."

Eureka looked back toward the gossipwitches, but they were gone. All that was left of them was a single orchid petal, glowing on the ground. "I wanted to thank them."

"Don't worry," a voice whispered in her deaf ear. It was the youngest gossipwitch, but she was nowhere Eureka could see. "Solon has a tab with us."

"Where do we go?" Ander shouted into the rain.

The witches' laughter shook the earth. Eureka felt something in her hand and looked down. A torch had appeared between her fingers. It had a long silver handle and widened into a broad fluted goblet near the top. A flame glowed from the goblet's center, unextinguished in the rain. Eureka gazed into the center of the torch, looking for the oil or coal that fueled its flame. Instead, she saw a little mound of glowing amethyst stones.

"You're welcome," the young witch's voice whispered in Eureka's deaf ear.

"Give Solon our worst!" the old one shouted.

There was more laughter, then silence, then rain.

Eureka paced the grove, looking for clues her new torch might illuminate. Just past the trunk of one of the trees she slammed into something hard. She rubbed her brow. Nothing unusual was visible before her—just more rotting, twisted trees. Yet she had walked into something as solid as a wall. She tried again, and slammed into it again, unable to take another step.

Ander traced the invisible force with his fingers. "It's wet. It feels like a cordon. It's real, I can feel it, but it isn't there."

"Guys." Claire waved from a few feet away. "Shouldn't we just use the door?"

Eureka squinted as something white blurred in the space in front of her sister. Claire rose on her toes to reach above her head, revisiting what seemed to be a tricky spot several times. At the edge of the grove, under the crooked elbow of a hazelnut branch, just past a flat stone bearing a patch of lichen shaped like Louisiana, a wall of porous white rock sharpened slowly, incredibly, before them.

Claire had finger-painted it into existence—or into visibility, for the rock had been there before its painter.

"Here it is." Claire's hands moved over a black portion of the rock like she was polishing a car. The rock looked more and more like a rounded doorway.

Eureka wished Rhoda were here to applaud. It made Eureka think about Heaven, which made her think about Diana, and she wondered if two souls interested in the same earthly subjects could gather in the same celestial place to look down on them. Were Rhoda and Diana together, somewhere out there, on a cloud? Did Heaven still lie beyond the gray smear of sadness above?

She looked upward for a sign. Rain fell in the same lonesome rhythm it had been beating out all day.

Ander knelt next to Claire. "How did you do that?"

"Kids see more than adults," Claire said matter-of-factly, and slipped through the door like a ghost.

7

FOR A SONG

Eureka turned to Ander. "Do you think this is really—"

"The Bitter Cloud." Ander's smile was the opposite of William's open grin. It was a smile at the border of weeping, a passport flashed and pocketed. It fascinated Eureka, and it frightened her to consider what it would mean to be Ander's girlfriend, to combine her enormous pain with his, to become a power couple of loss. They would understand each other's sorrow naturally—but who would lighten the mood?

"You're as sad as I am," she whispered. "Why?"

"I'm happier than I've ever been."

It made Eureka wish she'd known Ander forever, that she had as many memories of him as he had gathered of her over the years.

She touched the bright white rock. The Bitter Cloud. If this was Solon's cave, Eureka could see why he compared the travertine stone to a cloud. Even after Claire had revealed how solid it was, there was a lightness to the stone, like you could almost pass your fingers through it.

Eureka held out her torch and entered the cave. Her bad ear listened to the soft vibration of moth wings carrying her father behind her.

William saw his shadow stretching on the cave walls and drew closer to Eureka. "I'm afraid."

Eureka had to set the example that love was bigger than fear. "I'm with you."

The cave walls had a strange, mottled texture. Eureka held the torch near one. Her fingers tightened around the torch's silver wand.

There must have been a thousand skulls arranged along the walls. Had they been former residents? Trespassers like her? An earlier Eureka might have shuddered at the sight. The girl she was now leaned closer to the wall, peered into a skinless, grinning face. She sensed that the skull had belonged to a woman. Its eye sockets were large and low and perfectly rounded. Its teeth were intact along its delicate jaw. It was beautiful. Eureka thought about how intensely she used to want to die, how she'd aspired to be like this woman. She wondered where this lovely skull's soul had gone, and what pain it had left on earth.

She reached out. The skull's cheekbones were icy.

Eureka drew away, and the skull blended into the larger design. It was like stepping away from a telescope on a starry night. The skulls were separated here and there by other types of bones: femurs, ribs, kneecaps. Eureka knew from her archaeological digs with Diana that this room would have set her mother's mind spinning.

They walked deeper into the cave, Cat's stiletto heels clicking on the stone. The torch lit the space only a few feet ahead of Eureka and a few feet behind, so the others had to stay close. Stalactites dripped from the ceiling, like giant frozen fingers thawing. Cat pressed on Eureka's head to signal her to duck under a spear-shaped one.

Eureka tipped the torch in Cat's direction. The light made her friend's freckles stand out against her skin. She looked young and innocent—Cat's two least favorite qualities—which made Eureka think of Cat's parents, who would always see their daughter that way, even when Cat was sixty. She hoped Cat's family was safe.

"Be-fri." Eureka spoke her half of the heart-shaped best-friends puzzle-piece necklace she and Cat had won during a Cajun line-dancing contest at the Sugarcane Festival in ninth grade.

Cat automatically recited her half of the charm. "St-ends." She swung her hip out like they were still there, dancing in New Iberia, past Main Street's decorated storefronts, the fall night promising a new school year and football and cute boys with thick warm cardigans you could slide inside.

They didn't wear the necklaces anymore, but every once in a while, Eureka and Cat performed the familiar call-and-response. It was a way of checking in, of saying *I will always love you* and *You're the only one who gets me* and *Thanks.*

The cave smelled musty and ripe, the way Eureka's garage had smelled after Hurricane Rita. Its floor was surprisingly smooth, as if it had been sanded down. It was quiet except for the sound of water dripping from the stalactites into root-beer-colored pools. Pale tadpoles darted to and fro.

The most remarkable thing about the cave was the absence of rain. Eureka had grown accustomed to the constant sensation of storm on her skin. Under the cave's cover, her body felt numb and charged at the same time, unsure what to make of the lull.

The torch illuminated a dark space in the center of a small wall of swirling skulls at the far end of the passage. Eureka approached and saw that it was the entrance to a narrower passage. She pushed the witches' torch into the gloom.

More skulls lined this smaller path, which narrowed into dark endlessness. Eureka's claustrophobia awakened and her hand tightened around the torch.

Dad lifted his head from the mystical moth bower. He had talked his daughter down from panic attacks in elevators and

73

attics since she'd been a child. She saw recognition on his face and was relieved he was still cognizant enough to understand why she was frozen at the door.

Dad nodded toward the daunting darkness. "Gotta go through it to get through it." That had been his line in those bleary days after Diana died. Back then he was referring to grief. Eureka wondered if he knew what he was referring to now. No one knew what lay on the other side of darkness.

Dad's bayou drawl was more pronounced away from home. Eureka remembered that the only other time he'd left the country was when he and Diana went to Belize for their honeymoon. The sun-soaked photographs were imprinted on her brain. Her parents were young and golden and gorgeous, never smiling at the same time.

"Okay, Dad." Eureka let the walls embrace her.

The temperature dropped. The ceiling did, too. Lit candles flickered sporadically along the way. Their shallow light faded into long stretches of darkness before the next candle appeared. Eureka sensed her loved ones at her back. She had no idea what she was leading them toward.

Distant sounds echoed off the walls. Eureka stopped to listen. She could only hear them in her good ear, which she realized meant the voices were of her world, not Atlantis. They grew louder, closer.

Eureka widened her stance to shield the twins. She held

the torch with both hands like a bludgeon. She would strike whatever came.

She cried out and swung the torch—

At the edge of its light stood a small, dark-haired, barefoot child. He wore nothing but a pair of ragged brown shorts. His hands and face were grimy with something black and glossy.

He called to them in what could have been Turkish, but Eureka wasn't sure. His words sounded like the language of a nearby planet from a thousand years ago.

Slowly, William stepped out from behind Eureka's leg. He waved at the little boy. They were the same age, the same height.

The boy grinned. His teeth were small and white.

Eureka relaxed for half a second—and that was when the boy lurched forward, grabbed William's and Claire's hands, and dragged them into the darkness.

Eureka screamed and ran after them. She didn't realize she had dropped the torch until she'd run deep into blackness. She followed the sounds of her siblings' cries until somehow her fingers found the waist of the boy's shorts. She jerked him to the ground. Cat held the torch to light Eureka's struggle with the boy.

He was shockingly strong. She strained fiercely to pry the twins from his grip.

"Let go!" she shouted, not believing that anyone so small and young could be so strong.

Ander heaved the boy into the air, but the child wouldn't let go of the twins—he lifted them off the ground with him. William and Claire writhed and cried. Eureka wanted to dismember the boy and make his head part of the mosaic on the walls.

Neither she nor Ander could pry the boy's tiny fingers free. Claire's arm was swollen and red. The boy had worked himself out of Ander's hold, had slipped through Eureka's exhausted hands. He was dragging the twins away.

"Stop!" Eureka shouted, despite the absurd futility of the word. She had to *do* something. She scrambled after the three of them and, without knowing why, she began to sing:

"To know, know, know him is to love, love, love him."

It was a Teddy Bears song from the fifties. Diana had taught it to her, dancing on a humid porch in New Iberia.

The boy stopped, turned around, and stared at Eureka. He gaped like he'd never heard music before. By the end of the chorus, his iron grip had relaxed, and the twins slid away.

Eureka didn't know what to do but keep singing. She had reached the song's eerie bridge, with its one sharp note beyond her range. Cat joined in, nervously harmonizing; then her father's rich, deep voice met Eureka's, too.

The boy sat cross-legged before them, smiling dreamily. When he was sure the song was over, he rose to his feet, looked at Eureka, and disappeared into the recesses of the cave.

Eureka collapsed on the ground and pulled the twins to her. She closed her eyes, enjoying the fall of their breath against her chest.

"I take it that wasn't Solon," Dad said from his bower, and everyone managed to laugh.

"How did you do that?" Ander asked.

Eureka recognized the wonder in his eyes from a look that Diana had given her a few times. It was a look only someone who knew you really well could give, and only when they found themselves amazed to still be surprised by you.

Eureka wasn't sure how she had done what she'd done. "I used to sing that when the twins were babies," she said. "I don't know why it worked." She stared in the direction the boy had run. Her pulse raced from the victory, from the surprising, simple joy of singing.

It was the first time she'd sung since Diana died. She used to sing all the time, even make up her own songs. Back in seventh grade, when they'd still been friends, Maya Cayce had entered a school poetry contest using song lyrics lifted from Eureka's journal. When Eureka's stolen song won, neither girl mentioned it. Maya won twenty-five dollars, had her poem read over the intercom on Friday morning. It became the thing between them, a loaded glance over sleeping-bagged knees at slumber parties, and later, over kegs at house parties. Was Maya dead now? Had Eureka taken her life the way she'd taken Eureka's words?

"I think that boy wanted us for his friends," William said.

"I think we have our first fan." Cat handed the torch back to Eureka. "Now we need a band name. And a drummer." Cat brainstormed band names as they continued more cautiously down the narrow passage. Her rambling was comforting, even if Eureka couldn't afford the energy to attend to every manic idea darting catlike through her friend's mind.

White and dark blue tiles now paved the floor beneath their feet. Mounted on the wall was a marble plaque, into which were chiseled the words *Memento mori*.

"Thanks for the reminder," Cat quipped, and Eureka loved that Cat knew the sign meant "Remember that you must die" even though she hadn't been in the Latin class where Eureka had learned the phrase the year before.

"What does it mean?" William asked.

"A slave called it out to a Roman general who was going into battle," Eureka said, hearing her Latin teacher Mr. Piscadia's drawl in her mind. She wondered how he and his family had weathered her flood. Once she'd seen him and his son at a park walking a pair of brindle boxers. In her imagination, a giant wave washed away the memory. "It meant 'You are mighty today, but you're just a man, and you will fall.' When we studied it in Latin class, everyone got hung up on how it was about vanity and pride." Eureka sighed. "I remember thinking the words were comforting. Like, someday, all this will end."

She looked at the others, their surprised faces. Cat's sarcasm was a cover for her genuinely sunny disposition. Dad didn't want to consider that his daughter felt so much pain. The twins were too young to understand. That left Ander. She met his eyes and she knew he understood. He gazed at her and didn't have to say a word.

Ten steps later, the path dead-ended. They stopped before a crooked wooden door with brass hinges, an antique bell, and a second, silver plaque:

Lasciate ogni speranza, voi ch'entrate.

"Abandon all hope, ye who enter," Ander translated.

Cat stepped closer to the plaque. "This I like. Talk about a killer tramp stamp."

"What's a tramp stamp?" Claire asked.

Eureka was surprised. Ander had told her he had never gone to school, that Eureka herself was the only subject he'd ever studied. She wondered how he'd learned Italian. She imagined him sitting at a computer in a dark bedroom, practicing romantic phrases from an online course he listened to through his earbuds.

"It's from Dante's *Inferno*," he said.

Eureka wanted to know more. When had he read the *Inferno*? What had made him pick it up? Had he liked it, made his own lists of who belonged in which circle of hell the way Eureka had?

But this wasn't Neptune's Diner in Lafayette, where you hunkered down in a red vinyl booth with your crush and flirted your way into each other's secrets over cheese fries and chicken gumbo. She sensed that, like Mr. Piscadia's leisurely walks in the park, those kinds of dates now lay at the bottom of the sea.

She reached for the bell and rang.

8

TRIAL BY ORCHID

A panel in the door slid open.

Eureka's reflection greeted her. Her ombré hair was soaked and tangled. Her face was swollen and her lips were cracked. Her blue irises looked dull from exhaustion, but she couldn't tell if crying had made her eyes something they hadn't been before.

Cat pursed her lips at her mirror face. Her fingers scrambled to rebraid her pigtails. "I've looked worse. Usually in the context of more . . . pleasant circumstances, but I have looked worse."

Eureka watched Ander avert his eyes from the mirror. He was jiggling the doorknob, trying to get in.

"What's a mirror doing on a door in the middle of a cave?" Claire asked.

William raised a finger to the glass. A magician had visited his preschool a few months ago, and Eureka remembered that one of the things William had learned was how to detect a two-way mirror: a regular mirror had a small space between the reflective surface and its glass covering; a two-way mirror did not. If you pressed a finger to the glass and saw no gap in its reflection, someone was on the other side, watching you.

Eureka looked down at William's finger. There was no gap. He looked up at Eureka in the mirror.

A voice made them jump. "Who do you think you are?"

Eureka held William's shoulders as she spoke into the mirror. "My name is Eureka Boudreaux. We came from—"

"I didn't ask your name," the voice cut her off. It was soft and deep—a boy's voice—seasoned with the slightest German accent.

It was odd to be looking at herself, addressing a disembodied voice, and discussing the nature of identity.

"When who you are changes all the time," she said, "the only thing you have is your name."

"Good answer."

The door creaked open, but no one stood behind it. Ander led them through the doorway, into a grand, circular room. Rushing water echoed off a distant ceiling.

Eureka held her torch over the moth-wing bower. Dad had drifted to sleep, but his tightly clenched jaw told her that, even after the salve, his pain was severe. She hoped help was inside this cave.

A vast tile mosaic covered the floor. Its design depicted the Grim Reaper grinning through bloody fangs. A sickle sparkled in his left hand, and where his right hand ended, a fire pit had been built into the stone. Its blaze emanated from the Reaper's bony fingers.

Between the stacks of skulls, the walls were decorated with dark murals. Eureka stared at one depicting a great flood, victims drowning in a violent sea. A day ago it would have reminded Eureka of the Orozco murals she'd seen with Diana in Guadalajara. Now it could have been a window outside.

"We came all this way to end up in some freak's bachelor pad," Cat whispered in Eureka's good ear.

"Freaks can be valuable friends," Eureka said. "Look at us."

Near the far wall of the room, a spiral staircase made of stone curved up, to a floor above, and down, to another floor below. But as they walked farther into the room, Eureka saw that the far wall was moving, that it was a waterfall cascading from an unseen source down white stone. The ceiling opened up and the floor dropped off and there was a gap of several feet between the edge of the ground and the waterfall. It made Eureka claustrophobic and she didn't know why.

Just in front of the waterfall, a dark green slope-back leather chair stood atop a sleek fox-fur rug. A man sat in it, his back to them. He faced the waterfall, reading an ancient book and sipping something fizzy from a golden champagne flute.

"Hello?" Ander called.

The man in the chair was still.

Eureka stepped deeper into the room. "We're looking for someone named Solon."

The figure spun to face them, propping his elbows atop the studded back of the chair. He lifted his chin and surveyed his guests. He looked fifteen, but his expression had a serrated edge that told Eureka he was older. He wore suede moccasins and a maroon satin robe belted loosely at his waist.

"You've found him." His voice held an absence of hope. "Let's celebrate."

Cat tilted her head toward Eureka and whispered, *"Schwing."*

It hadn't occurred to Eureka that the boy was hot—though, now that Cat mentioned it, he was. Very. His eyes were a pale, spellbinding blue. His close-cropped hair was blond with intriguing black and brown leopard-print spots. The slinkiness of his robe suggested they had stumbled into his boudoir.

The Solon she'd heard about defected from the Seedbearers seventy-five years ago. Was this boy pretending? Was the real Seedbearer somewhere hidden away?

"You're Solon?" Eureka asked.

"Read 'em and weep." He glanced at Eureka. "Not literally, please."

They endured an awkward silence.

"Please don't take this personally," Solon said, "whatever *that* means, but I've been hoodwinked by those witches so many times that, before I welcome you into my salon, I require some proof of your quote-unquote identity."

Eureka felt her empty pockets. She had no means of identifying herself, other than her tears. "You might have to take my word for it."

"No, please keep that." The boy's blue eyes twinkled. "Do you see that flower at the top of the waterfall?"

He raised an index finger. Thirty feet above them, a vibrant fuchsia orchid grew out of the stone. It was stunning, undisturbed by the rushing water. It reminded Eureka of the gossipwitches' caftans. At least fifty bright-lobed blooms clung to the orchid's vine.

"I see it."

"If you are who they say you are," Solon said, "bring it to me."

"Who are 'they'?" Eureka asked.

"One vexed identity at a time. You first. The orchid . . ."

"Why should we believe *you* are who you say you are?" Cat asked. "You look like a freshman gamer too wimpy to carry my books."

"What Cat means is," Eureka said, "we were expecting someone older."

"Age is in the eye of the beholder," Solon said, and tipped his head toward Ander. "Wouldn't you agree?"

Ander looked paler than usual. "This is Solon."

"Fine," Cat said. "He's Solon, Eureka's Eureka, and the Cat's the Cat, not that you're interested. We're thirsty, and I'd like to know if my family's pushing clouds around or what. I take it you don't have a phone?"

"The orchid," Solon said. "Then we'll talk."

"This is ridiculous," Cat said.

"She shouldn't need to prove herself to you," Ander said. "We're here because—"

"I know why she's here," Solon said.

"If I bring you the orchid," Eureka said, "you'll help us?"

"I said we'll talk," Solon corrected. "You'll find that I'm an excellent conversationalist. No one has ever complained."

"We need water," Eureka said. "And my father's hurt."

"I said we'll talk," Solon repeated. "Unless you know someone else in the neighborhood who can give you what you seek?"

Eureka studied the waterfall, trying to determine the texture of the white rock wall behind it. The first step would be getting beyond the water to the rock. Then she'd have to worry about climbing.

She looked at Dad, but he was still asleep. She thought of the hundreds of trees she and Brooks had climbed throughout their childhood. Their favorite climbing time was dusk, so that when they nestled into the tallest branches, the stars would just be coming out. Eureka imagined attaching all those tree limbs onto one colossal trunk. She imagined it stretching into outer space, past the moon. Then she imagined a tree house on the moon, with Brooks waiting for her inside, floating in a space suit, biding his time by renaming constellations. Orion was the only one he knew.

She fixed her eyes on the surface of the waterfall. Fantasizing wouldn't help her now. Cat was right—this was ridiculous. She couldn't reach that orchid. Why was she even considering it?

Find your way out of a foxhole, girl.

Memories of Diana's voice filled Eureka's heart with longing. Her mother would say that belief in the impossible was the first step toward greatness. She would whisper in Eureka's ear: *Go and get it.*

When Eureka thought of Diana, her hand moved to her neck. As her fingers traced the locket, the yellow ribbon, and the thunderstone, she devised a plan. She handed Cat the torch. She slid her tote bag from her shoulder and gave it to Ander.

He gave her a smile that said, *You're really going for it?*

She hung in front of him, feeling the warmth of his fingers as he took her bag. Sweat formed on her brow. It was foolish to want a good-luck kiss, but she did.

"Go and get it," he whispered.

Eureka crouched into the starting pose she assumed before a race. She bent her knees and balled her fists. She was going to need a running start.

"Nice form." Solon drained the last of his drink. "Who knew she was trained?"

"Let's go, Boudreaux." Cat repeated the cheer she'd chanted at meets. But her voice sounded distant, like she couldn't believe what was happening.

Eureka had done the high jump for a season when she'd first started running. She stared at the waterfall, envisioning a horizontal beam of water for her body to clear when she leapt. Fear filled her, energy she told herself to exploit. From the back of the cave, she began to jog.

For the first few strides, her muscles were cold and tight, but soon she felt the loosening, the lightening. She inhaled deeply, drawing the strange, steamy air into her lungs, holding her breath until she felt immersed in the atmosphere. Her shoes stopped squishing. Her rib cage lifted. Her mind traveled to the highest branch on the moon. She didn't look down when the floor dropped out from under her. She pivoted in the air, arched her back, drew her hands up, and dove backward into the waterfall.

Cold water roared around her. She screamed as her body dropped twenty feet and was consumed by the fall. Then the thunderstone shield bloomed around her, an answered prayer bouncing her upward. She was weightless, protected. But the force of the waterfall was dragging her down.

She was going to have to swim up it.

Her body straightened. She did one breaststroke, then another.

It was hard work. Every burning stroke of her arms raised her only a half-inch higher. When she didn't strain against it, the water pushed her down. After a long, exhausting stretch, Eureka sensed that she was only now level with the cave's floor. She still had far to go.

Her arms thrust forward. She groaned as she strained to draw them back. She kicked her legs fiercely. She struggled up the waterfall, half-inches becoming inches, and then, impossibly, feet.

She was trembling from exhaustion when she saw the thin roots of the orchid tracing the side of the stone. Beyond the waterfall were wobbling broad green leaves, shimmering fuchsia blossoms. She was so excited that she lunged toward the orchid.

She moved too quickly. Her body passed through the waterfall before she realized her mistake: the instant the shield was exposed to air, it popped like a balloon.

Eureka's hand had been just inches from the flower, but now she lost propulsion. Her arms spun. Her legs bicycled in the air. She screamed, and her body dropped—

Then something brushed against her back. A force buffeted her in midair as she rose along the face of the waterfall. The orchid came within reach again.

The Zephyr. The sensation of Ander's breath surrounding her body was wonderful and intimate. It embraced her and pushed her higher in the sky. They were thirty feet apart, but Eureka felt as close as when they'd kissed.

She reached out and grasped the orchid. Her fingers closed around its reedy stem. She pulled it loose from the rock.

Below her, Ander whooped. The twins clapped and jumped. Cat catcalled. When Eureka turned to wave the flower triumphantly, she saw Solon frowning at Ander.

The wind changed directions, and the force that had been holding her up was ripped out from underneath her. Gravity returned. Eureka plunged down the face of the waterfall into distant darkness.

9

DIVER DOWN

Eureka plummeted through cold mist. She heard the twins scream. She reached out for the blur of their bodies as she hurtled downward, through the space in the floor of the cave and into a wide, shadowy chute.

Darkness swallowed her. She crossed her arms over her chest, clutching the orchid with one hand, her thunderstone with the other. The yellow ribbon slapped her chin to remind her she had failed that girl. She braced herself for whatever she would soon be crashing into. Every waterfall had an end.

She worried about plunging into water too shallow for her shield. She thought back to the rainy night her grandmother Sugar had died, the soles of her feet slowly turning blue, and the old woman's hoarse last word: *"Pray!"* For some reason, the memory was calming. She whispered, "I'm coming, Sugar," then, "I'm coming, Mom."

She fell faster. Then she did a somersault. If these were her final living moments, she wouldn't spend them like a mannequin.

She thought of a million things at once—a poem she'd read in the psych ward called "Falling," by James Dickey, a movie about people who committed suicide by jumping off the Golden Gate Bridge, her first taste of whipped cream on pancakes, the aching baroque sweetness of the world, the luxury of letting yourself feel lonesome and sad.

Suddenly the chute opened into a vast dim chamber and Eureka saw water below. From the movie about the Golden Gate suicides, she knew to assume a sitting position before she broke the water's surface.

She rocketed underwater as if strapped to an invisible chair. The shield sprang up around her. She gasped and whooped and looked beneath her. It had saved her from being impaled on a dense metropolis of stalagmites. Their spires had come within inches of her skin.

She collapsed against the surface of the shield. She tried to breathe, to slow her sprinting heart. She tried to recover what she'd been thinking as she fell, but those thoughts were flying up wherever dreams lived.

She heard shouting, her name being called. A great splash blew the shield backward. Ander swam toward her. He arrived in front of her shield and pressed his hands against its surface. He looked desperate to hold her.

Eureka released the orchid. She pressed her hands against the shield, her palms against Ander's. Then, slowly, she pressed her forehead and her shoulders against it. Ander lifted his chin, rapt, as she pressed her lips to the shield.

She gazed at him. His lips were slightly parted. He hesitated for a moment, then took his finger and traced her lips lightly through the shield. She could feel the subtle pressure of his touch but not the softness of his skin.

Heat coursed through Eureka. They were tantalizingly close—

They could swim to the surface and the shield would fall away, but Eureka suddenly sensed that a powerful force might always lie between them, teasing her, torturing her.

Ander had been underwater a long time without air. Within her shield, Eureka could breathe, but Ander's lungs must have ached. She pulled back from the edge of the shield and pointed toward the surface. When Ander nodded, she picked up the orchid and they kicked themselves higher, higher, until Eureka's head broke the surface and the shield shattered again.

They faced each other and tread water, which was as warm as a just-drawn bath. Her arm brushed Ander's thigh. His foot pedaled into her knee. Her guilt grazed his, then got lost in the dark water. Eureka didn't know how to stay connected and not sink.

"Don't mind me." Solon smirked at them from the edge of the pool.

Beyond Solon, Eureka saw a curved staircase built into the stone. Cat and the twins leapt from the bottom step and ran toward her. Dad's winged bower hovered at the foot of the stairs.

She waved the orchid to signal she was okay. She was still adjusting to the idea that she wasn't about to die.

The cave was darker down here, undecorated. Only a few stalagmite candelabra lit the yawning space, but Eureka sensed there was more to this underground cistern than she could see from the pool.

A spray of water erupted behind Eureka. She lunged forward.

"Just a little blowhole," Solon said. "It's not another test. Why don't you calm down and emerge? We have much to discuss."

Ander pulled himself out of the pool and turned to help Eureka. She was soaking; he was as dry as ever.

Solon tossed her a robe identical to his. She put it on over her wet clothes and wrung the water from her ponytail. Cat and the twins embraced her—her friend high up on her body, her siblings low.

"So. You passed," Solon said. He glanced at Ander. "With only some cheating."

Ander chested up against Solon. "She was almost killed."

Solon stumbled backward, amused. "Some would say that's the point. I'm sure you know who I mean." He turned back to Eureka. "Your friend is mad because when I realized he was using his Zephyr to aid you, I used mine to disengage his. That's when you fell." He used two fingers to mimic the flailing legs of a falling girl and whistled the sound of her descent.

"You *wanted* me to fall?" Eureka asked.

"*Want* is a strong word. Mostly, I *don't* want a Seedbearer paraded into my home."

"I'm not a Seedbearer anymore," Ander said. "My name is Ander. Like you, I turned my back—"

Solon scowled and shook his head impatiently. "Once a Seedbearer, always a Seedbearer. It is the most unfortunate aspect of a vividly unfortunate existence. And you are nothing like me." He paused. "Ander? After Leander?"

"Yes."

"Rather pretentious, isn't it?" Solon asked. "Have you had your Passage yet?"

Ander nodded. "I was eighteen in February."

Eureka's gaze darted between the two boys, trying to keep up. All of this was news to her. She imagined Ander's birthday months ago in Lafayette. Whom had he celebrated with? What kind of cake did he like? And what was a Passage?

"Whom did you replace?" Solon asked Ander. "Wait, don't tell me, I won't get stuck at that dysfunction junction just because some kid walks into my cave like a bad joke."

95

Eureka threw the orchid, striking Solon in the face. "Here's your flower, asshole."

"Blow it out your blowhole," Cat muttered.

Solon caught the orchid by its stem. He brought it to his chest and patted its petals. "How much time will you buy me?" he asked the flower.

When he looked up at Eureka, an eerie smile haunted his face. "Well, you're here now, aren't you? I might as well get used to it. Privacy and dignity are temporary states."

⋊

"Water, water, everyone?" Solon held out a copper carafe when they were back upstairs and dry, seated around his fire. He'd distributed alpaca blankets, which they all wrapped around their shoulders.

Cat flexed her feet in a pair of Solon's moccasins.

"These things will be the death of me," she'd told one of the skulls on the wall when she'd slipped off her red stilettos and hooked their heels through its eye sockets. "You feel me, right?"

Dad's moth-wing bower had begun to sag during Eureka's adventure with the orchid. The moths were dying. When the bower drooped all the way to the ground it unfurled, looking as magical as a drab gray quilt. As Solon and Ander carried Dad closer to the fire and propped him up on a mountain of pillows, Eureka fingered the bower's strange material. The moths' wings were changing, from thin, chalky sheets to dust.

She took the carafe from Solon, aching to down its contents in a few gulps. She held it to her father's lips.

He drank weakly. His dry throat made scraping noises as he strained to swallow. When he seemed too tired to drink any more he turned his eyes on Eureka. "I'm supposed to be taking care of you."

She wiped the corner of his mouth. "We take care of each other."

He tried to smile. "You look so much like your mother, but . . ."

"But what?"

Dad rarely brought up Diana. Eureka knew he was tired, but she wanted to stay in the moment, to keep him there with her. She wanted to learn as much as she could about the love that made her.

"But you're stronger."

Eureka was amazed. Diana had been the strongest person she knew.

"You aren't afraid to falter," Dad said, "or to be around others when they falter. That takes strength that Diana never had."

"I don't think I have a choice," Eureka said.

Dad touched her cheek. "Everybody's got a choice."

Solon, who had disappeared behind a hanging rug that must have led to a back room, returned carrying a wooden tray of tall ceramic mugs. "I also have prosecco, if you'd prefer. I do."

"What's prospecto?" William asked.

"Do you have popcorn?" Claire asked.

"Look at us"—Solon tossed an empty mug to Cat, who caught it by the handle with her pinky—"having a little party."

"My dad needs a doctor," Eureka said.

"Yes, yes," Solon said. "My assistant should be here presently. She makes the loveliest painkillers."

"His wound needs redressing, too," Eureka said. "We need gauze, antiseptic—"

"When Filiz gets here. She handles what I don't." Solon reached into his robe pocket and withdrew a hand-rolled cigarette. He put it in his mouth, leaned over the fire, and inhaled. He blew out a great puff of smoke that smelled like cloves. William coughed. Eureka fanned the smoke away from her brother's face.

"First," Solon said, "I must know which one of you saw through the witches' glaze into my cave?"

"Me," Claire said.

"Should have known," Solon said. "She's three foot two and exudes the knowledge that adults are full of crap. Her quirk is still quite strong."

"What's a quirk?" Cat asked, but Solon only smiled at Claire.

"Claire is my sister," Eureka explained. "She and William are twins."

Solon nodded at William, exhaled out the corner of his mouth to be polite. "What's your brand of magic?"

"I'm still deciding," William said. He didn't mean it as a joke—to William, magic was real.

The lost Seedbearer rested his cigarette on the stalagmite he was using as an ashtray. "I understand."

Ander picked up the cigarette and sniffed it as if he'd never seen one before. "How can you smoke?"

Solon snatched the cigarette. "I have forsaken a million pleasures, but I am faithful to this."

"But what about your Zephyr?" Ander asked. "How can you still—"

"My lungs are ruined." Solon took a puff and exhaled an enormous plume of smoke. "Derailing you a moment ago was the first I've used my Zephyr in ages. I suppose, if my death depended on it, I could still erect a cordon." He tapped the tip of the cigarette. "But I prefer this little buzz."

He turned away, cigarette dangling from his lips, and plucked the orchid petals from their branch. He dropped them into a glass soda bottle, counting the petals under his breath, as if they were precious gold coins.

"What are you going to do with those?" Claire asked.

Solon smiled and continued his weird work. When he had filled the bottle, he pulled a small black velvet pouch from his pocket and poured the remaining amethyst petals into it.

"I'll save these for a slightly less rainy day," he said.

"Now that you have your little flower," Cat said, "is there any chance I could use a phone, or hop on someone's Wi-Fi?"

"He's been living under a rock," Eureka said. "I doubt he's hooked up to broadband." She glanced at Solon. "Cat was separated from her family. She needs to reach them."

"We're off the grid down here," Solon said. "There used to be an Internet café a couple of miles to the west, but now all of that is waterworld, thanks to Eureka. The entire worldwide cobweb has been washed away."

Cat gaped at Eureka. "You killed the Internet."

"The witches may know where your family is," Solon continued, "but they don't provide information for free." He glanced at the petal-filled bottle. "I'd think thrice before becoming indebted to those beasts."

"We met them," Eureka said. "They helped us find you. They carried Dad and—"

"I know." Solon turned to the disintegrated bower. He ran his hand lightly over the moth-wing dust. "I would recognize the remains of my darlings anywhere."

"Can the witches really put Cat in touch with her family?" Eureka asked.

"They can do many things." Solon flung down the velvet pouch, reached for a burlap sack behind him. He spilled out a mass of colored stones and began sifting through them. "Scavenging vultures. Whorish harpies. You met Esme? The young one—very pretty?"

"We didn't catch their names," Eureka said.

"You never will—and you must never call her by it. Their

names are secret from everyone but other gossipwitches. Anyone who knows one must pretend that she does not."

"Then why tell me her name?" Eureka asked.

"Because Esme is the smartest and the loveliest and therefore the most terrible."

"What about the witches' glaze?" Claire scooted closer to Solon, who gave her an alarmed smile, as if no one had been close to him in years.

"I pay the hags to enchant the entrance to my cave. The glaze is a special camouflage so my family can't find me. It's imperceptible to the senses, or it's supposed to be. I shall demand a refund." He looked at Ander. "How *did* you get this far?"

"I have been planning to find you for a long time—"

"Easy to say that now, but you could never have found me on your own." Solon made a scary face at one of his skulls. Then he rose and disappeared again behind the hanging tapestry. Eureka heard sounds of cupboards being flung open and slammed shut.

"I am no threat to you, Solon," Ander called. "I hate them as much as you do."

"Impossible," Solon said when he returned a moment later, icy bottle of prosecco in one hand, champagne flute in the other. He jerked his head toward Eureka. "You have *her*. My Byblis is dead."

Eureka felt for her bag to make sure she still had *The Book of Love.* Byblis had been one of the previous owners of the book, and a Tearline girl. Ander had told Eureka that the Seedbearers had killed her.

Solon studied Eureka. "You resemble her."

"Byblis?"

"Your mother."

Dad raised his chin. "How'd you say you knew Diana?"

"She visited me here years ago." Solon popped the cork on his bottle. *"Opa!"* he shouted as it rocketed off one skull's forehead and lodged in the eye socket of another. There were more than a few skulls sporting cork eyeballs.

"My mother—" Eureka said.

"Diamond of a woman." Solon raised his glass, toasting Diana. He took a sip. "How is she?"

"She—" Eureka didn't know how to end that sentence.

"Damn them," Solon whispered, and Eureka realized that he knew about the Seedbearers' plans. "Did you know she had made a pact with them?"

"What?"

"She swore to keep you from crying," Solon said, "and to keep the truth of your lineage a secret from you. In exchange, they were supposed to let you live."

Diana had never mentioned a Seedbearer pact or a journey to the Bitter Cloud. She had never mentioned so many things. Diana had known what Eureka faced, but she hadn't borne Eureka's burden. She hadn't been a Tearline girl—not born on a day that didn't exist, not a motherless child and a childless mother, not raised to withhold her feelings until they exploded from within her. Diana had been Eureka's greatest ally, but she'd never really understood what it was like to be Eureka.

Still, her mother had had a gift for letting chaos swirl until its meaning took shape. Eureka touched her necklace and let the piercing sensation of missing her mother come.

"Diana knew we'd get along," Solon said.

Eureka squinted. "She did? Do we?"

"I believe her words were 'If you survive each other, you will become great friends,'" Solon said. "I should warn you I am very hard to kill."

"Same here," Eureka said. "Believe me, I've tried."

"Yes?" Solon looked admiringly at Eureka. "Now I know we'll become friends."

"I'm not suicidal now." Eureka didn't know why she said that—maybe it was for the twins, maybe for herself. In any case, it was true.

"What makes you want to live?" Solon asked. "Let me guess." He snapped his fingers. "You want to save the world."

"You think this is a joke?" she asked.

"Of course it's a joke." Solon jerked his thumb toward Ander. "Especially on him. He's in *love* with you."

"You don't know us," Ander said. "We came here for help defeating Atlas, not your twisted perspective on love. Diana must have made you promise to help Eureka. Are you going to or not?"

"You talk as if you're unique." Solon spoke like he knew his words stung and was enjoying it. "And the rest of you. You're the collateral damage of a deadly teenage fling that these two were too self-absorbed to prevent."

"Hey," Cat said. "I'm twice as self-absorbed as Eureka."

"But not a tenth as deadly," Solon said.

Behind Solon, snow-white water tumbled from the fall. Eureka studied the place where the orchid had been. She didn't know what she'd been expecting from Solon, but it certainly hadn't been this.

"Why did my mother think you could help me?"

"Because I can," Solon said, "and I should. I hope you're a fast learner. We have only until the full moon before this stupid world comes to its stupid end."

10

AS IT RELATES TO LOVE

"What happens on the full moon?" Eureka asked hours later when she, Solon, and Ander were alone before the fire pit.

Ever since his assistants had arrived that afternoon, Solon had been quiet. He would offer no further details on Eureka's Tearline while the redheaded girl Filiz passed in and out of alcoves, clearing dishes, making fires. She looked uneasy, like she'd gone to a party far from home and lost her friends.

Before Filiz left for the night, she'd redressed Dad's shoulder and brewed a potent pennyroyal tea that tucked him into sleep in the guest room behind the orange and red hanging tapestry. The twins slept on pallets at his side. Cat had refused food or rest until she reached her family, so Solon's other assistant, a boy introduced as "the Poet," escorted her to a veranda where there was a slim chance his phone might find reception.

The Poet was tall and sexy with the paint-stained finger-tips of a graffiti artist. He and Cat had appraised each other intensely. As they spiraled up the winding staircase, Cat had drawn an aerosol can of paint from his cargo pocket. "So, you're an *artiste. . . .*" Eureka assumed they'd be gone for hours.

At last, Solon led Eureka and Ander to a stone table in the center of his salon. The waterfall's mist reached Eureka's skin, dampened the maroon satin bathrobes she and Ander wore while their clothes dried over stones around the fire pit.

"The Tearline is tied to a lunar cycle," Solon said. "When you cried yesterday morning, you may have noticed the wax-ing crescent low in the sky? That was when the Rising began. It must complete before the full moon, nine days from now."

"And if it doesn't?" Ander asked.

Solon raised an eyebrow and disappeared into his kitchen. He returned a moment later carrying a tray filled with chipped, mismatched ceramic bowls of creamed spinach, egg noodles swimming in mushroom gravy, nuts and apricots drowned in honey, crunchy chickpeas, and a big wedge of dense, sugary baklava.

"If Atlantis does not rise before the next full moon, the Waking World will become a swamp of wasted dead. Atlas will return to the Sleeping World, where he must await the next generation of Tearline girl, should there be one."

"What do you mean—wasted dead?" Ander asked.

Solon held up an earthenware platter and offered it to Eureka. "Schnitzel?"

Eureka waved the plate away. "I assumed the rise was already complete."

"That depends on how many of your tears hit the ground," Solon said. "It is my belief that you shed only two, but you must enlighten me. The number will establish our position in this catastrophe."

"I'm not sure," she said. "I didn't know I was supposed to keep track."

Solon turned to Ander, slid a cutlet onto his plate. "What's your excuse?"

"I know each tear carries a unique weight," Ander said, "but I never knew the formula. I didn't know about the lunar cycle, either. The Seedbearers were secretive, even though I was family. After you left, they had to be careful who they trusted."

"They keep secrets because they are afraid." Solon swallowed a bite of meat and closed his eyes. His voice assumed a soft lilt as he began to sing.

"One tear to shatter the Waking World's skin.
A second to seep through Earth's roots within.

A *third to awaken the Sleeping World and let old*
kingdoms rebegin."

His eyes opened. " 'The Rubric of Tears' was the last song sung before the Flood. It's a metaphor, for life or death or—"

"Love," Eureka realized.

Solon tilted his head. "Go on."

Eureka didn't know where the idea had come from. She was no expert on love. But "The Rubric of Tears" reminded her of how she'd felt when she met Ander.

"Maybe the first tear," she said, "shattering our world's skin, represents attraction. When Cat likes a guy, she never calls it a crush. She says 'shatter' is more accurate."

"I know what she means," Ander said.

"But love at first sight doesn't lead anywhere," Eureka said, "unless the second sight goes deeper."

"So the second tear," Ander said, "the one that seeps into the roots—"

Eureka nodded. "That's getting to know someone. Their fears and dreams and passions. Their flaws." She thought of Dad's words earlier that day. "It's not being afraid to touch the other person's roots. It's the next thousand miles of falling in love." She paused. "But it still isn't love. It's infatuation, until—"

"The third tear," Solon said.

"The third tear reaches the Sleeping World," Ander said. "And awakens it." His cheeks flushed. "How is that like love?"

"Reciprocation," Eureka said. "When the person you love loves you back. When the connection becomes unbreakable. That's when there's no turning back."

She hadn't realized she was leaning toward Ander and he was leaning toward her until Solon wedged a hand between their faces.

"I see you haven't told her about us," Solon said to Ander.

"What about you?" Eureka asked.

"He means"—Ander turned back to his plate and cut a bite of schnitzel but didn't eat it—"the Seedbearers' role in stopping your tears."

Solon scoffed at Ander.

"I know about that," Eureka said. Ander might have turned against his family, but he still cared about the fate of her tears. She thought of the icy Zephyr against her frozen cheeks. "Ander has it," she realized.

"What?" Solon asked.

"The third tear. I cried again on the way here, but his breath froze my tears. They didn't hit the earth. They're safe inside his lachrymatory."

"Tearline tears are never safe," Solon said.

"They're safe with me." Ander showed Solon the little silver vial.

Solon rubbed his jaw. "You've been running with a bomb."

"Bombs can be disarmed," Eureka said. "Can't we dispose of my tears without—"

"No," Ander and Solon said together.

"I'll keep this." Solon snatched the lachrymatory and glared across the table. "I didn't stockpile all this food for it to go to waste. Eat! You should see what my neighbors have for dinner. Twigs! Each other!"

Eureka spooned some noodles onto her plate. She eyed the meat, which smelled like the kitchen of the Bon Creole Lunch Shack, whose crumpled, grease-stained takeout bags danced in the wind above the beds of most New Iberia pickup trucks. The scent awakened a nostalgia in her, and she wished she were straddling a sticky barstool at Victor's, where Dad used to fry oysters as small as quarters and as light as air.

Ander tucked forkfuls into his mouth rapidly, without tasting, as if the void within him might be filled.

Eureka was in awe of her own hunger. It had become a shape inside her, with edges sharp as broken glass. But Solon's words had made it hard to chew. She thought about Filiz's penetrating golden eyes.

"That's why you sent Filiz and the Poet away before you brought out the food."

"Did you really think a deluge of salt water could fall from the sky and not destroy the food chain?" Solon asked. "My assistants think I'm starving, just as they are starving. They must continue to think that. It wouldn't do for the neighbors to be crawling around on hands and knees, bumping their heads on my glaze. Understand?"

"Why don't you share with them?"

Solon picked up the pitcher, held it high over Eureka's empty glass, and poured a long stream of water to refill it. "Why don't you go back in time and not flood the world?"

Ander snatched the pitcher from Solon and slammed it on the table. Water sloshed onto Eureka's thighs.

"How very wasteful," Solon said.

"She's doing the best she can."

"She must do better than that," Solon said. "The third tear is in the world. Soon Atlas will get it."

"No," Eureka said. "We came here so you could help me stop him."

Solon dragged a finger down his plate and licked the grease from it. "This isn't a student council election. Atlas is the darkest force the Waking World has ever known."

"How? He's been trapped under the ocean for thousands of years," Eureka said.

Solon stared into the waterfall for a long time. His voice was faint when he spoke at last. "There was a boy who lived two blocks from Byblis when she was a girl in Munich. They took a painting class together. They were . . . friends. Then Atlas took him. He possessed the mind of an ordinary boy and set a devil loose. At a certain point, Byblis died, but never mind that. Atlas didn't leave his host's body for years." He waved a hand dismally. "The rest, unfortunately, is history. And if Atlantis rises, what the future holds is worse. You have no idea what you're up against. You won't understand until you're face to face with him at the Marais."

Eureka fingered Diana's locket. Inside, her mother had written the very same word. Eureka popped its clasp and pulled the chain taut to show Solon. "What happens at the Marais?"

"Time will tell," Solon said. "What do you know about the Marais?"

"It's the Cajun word for 'swamp.'" Eureka pictured the mythical city and its monster king rising from the bayou beyond her house. That didn't seem right.

"But a swamp could be anywhere," Ander said.

"Or everywhere," Solon said.

"You know where it is," Eureka said. "How do I get there?"

"The Marais is not on any map," Solon said. "True places never are. Man has frittered away millennia speculating about where Atlantis once was. Did it droop beyond marlins in Florida, or amid icy Swedish mermaids? Did it sink alongside Antarctic seals? Is it undulating under Bahamian yachts, oozing beneath ouzo bottles in Santorini, wafting like palm fronds off the coast of Palestine?"

From the bedroom behind the tapestry, William whimpered in his sleep. Eureka rose to go to her brother, who often needed soothing from bad dreams, but the boy grew quiet again.

Solon lowered his voice. "Or maybe the whole continent just drifted, disinclined to settle down. No one knows."

"In other words," Ander said, "Atlantis could rise from anywhere."

"Not at all." Solon refilled his glass of prosecco. "Over the years the Marais's latitude and longitude in the Waking World has shifted, but it is and always has been the place from where Atlantis must rise. The seafloor beneath the Marais is pliant in the exact shape of the lost continent. From there, Atlas can bring Atlantis up whole. A successful exhumation."

"So it matters where the third tear hits the earth—" Ander said.

"*If* the third tear hits the earth," Eureka said.

"Wherever the third tear hits, Atlantis will still rise," Solon said, "but unless it falls on the Marais, it rises piecemeal, in jagged shards, like teeth growing in already decayed. Atlas would have ugly work to do to reunite his empire." He grimaced. "And he would rather focus on . . . other things."

"The Filling," Ander said quietly.

"What is the Filling?" Eureka asked.

"You are far from ready to comprehend that," Solon said. "The Marais is where Eureka must face the Evil One. He will be waiting there."

Eureka remembered that vision of Brooks swimming toward her near the Turkish shore. It hadn't been a vision. And it hadn't been Brooks coming for her. It had been Atlas.

"No," she said. "I think he's here."

Solon glanced around his cave and furrowed his brow at Eureka.

"Eureka's confused," Ander said. "On our way here she thought she saw the boy Atlas possessed. I told her it couldn't be him—"

"You told her wrong." Solon studied the lachrymatory in his fist. He slipped it inside his robe pocket. "Coming for the Tearline girl himself. Hiding somewhere in these mountains. One must admire Atlas's commitment. It is essential, Eureka, that you keep your distance from him until you are prepared."

"Obviously," Eureka said, but she looked down at her plate so they wouldn't see her eyes. If Atlas was here, Brooks was here. If he was here, she could still save him.

"If he's here," Ander said, "we have to kill him."

"No one is touching Brooks," Eureka said.

"*Brooks* is gone," Ander said, and looked to Solon. "Tell her."

"For now, the boy you knew still exists inside his body," Solon said, "but once one is taken by Atlas, there is no way out. Were you sentimental about this mortal coil?"

"He's my best friend."

"Eureka." Ander reached for her hand. "When you shed the first two tears in your backyard, what were you crying about?"

"It's complicated. It wasn't just one thing."

But it wasn't complicated at all. It was the simplest thing.

She'd been thinking about a pecan tree in Sugar's backyard. Her mind had climbed the branches, searching for Brooks. He was always there in her happiest childhood memories, always laughing, always making her laugh.

Eureka realized Ander already knew what she was about to say. "I cried because I thought he was gone."

"And you were right"—Solon raised his glass—"so let's move on."

"That was before I saw him swimming toward me this morning," Eureka said. "As long as Brooks's body exists, as long as his lungs still draw breath and his heart still beats, I won't give up on my friend."

"Your friend is but a tool now," Solon said. "Atlas will use the boy's memories to manipulate you. When he is done, he will take the boy's soul with him."

No. There had to be a way to stop the world's worst enemy without ending her best friend. "What if I refuse to go to the Marais altogether? I'll stay here until the full moon wanes, and Atlas will have to go back to the Sleeping World. He'll leave Brooks's body and go home."

"That's no better than Ander's absurd idea to kill Brooks. Atlas's mind would return to Atlantis. On his way he will discard your friend's body and steal his soul," Solon said. "In either case, you would be avoiding the one thing you must do. You must face Atlas. You must destroy the Evil One."

"But Eureka has a point," Ander said. "Under your cave's

115

glaze she would be safe from the Seedbearers and Atlas. Why can't we just ride out the storm until he sinks again?"

"Just kick the can down the road to the next Tearline girl?" Solon said. "And leave this world rotting with wasted dead while you're at it?"

Shame washed over Eureka. She had started this rise. She would finish it once and for all. "Solon is right. This ends with me."

"Now, there's the girl Diana spoke of." Solon's eyes filled with boyish excitement.

Eureka studied the smoothness of his skin, the youthfulness of his dyed leopard-spotted hair, the vivid brightness of his pale blue eyes. But Solon was exiled from the Seedbearers seventy-five years ago. Nothing made sense anymore.

"Why aren't you old?" The question escaped her before she realized it was rude.

Solon set down his mug and cast a wide-eyed gaze at Ander. "Do you want to field this one?"

"We should be talking about Eureka's preparation to go to the Marais, not—"

"Not what?" Solon asked, beginning to stack their plates. "Your secret?"

"What secret?" Eureka asked.

"Don't do this," Ander said.

"It won't take a minute. I have the story well rehearsed." Solon grinned, gathering silverware from the table. "You really want to know how I stay so vibrantly young?"

"Yes," Eureka said.

"Monkey glands. Injected straight into the—"

Eureka groaned. "I'm not kidding, Solon—"

"I! Feel! Nothing!" Solon flung out his arms and shouted at the waterfall. "No joy. No desire. No empathy. And certainly not"—he stared at her entrancingly—"love." Solon tapped her bag containing *The Book of Love*. "Don't you know the story of Leander and Delphine?"

"You mean Leander and Selene?" Eureka asked. Selene was her ancestor; Leander was Ander's ancestor. Long ago, they had been deeply in love and escaped Atlantis so they could love each other freely—but they were shipwrecked and separated by a storm.

Solon shook his head. "Before Selene, there was Delphine."

Eureka remembered. "Okay, but Leander left Delphine because he wanted Selene." It sounded like locker-room gossip.

Solon had moved to a cupboard behind the table. He poured himself a shot of ruby-colored port. "You're familiar with the expression, 'Hell hath no fury like a woman scorned'?"

Eureka nodded. "Ander, what is he talking about?"

"Imagine a sorceress scorned," Solon said. "Imagine the blackest heart scorched into deeper blackness. Quadruple it. That is Delphine scorned."

"This is not the way Eureka should—" Ander protested.

"I'm just getting to the good part," Solon said. "Delphine couldn't stop Leander from falling in love with another, but she could ensure that his love would lead to misery. She cast a spell on him, one inherited by all his future descendants. Your boyfriend and I both endure under that spell: love drains our life away. Love ages us rapidly, decades in a moment."

Eureka looked from Ander to Solon and back again. They both were just boys. "I don't get it. You said you were once in love—"

"Oh, I was," Solon said fiercely. He swallowed the last drop of port. "There was no way to stop our love. It's fate—Seedbearer boys always fall for Tearline girls. We have Tearline fever."

Eureka looked at Ander. "This has happened other times?"

"No," Solon said sarcastically. "All of this began the moment you started paying attention to it. Good God, girls are dumb."

"It's different with us," Ander said. "We're not like—"

"Not like me?" Solon said. "Not like a murderer?"

It hit Eureka then, what had happened to Byblis. She shivered, then began to sweat. "You killed her."

Seedbearers were supposed to kill Tearline girls. Ander was supposed to have killed Eureka. But Solon had actually gone through with it. He had murdered his true love.

Ander reached for Eureka. "What we feel for each other is real."

"What happened with Byblis?" Eureka asked.

"After one astonishing and amorous month together"—Solon leaned back in his chair, hands clasped over his chest—"we were sitting at a riverside café, our bodies turned toward each other, much like yours are now." Solon gestured at Eureka's and Ander's knees brushing under the table.

"I reached my feeble hand across the table to caress her flowing hair," Solon said. "I stared into her midnight eyes. I gathered all my waning strength and I told her I loved her." He held out his hand and swallowed, drawing his fingers into a fist. "Then I broke her neck, as I had been raised to do." He stared into space, his fist still raised. "I was an old man then, decrepit with the age that love had brought me."

"That's horrible," Eureka said.

"But there's a happy ending," Solon said. "As soon as she was gone, my arthritis faded. My cataracts melted away. I could walk upright. I could run." He smirked at Ander. "But I'm sure my story sounds nothing like yours." He touched Ander's eyes. "Not even in the pitter-patter of your crow's-feet."

Ander swatted Solon's hand.

"Is it true?" Eureka asked.

Ander avoided her eyes. "Yes."

"You weren't going to tell me." Eureka stared at his face, noticing lines she hadn't seen before. She imagined him hobbling and wizened, walking feebly with a cane.

Solon said something, but Eureka's bad ear had been turned to him, so she didn't hear it. She spun around. "What did you say?"

"I said as long as he loves you, Ander will age. The more

intensely he feels, the more quickly it will happen. And on the off chance you're *not* one of those entirely superficial girls—age will affect more than his body. His mind will go as swiftly as the rest. He will grow incredibly, miserably old—and stay that way. Unlike mortal aging, Seedbearer aging leads not to the sweet freedom of death."

"What if he were to stop . . . loving me?"

"Then, my darling," Solon said, "he would remain the strapping, frowning boy you see forever. Interesting dilemma, isn't it?"

11

STAY, ILLUSION

"I need air," Eureka said. The cave seemed to be shrinking, a hand tightening into a fist. "How do I get out?"

There's no way out, Solon had said about Brooks. She sensed the same was true for her. She was trapped inside the Bitter Cloud, trapped in love with a boy who should not love.

"Eureka—" Ander said.

"Don't." She left them at the table and took the staircase down to the lower level. The waterfall's roar grew deafening. She didn't want to hear herself think. She wanted to dive into the pool and let the fall pummel her until she couldn't feel angry or lost or betrayed.

To the right of the waterfall, around the back of the curved staircase, was a heavy black and gray tapestry. She slipped behind the staircase. At the far edge of the pool she steadied herself against the wall and lifted the tapestry's corner.

A channel of water ran beneath it, leading from the pool to a dark, narrow infinity. Lifting the tapestry higher, she saw an aluminum canoe tethered to a post a few feet inside the watery tunnel.

The canoe was heavily dented and bore a cartoon profile of a Native American on the hull. A wooden paddle lay beneath its built-in seat, and a lit torch with a glowing amethyst base was inset in a groove in the prow. The current was lazy, gently undulating.

Eureka wanted to paddle to the unflooded brown bayou behind her house, glide beneath the arms of weeping willows, past jonquils sprouting from the banks, all the way back in time to when the world was still alive.

She climbed inside the canoe, untethered it, and raised the paddle. She was thrilled by her recklessness. She didn't know where this tunnel led. She imagined Seedbearers tasting her in the wind. And Atlas inside Brooks tracking her in the mountains. It didn't stop her. As the slosh of her paddle became the only sound Eureka heard, she watched the shadow show the torch cast on the walls around her. Her silhouette was a haunted abstraction, her arms grotesquely long. Peculiar shapes passed through her form like ghosts.

She thought of Ander's body, the unfair shapes love would sculpt it into. What if Ander aged into an old man before Eureka turned eighteen?

The narrow tunnel opened and Eureka entered a walled pond. Rain fell on her skin. Its salt tasted like the lightest kiss of poison. She was surrounded by white peaks of rock pinching a purple-clouded night sky. Stars twinkled between the clouds.

Once, a few months after Eureka's parents got divorced, Diana had taken her canoeing on the Red River. For three days it was just the two of them, earning sunburns on their shoulders, paddling in time to soul songs, camping on the riverbank, eating only the fish they caught. They'd borrowed Uncle Beau's tent but ended up sleeping in the open, at the bottom of an ocean of stars. Eureka had never seen stars so bright. Diana told her to pick one and she would pick one, too. They named their star after each other so whenever they were apart they could look at the sky and—even if they couldn't see the Diana-Star or Eureka-Star, even if Dad married another woman and moved her to a town where no one had ever been in love—Eureka could see her mother's presence, stand in her mother's glow.

She looked up now and tried to feel Diana through the spaces in the rain. It was hard. She wiped her eyes and lowered her head and remembered something she wished she'd never known Diana said—

Today I saw the boy who's going to break Eureka's heart.

Dad had quoted Diana's line the other day when Eureka introduced him to Ander. Diana had even sketched a picture of a boy who looked like Ander.

Eureka had dismissed Dad. He didn't know the whole story.

But how much of the story did she know? Ander was a Seedbearer, but he wasn't like his family. She thought she'd understood that. Now she was ashamed for doubting her parents. Diana had known that someday, some way, Eureka and Ander would care for each other. She had known that this affection would drain the life from him. She had known that this predicament would crush Eureka's heart. Why hadn't she warned Eureka? Why had she told her not to cry but never told her not to love?

"Mom—" she moaned into the rainy darkness.

A pack of coyotes howled in response. She wished she hadn't left the cave. The lonely pond looked ominous when she wasn't imagining Diana in the sky.

Candles lit portions of the rock opposite the Bitter Cloud. Other caves, Eureka realized. Other people awake and alive. Was that where Solon's assistants lived? She realized this pond was new. She must have cried it. Her rain had filled what used to be a valley connecting Solon to his neighbors. It was a Tearline pond. She wondered how Filiz and the Poet reached Solon's cave now that she'd washed out their path.

She let the canoe drift, lifted the torch from the prow. She held it toward the other caves. The light revealed evidence of desperation: remains of bonfires, abandoned fishing lines, carcasses of animals, bones picked clean of flesh.

She spiraled downward, caught in depression's seductive pull. The boy she'd trusted couldn't help her without loving her, couldn't love her without hurtling toward senility. She would have to give him up. She would have to face Atlas alone.

"Hey, Cuttlefish."

Eureka scanned the rocks. Her heart pounded as she tried to trace the sound's origin. A shadow crossed a rock on the other side of the pond. She lowered the torch into its clip and let the stars light the silhouette of a teenage boy. Dark hair was matted to his forehead. His hand was raised toward her. His face was obscured by shadows, and he wore an unfamiliar raincoat, but Eureka knew it was Brooks.

And inside Brooks was Atlas.

A shiver spread through her. She became afraid. She picked up her paddle. She hadn't been thinking when she left the Bitter Cloud. Why had she abandoned the safety of its glaze? She dragged the paddle through the water, away from Atlas. Brooks.

Until he laughed. Throaty and deep, bright with shared secrets, it was the way Brooks always laughed at their many thousands of inside jokes.

"Trying to get away from me?"

She couldn't leave Brooks. Her arms reversed to paddle backward. If she left now she'd regret it forever. She'd lose her chance to see whether Brooks was alive or a ghost.

"That's more like it." A smile lit his voice. Eureka yearned to see it on his face.

She drew closer. Gray starlight touched his skin, the white of his teeth. She remembered the last moment they'd shared before Brooks had been taken. She wanted to go back there and stay, even though she'd felt depressed and afraid. Those final moments with uncorrupted Brooks shone in her memory like gold. They'd been lying on the beach under a haze of coconut sunscreen. Brooks was drinking a can of Coke. They had sand on their skin, salt on their lips. She heard the swish of his bathing suit when he rose to swim to the breakers. Then he was gone.

He looked the same now. Freckles dotted his cheeks. His brow cast shadows over his dark eyes. He'd come all the way around the world for her. She knew that was Atlas, but it was Brooks, too.

"Are you there?" she asked.

"I'm here."

Atlas controlled his voice, but couldn't Brooks still hear her?

"I know what happened to you," she said.

"And I know what's going to happen to you." He crouched on the ledge so their faces were closer. He held out his hand. "I've got my boat. I know a safe place. We can bring the twins, your dad, and Cat. I'll take care of you."

This was a trick, of course, but the voice that spoke it sounded sincere. She met his eyes, torn by all she found in them—enemy, friend, failure, redemption. If Eureka could not separate Brooks from Atlas, she should take advantage of being this close to the Evil One. "Tell me what the Filling is."

His smile caught her off guard. She looked away.

"Who's been filling your head with ghost stories?" he asked.

"Eureka." Ander's voice called from a dark distance.

She spun around. She couldn't see him on the other side of the pond. Because of the witches' glaze, she couldn't even see the cave from which she'd come. He must have noticed the light of her torch, but could he see her? Could he see Brooks?

Brooks squinted, also unable to see through the witches' glaze. "Where is he?"

"Stay here," Eureka said to Brooks. "He has a gun. He'll kill you." She didn't know if Ander still had that gun, or whether the eerie green artemisia bullets harmed anyone besides Seedbearers. But she would do anything to keep the two—three—boys apart.

Brooks rose to his feet. "That would be interesting."

"I'm serious," she whispered. "I say one word and you're dead." She narrowed her eyes, addressing Atlas. "You'd be sent back to the Sleeping World for who knows how long. I know you don't want that."

Eureka heard the click of a gun being cocked. Brooks held a black pistol to his temple. "Should I save him the trouble?"

"No!" She stood up in the canoe and reached for Brooks, needing that gun far from his head. She thought he was reaching for her. Instead he handed her the gun. The weight of it surprised her. It was warm from being in his hand. She darted a glance back in Ander's direction. She hoped he hadn't heard her. "What are you doing?"

"You said you knew what happened to me. Maybe"—he grinned—"you think I'm dangerous? Here's your chance. Stop me."

She stared at the gun.

"Eureka!" Ander called again.

"That's not what I want," she whispered.

"Now we're getting to the heart of things." Brooks touched her shoulder, steadying her in the canoe. "You want something. Let me help."

The tumble of rocks behind her made Eureka spin around again. Ander was closer, outside the glaze. The sudden sight of him tugged at her and she couldn't help wanting to be closer. He was climbing down a path that ended at a shallow ledge twenty feet above the pond.

"I have to go." Eureka used her paddle to push off Brooks's rock.

"Stay with me," he said.

"I'll find you when I can," Eureka said. "Now go." She sat back in the canoe and paddled away from the ledge, toward the center of the pond. "Ander." She waved. "Over here."

Ander's eyes found her in the water. He arched his arms over his head, bent his knees, and dove. She watched him glide downward, his blond hair rippling, his toes pointed to the sky. When his body broke the surface, it made no splash. Eureka held her breath as he disappeared into her tears.

She looked to the rock where Brooks had been, but he was gone. Had their exchange been real? It felt like a nightmare where nothing happened but the atmosphere was deadly. She slipped the gun into the pond. As it sank, she imagined it coming to rest at the bottom of the flooded valley in the hand of a drowned Turk.

A splash arose from the pond. Eureka ducked—then saw that Ander had risen with it. He stood atop a towering, starlit waterspout like he was a magnetizing moon.

He had dragged much of the water from the pond under him. As her canoe grazed the bottom, Eureka saw the muddy ghost of the path that had once connected Solon's cave to his neighbors'. This was what it had looked like before Eureka's tears. She tried to memorize every detail of the unflooded land below, imagining a past Poet and Filiz walking through it on their way to work, the Poet picking a bud from a drowned olive tree. She didn't see the gun.

Ander's waterspout subsided gently, refilling the valley with tears until he was level with the pond. Then he was hovering on a small wave alongside Eureka's canoe.

"Were you talking to someone?"

"My mom. Old habit." She held out her hand and he climbed into the canoe.

"I never wanted you to find out like this," he said.

"You didn't want me to find out at all."

"When you didn't know, I could pretend it wasn't happening."

Eureka shivered and looked around. The clouds had covered all the stars and Brooks was nowhere. "Everything is happening."

She searched Ander's face for signs of aging. She wouldn't mind him having wrinkles or gray hair, but she refused to be the cause of his old age. Falling more deeply in love would drain Ander's life away. They shouldn't even have let it go this far.

"I trusted you," she said.

"You should."

"But why don't you trust me? You've known my secrets longer than I have. I don't know any of yours. I don't know if you've been in love before. I don't even know your favorite song or what you want to be when you grow up or who your best friend is."

Ander looked at his rain-blurred reflection in the water. He thought for a long time before saying, "I used to have a dog. Shiloh was my best friend." He smashed a fist into his reflection. "I had to let him go."

"Why?"

"It was part of my Passage. Until recently, I aged like any other boy, day by day, season after season, adding inches and scars to my body. But on my eighteenth birthday, I was inducted in a family ceremony." He gazed up, remembering. "I was supposed to repudiate everything I cared about. They said I'd live forever. When Seedbearers do something cruel, our bodies grow younger, like we're traveling back in time. I gave up Shiloh, but I couldn't give up loving you because it's all I am."

"I thought love was supposed to make a person *more* alive," Eureka said. "Your love is . . . like I used to be—suicidal."

"Love is an endless drive on a winding road. You can't see everything about another person all at once." Ander leaned forward in the swaying canoe and inhaled. When he let out his breath, Eureka felt something warm curl around her body. He'd generated a gentle Zephyr that pulled her toward him. Her hands slid up his arms, then clasped around his neck. She couldn't deny how good it felt being pinned against him. She absorbed the tension in his muscles, his body heat, and, before she knew it, his lips.

But then a feeling crept over Eureka like ivy. Somewhere in the darkness Brooks and Atlas were watching them.

"Wait," she said.

But Ander didn't. He held her close and kissed her deeply. Her body was wet and Ander's was dry and not even the rain seemed to know what to do when it touched the places they overlapped. She gave in for a moment, felt his tongue touch hers. Her heart swelled. Her lips tingled.

She forced herself to pull away. She didn't care what Atlas

saw, but she didn't want Brooks watching her kiss a boy like she hadn't flooded the world, like her best friend was not possessed. She pressed her hand against Ander's chest and felt his heartbeat. Hers was racing—with fear and guilt and desire.

"What is it?" Ander asked.

She wanted to trust him, but everything was muddy. Ander saw Brooks only as Atlas, the enemy. He wouldn't understand that Eureka loved and needed part of the enemy to survive. Her encounter with Brooks had to be a secret, at least until she was clear on how to save her friend.

"You can't love me without growing old," she finally said. "And I can't know that about you without wanting to cry. And my tears are the end of the world."

Ander touched the corners of her eyes with his lips to reassure her they were dry. "Please don't be afraid of my love."

He took the oar and paddled twice to spin the canoe around. His soft breath sent them gliding toward the entrance to the tunnel, back to the Bitter Cloud. Just before the rock swallowed them, Eureka looked back to where she'd seen Brooks. Atlas. The ledge he'd stood on was invisible. Low clouds had reclaimed the sky and were busy covering the world in darkness.

12

OCCUPY ATLANTIS

That night the Poet caught up with Filiz on her new, more arduous route home from work, all the way around the new pond. That Filiz no longer thought of the Poet by his given Celan name—Basil—suggested the impact Solon had on Filiz's way of thinking.

The Poet listened to a Discman as he walked—so prehistoric—an old country song twanging in his earbuds when he took them out to call her name. His lips had been swollen and she knew he'd been kissing the Tearline girl's friend. It made Filiz jealous, not because she wanted to kiss the Poet, but because she had never kissed anyone.

He tossed her a parchment-wrapped package. It was the size of the loaves of bread Filiz's mother used to bake when she was a girl and hunger was a greedy pleasure, dispelled by a ready meal. The Poet had another package under his arm.

"This is what Solon offers special guests," he said in their native tongue.

They were the first comprehensible words she'd heard him say in months. She unwrapped the package.

It was *food*—warm, fried meat next to a mound of honey-glazed nuts and dried fruit the color of jewels. Something gooey smelled like paradise. Baklava.

It was all Filiz could do not to devour the entire contents of the package on the path in the rain. But she thought of her mother's bony face.

"He's been building a hidden stash for months," the Poet said. "This was what I snuck today. But tomorrow . . ."

He trailed off, and Filiz knew that everything was about to change. As soon as she shared this food with her family, and the Poet with his, the whole community would know. Solon's cave would no longer be a haven for Filiz—or anyone else.

"They'll kill him," Filiz whispered. She felt protective of Solon—or, at least, of the pleasure she derived from working in his cave. She knew it was selfish, but she didn't want to lose the only touch of glamour in her life.

But her people were starving, so Filiz looked away from the Poet and said, "See you at Assembly."

※

Back at the cave where she lived with her mother and grandmother, Filiz pulled a handful of branches from her coat and dropped them in the center of the floor. She snapped her fingers, igniting a flame from the tips of her chipped blue nails.

Not long ago, they'd had enough wood to keep a fire always burning. Now it was dark and cold when Filiz came home, and she knew it had been like that all day.

The branches crackled, hissed, smoked. Burning wet wood was like forcing love, but since the Tearline girl had cried, nothing was dry. The entire world was dark and cold and wet. The flickering light warmed Filiz's mind and illuminated her sleeping mother. People said Filiz looked like her, even though Filiz dyed her hair and wore heavy makeup she stole from a drugstore in Kusadasi. She saw nothing of herself in her mother's weary face.

Her mother opened her eyes. They were the same soft brown as Filiz's.

"How was work?" Her mother spoke in the rolling, melodic Celan tongue, a mélange of Greek and Turkish and, some said, Atlantean. It was spoken only on these two square miles of earth.

Filiz's mother searched her skin, looking for injuries, as she did every night. She used to perform the same nightly scan on Filiz's father when he'd been alive.

"Fine." When Filiz was a child, she loved the heavy, soothing feel of her mother's gaze upon her skin. By the time the woman's eyes left Filiz's body, her every scratch was healed. It was her mother's quirk, the unique gift of magic every human being was born with. Growing up, Filiz had heard stories about people outside their community who lost their quirks as they matured. She hadn't believed the stories until last summer, when she got a job in Kusadasi as a cruise-ship tour guide. The pale tourists she guided were often friendly but always vacant, little more than polite zombies who saw the world through camera lenses. Their quirks were so long forgotten that Filiz took to imagining what their gifts had been— maybe this banker used to travel back in time, or that real estate agent could communicate with horses. Only the tourists' children's fading quirks were recognizable. It depressed Filiz to watch them being raised to lose them, too.

For the Celans, the quirk was the last thing to go, after the heart stopped beating. The elderly could lose every other faculty—hearing, sight, memory—but their quirks would stay with them until just after their dying breaths. Filiz would never lose her quirk. If her fingers were unable to make fire, she would no longer be Filiz.

She slid away from her mother's gaze, which felt babying and oppressive. Sometimes it was nice to leave a minor scratch alone. None of her deep wounds were on the surface anyway. She put her heavy bag down, not ready to address what it contained. She planned to play Gülle Oyunu, the game of marbles her father had taught her.

136

But she couldn't take her eyes off the bag on the floor, the way the firelight played over it. She'd wolfed down a third of its contents before she got home. She wanted to offer her mother and grandmother the rest, but she was afraid of what it would unleash among her people, who had long looked upon Filiz with distrust. Of course, the Poet would be feeding his own family in his own cave, so there really wasn't any avoiding the inevitable.

Her mother was watching her, full of questions. Lately there had been whispers about a visitor Solon would receive in the cave that all the Celans knew existed but none of them could see. Filiz knew her mother wanted to ask about it.

"She is here." Filiz avoided the wild look in her mother's eyes. She took off her sweatshirt and straightened her tight blue T-shirt. The fashions she had stolen in Kusadasi earned strange looks from the community, but Filiz hated the rough woven cloaks that were their style. Kusadasi had shown her how rural her home was. Now Kusadasi's cutting-edge shops and sparkly hotels lay a mile underwater.

Filiz's people had lived in these caves for thousands of years, since before Atlantis sank. Every generation prayed that Atlantis would not rise in their lifetime or in their children's children's. Now the girl who would bring it back was a hundred yards away.

"Eat." Her mother put a kettle on the fire. "Eat, then speak. The Assembly is beginning next door."

It should have been easy to present her starving mother with the stolen food, but her family's hunger was so great Filiz feared a limited amount of food would only make them more miserable.

She eyed the kettle. "What is it?"

"Soup," her mother said. "Grandma made it."

"You're lying," Filiz said. "It's boiled water from the sky."

"I didn't say what kind of soup it is. It tastes good. Salty, like a broth."

"You ate this already?" She stared at her mother, noticing her sunken eyes. "You can't eat this!"

"We have to eat something."

Filiz grabbed the kettle handle, which burned her in a way the fires she ignited never did. She cursed and dropped the kettle, spilling its contents on the floor.

Her mother fell on her knees, scooped water in her hand, brought it to her lips.

"Stop it!" Filiz fell on her mother, wrenching her hands from her mouth. She grabbed her bag and produced a wedge of baklava, a greasy veal cutlet. She pressed the food into her mother's hands. Her mother gaped at the food as if her hands were on fire. Then she started eating.

Filiz watched her mother scarf half of the cutlet down. "Is there more?" she whispered.

Filiz shook her head.

"We are dying."

The Assembly took place in Filiz's great-uncle Yusuf's cave. After Solon's cave, which none of the others had ever been allowed to see, let alone enter, Yusuf's cave had the largest room for gathering. The fire was dwindling, Filiz's pet peeve. A large painted evil eye watched them from the back wall. Filiz wondered if the eye was blind; it hadn't protected her people in a long time.

She had not been to an Assembly in years, since before her father died. She went tonight because she knew the Poet was going to rat out Solon and his food. She wanted to do what she could to temper the Celans' reactions.

"It is happening." Yusuf furrowed his wiry white eyebrows as Filiz entered the room. His skin reminded Filiz of a pan-fried quail, brown and tight and cracking from sun. "The animals we have long hunted now hunt us. Our home has become treacherous as everything around us starves."

The group was small that night, less than twenty of her neighbors. They looked haggard and feral. She knew that these were the healthiest of them, that everybody absent lay in a nearby cave, too malnourished to move.

The Poet was there, sitting between two other boys his age. The boys' dark skin had a strange white tint. It took Filiz a moment to realize that their skin was caked with salt. They must have been out in the rain all day building the arks. It was an old project of the Celans, in preparation for the flood that generations of them had feared. There were many ancient stories of heroes riding out past floods in sturdy arks. Few took their construction seriously, even stealing the food the ark builders had begun to stockpile when the famine hit last year. But everything was different now that the tear rain fell from the sky. Filiz didn't know where the Celans thought they'd sail to, or how they would survive at sea, but many were convinced the arks would be their salvation.

Filiz had grown up with the Poet and the other boys, but since she'd been to Kusadasi she felt like an alien all the time—too rural for the city, too cosmopolitan for home. Before the flood, she'd concluded that to be happy she must sever ties with the mountains, that one should not hold on to situations out of guilt.

Her grandmother Seyma sat atop a cushion next to Yusuf. Her white hair cascaded past her knees. Seyma claimed her quirk worked only when she was sleeping—she could visit others' dreams—but Filiz knew she could snake inside another's mind at any time of day.

Her neighbors made room as Filiz stepped toward the center of the Assembly. She knelt down before the fire, snapped her fingers, and brought the flame roaring back to life. She never thought much of her quirk until moments like these, when its value became obvious. All the Poet could do was sing and whistle like a bird, a useless gift. Birds never had anything comprehensible to say.

Filiz sat next to a child named Pergamon. He was like a silent shadow, always following her around. His quirk was the otherworldly power of his grip. Filiz had often heard his parents shrieking when Pergamon held their hands. Now he was napping, his soft cheek resting on his arm.

Everyone here had a magical talent, but no one could cause food or drinking water to appear out of thin air. A person with a quirk like that could rule the world.

When the storm began the other day, it had not rained for months. Some Celans had wept happy, foolish tears. Some had fallen on their knees, thanking God, drinking rain. Though most were wise enough to spit it out at the taste of the salt, there was one boy who had been so thirsty he couldn't stop drinking until his body convulsed with seizures. Even those with healing quirks like Filiz's mother could not ease his dehydration. And the salt in the rain had tainted what little drinking water they still had.

The boy died. Filiz had gone to the small service for him that afternoon, just before she went to work. Then she'd entered Solon's cave and met the girl responsible for his death. Solon had watched her reaction, but he must have known she wouldn't say or do anything. Now that the tear rain was falling, the girl was their only hope if Atlantis rose.

That was what Solon said anyway. How the Tearline girl would succeed was Filiz's greatest question. Perhaps her people were right—they should build their arks and prepare for the worst.

Filiz felt her neighbors' eyes on her and wondered whether the Poet had told them yet. Then she saw a plate of food being passed around. Men and women were slapping the Poet's back and laughing. The Poet, the hero. Filiz watched him bask in the glow. What good would it do a roomful of starving people to have a single bite of food? Maybe they were too hungry to ask now, but as soon as the food was gone, wouldn't they demand to know where it had come from, how to get more?

She wasn't angry at the Poet, she realized. She was angry at Eureka. She watched Pergamon sleepily place a bite of spinach in his mouth. The boy next to him took the plate and licked it clean.

The Poet watched Filiz with as much suspicion as she felt for him. He used to ask her why she avoided the Assemblies. Now he clearly wished she wasn't there.

"You met Solon's visitor this afternoon?" Yusuf said. All eyes turned to Filiz.

"She is here with two children, her father, and two friends," the Poet said. "They are kind people, tired from their journey. One girl is named Cat and she is very—"

"Enough about the others," someone called from the back. "What about *her*?"

"She is a selfish brat," Filiz said, and wondered why. Perhaps it was because the Poet had brought food and she also wanted to give the people something they hungered for. They desired an enemy, a common cause—someone to blame.

"Did she care about the innocent people who would die

because of her?" Filiz shook her head. "She thought her pain was more important than your lives. Now Atlantis will rise and wash us away. We are powerless." Her voice grew louder as she went on. "We sit and wait and starve."

"I've always wanted to visit Atlantis," someone said in the back.

"Hush, boy," Filiz's grandmother said. "We have no food, no water to drink. My daughter is dying. And my granddaughter . . ." She looked away as the others finished her sentence in their minds.

"There is more food," Filiz said, because she resented the distrust on her grandmother's face. She was tired of feeling like an outsider among her people.

The room grew silent. Eyes like saucers watched Filiz. The Poet offered her no help. She wished she hadn't said it— she was giving up her life's one remaining pleasure, the time she spent with Solon in his cave—because now she had no choice but to explain.

"Solon has food. He has been preparing for this storm, stocking up. The Tearline girl feasted tonight as you starved."

"And water?" a salt-boy beside the Poet asked.

"He has water, too." Filiz glanced at the Poet. "We discovered this only tonight."

"You will take us there tomorrow," Filiz's grandmother ordered.

"It's not that easy," the Poet said. "You know his home is protected."

143

The gossipwitches had no interest in the Celans, so most in Filiz's community had never personally encountered the strange, orchid-clad women, but they had heard the buzzing bees and felt the presence of magic in the nearby rocks. Once Pergamon had found a gossipwitch honeycomb, though he never told anyone where. Most Celans wouldn't admit it, but Filiz knew they were afraid of all they did not know about the gossipwitches.

"We will bring you more food tomorrow," the Poet promised.

"No. You will get us inside that cave," Filiz's grandmother said. "And we will see what is so special about this Tearline girl."

13

EYE OF THE STORM

"Enjoying the view?"

Eureka jumped at Solon's voice behind her the next morning. She thought she'd been alone on the Bitter Cloud's roof.

She'd climbed the stairs to the veranda at sunrise, curious about the view Ander had seen the night before when he came looking for her. Everything was silver in the morning cloudlight. The Tearline pond had risen, and Eureka didn't think Brooks's rock was still above the surface. She relived dropping that gun into the water, kissing Ander in the canoe, confronting the monster she was supposed to fear. She did fear him, and hate him, and love him.

He was—they were both—out there somewhere, hidden along the banks. She could feel them, the way she could still feel the nightmare from which she'd just awoken.

She'd dreamt she was scaling a mountain in the rain. Near the summit, the earth shifted beneath her. She grabbed hold of something slick and spongy, but it disintegrated in her fingers. Then the whole mountain crumbled, a dangerous rockslide under her feet. As Eureka succumbed to the avalanche, she realized she had not been climbing a mountain, but a vast heap of rotting arms and moldy legs and decomposing heads.

She had been climbing the wasted dead.

"I must admit"—Solon gazed at the pond—"your tears have improved this vista. It's like how sunsets are more beautiful in polluted air."

Eureka could no longer feel the rain. Droplets gathered twenty feet above her but never reached the white stone veranda. Solon must have pitched a cordon over them, though he'd said he rarely used his Zephyr anymore. He coughed and wheezed and lit a clove cigarette with a silver lighter.

"Sleep well?" He eyed her as if he'd asked a more personal question.

"Not really." She felt Atlas spying on their conversation, observing every nuance of her body language. Goose bumps rose on her skin.

Solon would want to know about Eureka's encounter last night, but she could never tell him here, with Atlas possibly within earshot. She could never tell him anywhere if she planned on seeing Brooks again. It had to stay her secret.

"The gang rises," Solon said as the twins bounded onto the veranda.

"What's for breakfast?" William swung from the barren branch of a tree in the center of the veranda.

"There was supposed to be coffee," Solon said, "but apparently my employees have quit."

"I had the craziest dream." Cat appeared at the top of the stairs. "My brother and I were driving my dad's old Trans-Am across the ocean through all these giant schools of fish." She rested her head on Eureka's shoulder with un-Cat-like lethargy. She still hadn't reached her family.

A moment later, Dad mounted the stairs, his weight steadied by Ander. Eureka touched the bandage around his shoulder. It was clean and tight.

"Better today," he said before she could ask. The bruise spreading from his temple was green.

"You should be resting," she said.

"He was worried about you," Ander said. "We didn't know where you were."

"I'm fine—"

"Claire!" Dad shouted. "Get down!"

Claire had climbed atop the veranda's stone rail. She leaned for a branch of pink bougainvillea, its petals bordered with brown.

"I want to get the flower like Eureka."

She leaned too far. Her foot slid across the wet stone,

and she tumbled forward, over the rail. Everyone scrambled toward her, but William, who was always already next to Claire, was first.

His arm shot over the rail. His open hand reached out. By the time Eureka got there, William was holding Claire.

Except he wasn't. Their hands didn't even touch. Five feet of air separated the twins. Claire dangled over a steep drop, held aloft by an invisible force. As William reached down and Claire reached up, some kind of energy in the space between connected them and kept her from falling. She looked beneath her feet at nothing. She began to cry.

"I've got you." William's forehead beaded with sweat. His body was still except for his twitching fingers. Claire began to rise.

The rest of them watched as Claire slowly floated toward her brother's hand. Soon, their fingertips connected, then each grasped the other's wrist. Then Ander and Solon were hauling Claire up the rest of the way, onto the veranda.

"Thanks." She shrugged at William after she was upright, safe.

"Sure." He shrugged back as Claire ran to Dad to wipe her tears.

Eureka knelt before William. "How did you do that?"

"I just wanted to bring her back where she belonged," William said. "With us."

"Try it again," Solon said.

"I don't think so," Dad said.

"Throw something in the air," Solon said to Claire. "Anything. But let William be the one to catch it."

Claire glanced around the veranda. Her gaze settled on the purple bag Eureka had set by the head of the stairs. *The Book of Love* peeked from its top.

"No!" Eureka warned, but Claire already held the book in her hands.

She hurled it into the sky. There was a small gray burst as the cordon became visible where the book pierced it. Wind and rain ripped through the hole it created. Eureka heard a loud buzz, like a riot of bees, then a tiny purple mushroom cloud bloomed in the sky. The book sailed over the Tearline pond below the veranda. It moved through the rain like it would never stop, like the answers to Eureka's heritage would always be further and further away. After what seemed like half an eternity, *The Book of Love* struck a high peak of white stone and fell open on the face of a rock.

"My book," Eureka murmured.

"I'll get it back," Ander said.

"The little thing has pierced my cordon *and* compromised the witches' glaze." Solon scratched his chin, horrified. His gaze darted around the Tearline pond, like he could suddenly sense Atlas, too. "Everybody run!"

"Wait." William edged forward and rested his elbows on the veranda's rail. He focused on the book across the pond.

After a moment, it rose from the stone, thumped closed, and sliced backward through the air. A purple shimmer blinked in the sky as the book passed through the glaze. Then came the gray burst at the cordon's boundary. Everybody ducked as *The Book of Love* soared back to the veranda. It shot into William's arms and knocked him off his feet.

"Amazing." Solon helped William up, then hopped atop the veranda's rail and examined his cordon, through which rain no longer fell. "It must be a counterquirk."

"A what?" Eureka returned her book to her bag, and her bag to her shoulder.

"Yesterday, Claire trespassed the border of the witches' glaze to enter the Bitter Cloud. Today, William does the opposite. He said it beautifully: he brings things back where they belong. The twins' quirks are counterpoints. Counterquirks."

"What is a quirk?" Eureka asked.

"The quirk—it's . . ." Solon glanced at the others. "No one knows? Really?"

"Eureka killed Google," Cat explained.

"A quirk is an enchanted inkling," Solon said, "a fragment of magic with which every mortal soul is born. Most people never learn how to harness theirs, and die with their quirks still dormant. Quirks are as fragile as one's sense of self. Unless one's quirk is protected to survive the chilling effects of growing older, it disappears. A true pity, because even the most absurd quirks become essential in the proper context."

"Do we get only one?" William asked.

"Ambitious lad," Solon said. "Well, why should there be a limit? One quirk is a miracle, but don't let me stand in your way. Quirk out as much as you like."

"Do you have a quirk?" Claire asked Solon.

"Yes," Cat answered for him. "Being a dick."

"I possess the Seedbearer's global quirk," Solon said, "the Zephyr. Ander shares it, too. Groups often have global quirks, and sometimes counterquirks, like the twins. My neighbors, the Celans, can visit the dead in their dreams. But quirks don't have to rely on heritage or who your parents were. Each of us has magic within us. We take our quirks from the universal store." He paused. "William and Claire have already awakened their quirks. Perhaps the time has come for the rest of you to do the same."

Eureka approached Solon. "You're supposed to prepare me to go to the Marais," she said. "We have eight days before the full moon."

"Says the girl who disappeared last night when we could have been working."

"She left because you dropped a bomb on her," Ander said.

"A bomb I wouldn't have had to drop if you had been honest," Solon said.

"A bomb went off last night?" William asked.

"Everything good happens when we're asleep," Claire said, and crossed her arms.

"Eureka's right," Ander said. "This isn't the time for magic tricks. Our enemy is out there. Teach us how to fight him."

"Not us. Me. This is my fight," Eureka said to Solon, to Ander, to Atlas wherever he was.

"If I were facing the darkest force in the universe," Solon said, "I'd want all the help I could get."

"Yeah, well, some people have less to lose than others," Eureka said.

"Meaning?" Solon asked.

"You don't love anyone, so you don't care who gets hurt," Eureka said. "When I go to the Marais, I'll go alone."

Solon snorted. "The day you're ready to go to the Marais alone is the day I keel over and die!"

"Finally, you've given me a goal!" Eureka shouted.

A hint of green in the corner of Eureka's vision grabbed her attention. Cat sat with her back against the trunk of the tree, which wasn't barren anymore. Its branches sprouted tender green leaves, then flowered into a thousand pale pink cherry blossoms. Petals floated to the ground, showering Cat's braids, as ripe red cherries swelled from the branches' buds. The twins started laughing, leaping to pluck the fruit from the tree. Its branches curved forward, embracing Cat in what almost seemed like a gentle, grateful hug.

"How did you do that?" Eureka asked.

"Diana said you and Solon were supposed to be great friends," Cat said. "I didn't want you to fight. So I sat down and focused on the love Diana felt for both of you. I was hoping you'd feel it for each other."

"Cat." Eureka sank to her knees. "Why do you love fixing people up so much?"

Cat ran her hands through the carpet of cherry blossoms around her feet. "I want everyone to fall in love."

"But why?"

"Love makes people the best versions of themselves."

Eureka plucked a cherry, handed it to her friend. "I think you found your quirk."

"Eat one, Reka," William said, dumping a fistful in her lap.

Eureka slipped a cherry in her mouth. As she chewed she found it difficult to stay angry at Solon. There was love inside the fruit. Love that was bigger than fear.

"I'm sorry," she told Solon. "I'm just worried that I'm running out of time."

"Now you have to say you're sorry, too." Claire held out a cherry to Solon.

"I regret nothing," Solon said, and turned away. "Trenton, you're next."

"Wait," Cat said. "I could do more. If we went back to those hazelnut trees, I could revive them. My grandfather grew pecans—one tree produces six hundred pounds of nuts per year. Say there were fifty trees in that grove. That's three hundred thousand pounds of food. The Poet said his family is starving. I could help."

"None of you will leave the protection of the glaze," Solon said.

"My family could be starving right now," Cat said. "If there was something someone could do to help them—"

"You cannot handle what is out there." Solon glared at Eureka, making her wonder if he knew where she had been last night.

Dad approached Solon. "I'll give it a shot. What do I do?"

"You don't have to, Dad," Eureka said. "You're not well."

Solon looked hard at Dad. "Your quirk is likely buried very deep within you. But it's there. It's always there. Perhaps a tool might help. Ander, the orichalcum?"

Ander unzipped his backpack and withdrew three silver objects. First was the delicate anchor they'd used yesterday to make landfall. It gleamed as if recently polished, as all the objects did. There was also a sheath, six inches long, and made of thinly hammered silver. From it Solon drew a futuristic-looking spear that was, amazingly, many times longer than the sheath. It was nearly four feet long, with a thin serrated blade.

The last object was a small rectangular chest about the size of a jewelry box. It contained Atlantean artemisia, a substance deadly to Seedbearers. Ander had flashed that chest at his family when they tried to run Eureka off the country road in Breaux Bridge. Its green glow had scared them off. Solon eyed it greedily.

"The objects before you are made of orichalcum," he said

154

to Dad. "Before Ander brought them here, I had not seen them in three-quarters of a century and was beginning to think they were mystical aspects of my imagination. Orichalcum is an ancient metal. It is also an indentured metal, which means it works for its owner. You may choose one—which is to say one may choose you—as a talisman to help uncover your quirk."

Dad stared at the objects. "I don't understand."

"Can we please stop trying to make sense of things?" Solon said. "It's supposed to be natural, like it was for your children. For example, this one speaks to me." He lifted the chest's lid and gave a deep, sensual sniff.

Ander snapped the lid shut. "Are you suicidal?"

"Of course I'm suicidal," Solon said, laughing. "What kind of insane lunatic isn't suicidal?"

"If you die, I die," Ander muttered. "I won't abandon Eureka because you're too much of a coward to live."

Solon raised an eyebrow. "That remains to be seen."

"Dad, take the chest," Eureka said.

"Yeah, I like this one." Dad eased the chest from Ander's and Solon's grips. He opened the lid and recoiled at the sharp odor. Solon leaned forward, breathing in, enchanted. Eureka noticed that Ander leaned forward, too. Seedbearers couldn't resist artemisia.

As Solon bent over in another consuming coughing spell, Dad watched with a concern that Eureka recognized. He'd looked at her that way all her life.

"You have cancer," he said.

Solon straightened, stared at Dad. "What?"

"Your lungs. I see it clearly. There's darkness here"—he gestured toward Solon's heart—"and here, and here." He pointed at two other places along Solon's lower ribs. "Artemisia could help. The herb eases inflammation."

"Hear that, Ander?" Solon laughed.

"This artemisia comes from Atlantis," Ander said. "It's far more potent than any herb you are familiar with."

"Dad," Eureka tried to explain, "Solon can't inhale artemisia without dying from it, without killing Ander, too."

"There are other homeopathic remedies," Dad said, pacing, excited. "If we could get our hands on some Venus flytrap extract, I could make a tea."

"There's a health-food store about a mile underwater," Solon said.

"You've always had your quirk," Eureka said to Dad. "That's why you try to heal us all with food. You can see what's wrong inside us."

"And you want us to get better," William said.

"Your mother always said I could see the best in people," Dad said.

"Which one?" Eureka asked. "Rhoda or Diana?"

"Both."

"Now it's Eureka's turn," Claire said.

"I think my quirk is my sadness," Eureka said. "And I've already used it enough."

Solon frowned. "Your mind is much narrower than Diana's."

"What do you mean?"

"There *is* a wider spectrum of emotions than just sorrow and desolation. Have you ever considered what might transpire if you allowed yourself to feel"—Solon's eyes widened—"joy?"

Eureka looked at William and Claire, who were waiting for her response. She recalled a quote she'd once seen tattooed on a boy's neck as he fought with another kid at Wade's Hole:

A LEADER IS A DEALER IN HOPE.

At some point, Eureka had become Cat, Dad, and the twins' leader. She wanted to give them hope. But how?

She thought of a popular phrase in the chat rooms she had trolled after Diana died: "It gets better." Eureka knew it was originally offered as encouragement to gay kids, but if there was one thing she'd learned since Diana's death, it was that emotions didn't travel in a straight line. Sometimes it would get better, sometimes it would get worse. Sure, Eureka had known joy—in the tops of live oak trees, in dilapidated boats cruising the bayou, on long runs through shady groves, and in peals of laughter with Brooks and Cat—but the sensation was usually so fleeting, a commercial in the drama of her life, that she'd never put much stock in it.

"How would joy help me defeat Atlas?" Eureka wondered aloud.

"Solon!" a voice called from behind them. The Poet

157

appeared at the top of the stairs. He looked terrified. "I tried to stop them . . . but beggars must be choosers."

"What are you talking about?" Solon asked.

From behind the Poet an enraged voice shouted something Eureka didn't understand. A young man with a stubbly beard joined the Poet on the stairs. Every muscle in his body was tensed, as if he were in shock. His chest heaved and his eyes were wild. He pointed a trembling finger at Eureka.

"Yes," the Poet said with heavy regret. "She is the one the dead speak of in our dreams."

14

STORMING A STORM

"Stay there!" Solon shouted at Eureka. His silk robe trailed behind him as he rushed past the Poet and down the stairs. Without the protection of his cordon, rain returned to the veranda.

"What's going on?" Cat asked the Poet.

The other boy moved quickly across the veranda, splashing through puddles, trampling on swirls of cherry blossoms, heading for Eureka.

A silver flash caught her eye as the orichalcum chain of Ander's anchor tightly encircled the boy's bony rib cage. He grunted, struggling to breathe.

Ander held the shank of the anchor over his shoulder, the chain coiled around his wrist. He shoved the bearded boy and the Poet against the veranda's rail. He pressed their necks over the overlook. A sheet of mist spread toward them and the boys slipped in and out of foggy, white obscurity.

"Who's down there?" Ander's grip tightened on both boys' necks. "How many?"

"Don't hurt him!" Cat said.

"Let go, please," the Poet grunted. "We come in pieces."

"Liar," Ander said. Lightning split the sky, illuminating his shoulder muscles through his T-shirt. "They want her."

"They want food." The Poet gasped and struggled to break free.

The Poet's companion began whipping his head back in violent jerks, trying to strike Ander's face.

Claire tugged on the sleeve of Dad's jean jacket. "Should I spear that boy?"

Dad locked eyes with Eureka. Both of them had noticed the orichalcum sheath in Claire's hand. Dad lifted it from one daughter and passed it to the other. Eureka slipped it through the belt loop of her jeans as Dad tucked the orichalcum chest inside his jacket.

A series of thumps drew Eureka's attention to Ander and the boys. The sharp point of Ander's elbow snapped into the back of the bearded boy's head, over and over, until the boy grunted and finally went limp.

Dad tried to shield the twins from the violent sight, and Eureka was surprised she hadn't thought to do the same. It hadn't shocked her the way it would have once. Now violence was ordinary, like the ache of hunger and the dull edge of regret.

Dad moved the twins toward the staircase. Something in Eureka lightened as they slipped away. The sensation came and went quickly, and she couldn't put it into words, but it made her wonder whether she would rather be like Cat, with no knowledge of her family, with no special responsibility to protect them.

A crash below made Dad jump away from the head of the stairs. There was nowhere safe to go.

"Stay up here!" Eureka called.

Behind her, the Poet was on his knees, lightly slapping the unconscious boy's cheeks, murmuring something in their language.

"Take this to your family," Cat said, her crossed arms full of cherries. The Poet gave her a grateful nod and a shy smile that belonged on the outskirts of a high school football game—not over an unconscious body somewhere near the end of the world.

"We have more food," Eureka heard herself say.

Ander moved next to her. She felt his heat pulse near her body. He was bleeding above his eyebrow where the boy's head had struck him.

"If we feed them," Ander said to the Poet, "do you swear they'll leave her alone?"

Another crash sounded below. Eureka heard Solon wheeze: "I said *hit* me, you pathetic weaklings!"

"Solon, you idiot," she muttered as she rushed for the stairs.

Dad's arm shot out, trying to block her. "This isn't your fight, Reka."

"It's only my fight," she said. "Don't go down there."

Dad started to argue, then realized he couldn't stop her, or change her mind, or change the person she'd become. He kissed her forehead lightly, between her eyes, the way he used to after her nightmares. *You're awake now,* his soft voice once reassured her. *Nothing's gonna get you.*

She was awake now, to a nightmare never more real or more dangerous. She thundered down the stairs. "Solon!"

The cave was unrecognizable. A giant crack split the overturned dining table. The fire pit had been crushed, the tile mosaic on the floor melted by a burning log. Eureka slipped behind a rough-hewn pine bookcase and watched as a dozen gaunt and haggard men prowled through Solon's things. She felt the spear's hilt against her hip. Maybe it was precious and magical, but it must also be deadly. She would use it if she had to.

A dark-haired boy about her age ran his hands along Solon's mural-painted walls. His eyes were closed. He paused at a portion of the mural that depicted a snake belching a fireball. He leaned against the wall and sniffed. Then he raised a crowbar and struck the mural. Shards of rock flew aside, revealing a closet stocked with canned goods.

A heightened sense of smell must have been his quirk. Eureka looked around to see how the other raiders were using theirs.

A man rushed to the exposed closet, but instead of grabbing cans with his hands, he held up a burlap sack. The entire contents of the pantry glided swiftly into the sack. When it was filled, the little boy who'd tried to run off with William and Claire cinched the sack tightly in his fists. Eureka knew there would be no prying his small fingers free.

If she sang to him again, would he drop the food? Did she want him to? She didn't want him to starve. She thought about William and Claire and Dad at the top of the stairs. She didn't want them starving, either.

In the center of the room, a tall man brandishing a J-shaped knife circled Solon. Solon was swinging something long and white—a femur he had snatched from a wall. He wheezed as he swung the bone. He was trying to use his Zephyr to fend off the attacker, but it did nothing more than rustle the man's hair. The cordon he'd made earlier must have exhausted his powers. He coughed and spat some phlegm in his opponent's face.

"There are other ways to ask for a raise!" Solon yelled over his shoulder at Filiz.

"I'm sorry, Solon." Filiz's voice trembled. "I didn't—"

Solon's hacking cough cut his assistant off. He lunged and swung the femur at the intruder. He landed a blow to the side of the slower, malnourished man's head. When the man fell to his knees, Solon stood over him, quizzically triumphant.

Eureka heard a cry behind her and turned to see William, Claire, and Dad at the bottom of the stairs. Her heart sank.

"I told you to stay on the veranda!"

One of the men held Claire by the arm. Dad's fists were white-knuckled and clenched tight, ready to punch. Eureka reached for the handle of the spear. Then she heard a snap, then saw a burst of fire erupt behind Claire's attacker.

The man dropped Claire and swatted at his smoking head.

"Do not touch the children," Filiz commanded.

Solon's assistant had ignited a fireball with a snap of her fingers. Her quirk.

"Thank you," Eureka said.

But Filiz was tending to the man's burns and wouldn't meet Eureka's eyes.

Someone had discovered Solon's booze. Men yanked open the drawers of a chest disguised as a rock. Corks popped like it was New Year's Eve. One man held up a bottle of deep green liquid.

"Not my Swiss absinthe!" Solon shouted. "That bottle is one hundred and fifty-four years old. It was a gift from Gauguin."

The largest of the raiders launched an empty prosecco bottle at Solon's ducking head. The tall man with the knife rose slowly to his knees. He said something to Filiz.

"They say they are starving," Filiz translated. "They want to know why you feed the girl who made it so."

"I planned to share all this with them as soon as the girl was gone," Solon said. He grabbed a bottle from one of the raiders and took a liberal swig. When the man swung at him, Solon casually smashed the bottle over his opponent's head. "But you must tell them if the girl starves to death before she fixes things, no one will ever eat again!"

Eureka imagined each of these raiders with a full belly and a long drink of water. The ferocity in their eyes would soften. Their voices would smooth out. These were good people, driven to violence because of hunger and thirst. Because of her. She wanted to share the food.

"Filiz," Eureka said, "will you translate for me?"

The raiders crowded Eureka. They leered at her, studying her face. Their breath was sour, hot. One of them reached toward her eyes, then growled when she swatted him away. They all began to speak at once.

"They want to know if you're the one!" Filiz called over the cacophony of voices.

The one the dead speak of in our dreams, the Poet had said.

Eureka was on trial, not just for her tears but for every mistake she'd ever made, every choice that had brought her to this moment.

A deep buzzing filled her good ear. She flinched as a swarm of insects spilled into the salon. A million butterflies, bees, moths, and baby hummingbirds swirled around in mad circles.

"They raided my butterfly room," Solon said. "What next?" He thought of something, then froze. A look of panic washed over his face. "Ovid." He shoved a raider aside and hurried down the spiral staircase to the lower level of his cave.

"Who's Ovid?" Eureka asked, ducking under a cloud of wings.

"Don't be a fool!" Filiz called after Solon. "No one cares about that."

At the far end of the room, as hummingbirds whizzed and butterflies bumped against the ceiling, Dad snapped a sharp stalactite from the ceiling and followed a man carrying Solon's last jugs of water toward the cave entrance.

Someone shouted a warning, and as the man with the water spun around, he knocked the stalactite from Dad's hand. Eureka saw another raider pick it up.

She was old, with bushy white eyebrows and a dirty apron. She held the stalactite like a dart and faced Eureka's dad. She swatted a moth from her face and bared a mouthful of small, crooked teeth.

What happened next happened quickly. The woman plunged the sharp rock into Dad's stomach. He sputtered in shock and doubled over.

Eureka screamed as the woman kicked Dad onto his back, withdrew the stalactite, and raised it over Dad's chest. Eureka ran toward them, batting wings out of her way. They could have the food and water, but they could not take her father.

She was too late. The stalactite plunged deeply into her father's chest. Blood spread over his rib cage. Dad lifted his hand toward Eureka, but it stilled in the air, an interrupted wave. She fell upon her father.

"No," she whispered as blood soaked her fingers and her shirt. "No, no."

"Reka," Dad's voice strained.

"Dad."

He fell silent. She laid her good ear against his chest. The maelstrom of the raid grew distant. She imagined the twins wailing, the cacophony of beating wings, the shattering of more glass, but she couldn't hear anything.

Her eyes fixed on the dirty apron hem of the woman who'd stabbed her father. She looked up and saw her face. The woman muttered something at Eureka, then shouted something at Filiz, who drew closer. After a moment, she repeated her words to Filiz.

"My grandmother says you are the world's worst dream come true," Filiz whispered.

Eureka rose from Dad's bloody chest. Something inside her snapped. She leapt onto the old woman. Her fingers clenched white hair and yanked. Her fists rained down on the woman. Eureka kept her thumbs outside her fists, like Dad had taught her, so she wouldn't hit like a girl.

Filiz screamed and tried to drag her off, but Eureka kicked Filiz away. She didn't know what she was going to do, but nothing was going to stop her from doing it. She felt the old woman buckle underneath her. Wings clouded her vision. The image of Dad's still hand waving goodbye flooded her mind. She had stopped thinking; she had stopped feeling. She had become her rage.

Blood spurted from someplace on the woman's face, splattered across Eureka's chest, into her mouth. She spat, and hit harder, shattering the brittle bone that formed the woman's temple. She felt the squish of an eye socket caving in.

"She begs for mercy!" she heard Filiz shout behind her, but Eureka didn't know how to stop. She didn't know how she'd gotten there. Her knee was against the woman's windpipe. Her bloody fist was in the air. She had not even thought to use the spear.

"Eureka, stop!" Cat's voice was horrified.

Eureka stopped. She was panting. She studied her bloody hands and the body beneath her. What had she done?

A crowd of raiders drew near, some horrified, some with murderous expressions on their faces. They shouted words she didn't understand.

Ander moved toward her. The shock in his blue eyes made her want to flee and never be seen by anyone she loved again. She forced herself to see her bloody hands and the woman's caved-in cheekbone, her vacant, blood-filled eyes.

When one of the raiders tried to grab Eureka the cave filled with the strange whistle of wind. Everyone ducked and shielded their eyes. Ander was exhaling a great stream of breath. It flew around the cave like a helicopter landing. It drew every winged creature into its realm, like a lantern in a dark sky. The birds and insects still flew, but they flew in place, manipulated by Ander's breath.

Ander's Zephyr had constructed a transparent wall of wind and wings that split the cave in two. On one side, close to the cave's entrance, stood the stunned intruders. On the other side, near the waterfall at the back of the salon, stood Cat, the twins, Ander, and, hunched over the old woman's body, Eureka.

Ander's breath protected her from the Celans' revenge. They couldn't reach her on the other side of the beating, winged wall. They couldn't do to her what she had done to Filiz's grandmother, what Filiz's grandmother had done to Dad. Ander's breath had forged a temporary truce. Maybe he was the dealer in hope.

But how long would it take for what she'd done to sink into Ander, into the hearts and minds of everyone she loved? How long until everyone turned away?

Eureka hadn't had a choice. She saw her father die and she reacted without thinking. It was instinctual. But what would happen now? Were there still laws in this drowning world?

"Take the food," Eureka heard herself tell Filiz. She gestured at the cans and packages scattered on the other side of the cave.

This murder was a rift in Eureka's identity. She no longer

belonged in the world she was trying to fix. She no longer recognized the girl who had come from there. She could never return home. The best she could hope for was that other people could return there.

A shadow fell across her body. If it was Cat or the twins, Eureka would lose it. They would need consoling, and how could she console anyone after what she'd done?

"Eureka." It was Solon.

"If you want me to go, I'll understand."

"Of course I want you to go."

Eureka nodded. She had ruined everything, again.

"I want you to go to the Marais," Solon whispered in her good ear. "Suddenly I think you might actually pull this off."

15

MOURNING BROKEN

Murderer.

The voice inside Eureka's mind that night was full of loathing. It had taunted her all day as she prepared Dad for a burial he wouldn't receive.

There was no soil in the Bitter Cloud, and Solon wouldn't let them venture farther than the reaches of the witches' glaze. Instead, he suggested they give Dad a Viking funeral, sending his body out to sea in a blazing pyre.

"But how—" Eureka had started to ask.

Solon pointed at the watery tunnel Eureka had paddled down the night before. The aluminum canoe bobbed inside. "This channel is many-fingered," he said, and spread the fingers on his hand. "This finger leads swiftly to the ocean." He wiggled his ring finger. "It's really very dignified."

"You just want everything to be as morbid as possible, all the time," Cat had said, helping Ander line the canoe with collapsed wooden prosecco crates. She had been raised to be superstitious about rites of passage, mindful of the fate of spirits, wary of forlorn ghosts.

Murderer.

Ander tried to catch her eye. "Eureka—"

"Don't," she said. "Don't be tender anymore."

"You were avenging your father," he said. "You lost control."

She turned away from Ander and envisioned Dad's imminent conflagration. She liked that there would be no claustrophobic coffins involved, no dishonest formaldehyde embalming. Maybe out in the ocean Dad's ashes would find a piece of Diana and they would twirl together for a moment before drifting on.

If Dad had known he was about to die, he would have written out a menu and started a roux. He would have wanted no memorial without an accompanying good meal. But they were down to two carafes of water, a small bag of bruised apples, a tub of salad dressing, a box of Weetabix, and a few bottles of prosecco that Solon had stashed in an ice bucket in his bedroom. Eating out of ceremony was impossible now that Eureka had met her starving neighbors.

At least she could clean Dad up. So she started with his feet, stripping off his boots and socks, scrubbing his skin with water from the salty spring. The twins sat next to her, watching, silent tears cleaning their dirty cheeks as Eureka carefully groomed

172

under Dad's nails with a knife. She borrowed an ornate Victorian razor from Solon and shaved the stubble on Dad's face. She smoothed the frown lines around his mouth. She cleaned his wounds, working lightly around the bruise at his temple.

She found it easier to focus on Dad than on William and Claire or Cat and Ander. The dead let you help them any way you wanted to.

When she'd made Dad look as peaceful as she could, Eureka turned to the woman she had killed. She knew the Celans would be back for the body and she wanted to show her respect. She removed the woman's filthy apron. Blood drained in a long red wash along the mosaic tiles on the floor. It became a gentle river, mingling with Dad's blood. Eureka mopped it up, as careful as she had been wild when the blood was spilled. She straightened the woman's hair, hating her for killing Dad, hating her for being pretty, hating her for being dead.

A blaze of light drew near Eureka. She ducked to the left to avoid being singed as a sphere of fire the size of a baseball swerved past her face and struck a skull on the wall behind her.

"Don't touch Seyma," Filiz said. A second sphere of fire burned at the tips of her fingers.

"I was just—"

"She was my grandmother."

Eureka rose to give Filiz space with the dead woman. After a moment, she asked: "Do you believe in Heaven?"

"I believe you have made it very crowded."

The Poet appeared and slipped one hand under Seyma's back, another beneath her stout knees. He lifted the old woman up, and Filiz followed him out of the demolished cave.

Cat stood over Dad's body. "We don't have a rosary."

"Any necklace will do," Solon said.

"No, it won't." Cat's brow was damp. "Trenton was Catholic. Someone should say the Lord's Prayer, but I can't get my teeth to stop chattering. And we don't have holy water for the blessing. If we don't do these things, he'll—"

"Dad was a good man, Cat. He's going to get there no matter what we do."

She knew Cat wasn't really upset about the rosary. Dad's death represented all the other losses they hadn't had time to mourn. His death had become everydeath, and Cat wanted to make it right.

"Is Dad going to Heaven?" William tilted his head as he looked at his father.

"Yes."

"With Mom?" he asked.

"Yes."

"Will he come back?" Claire asked.

"No," Eureka said.

"Is there room for him up there?" William asked.

"It's like the country roads between New Iberia and Lafayette," Claire explained. "Wide open and full of room for everyone."

Eureka knew the reality of Dad's death would bloom

slowly and painfully for the rest of the twins' lives. Their bodies caved the way they did right before they cried, so she enveloped them—

Murderer.

She hummed an old hymn to silence the voice. She stared at Dad's restful expression and prayed for the strength to take care of the twins with as much courage as their parents had.

" 'Yea, though I walk through the valley of the shadow of death, I will fear no evil,' " Solon said. "Isn't that how it goes?"

The psalm used to thrill Eureka. It was one thing to walk through the valley of death—but to walk through death's shadow meant that you didn't know where death was, or what light behind it made its shadow. The psalm made death sound like a secret second moon in the sky, orbiting everything, making every minute night.

On many nights, not long ago, Eureka had bargained with God to take her life and bring back Diana. She didn't want that anymore. She didn't look at Dad's body and wish she were in his place. In a way, she already was in his place, and in the place of everyone she had killed, regardless of whether she knew their names. Part of Eureka had died, was always dying now, and becoming part of her strength. This was a muscle she sensed she would use when the time came to defeat Atlas and redeem herself.

" 'For thou art with me,' " she finished the psalm. " 'Thy rod and thy staff they comfort me.' "

"You couldn't cry at Diana's funeral, either." Solon took

a seat on an antique cockfighting chair, sipping prosecco carefully from a glass with a broken handle. "What gets you through it? God?"

Eureka stared at Solon's broken glass and remembered the window shattering above her head the night Diana left her family. She remembered the water heater bursting in the hallway, the storm entering their living room. She remembered being unable to tell what was hail against her skin and what was glass. She remembered her feet on the soaked and shaggy carpet on the stairs. Then sobbing. Then Diana's slap across her cheek.

Never, ever cry.

Solon was watching her as if he knew all about it.

"She wanted to protect you," he said.

"You can't control the way somebody feels," Eureka said.

"No, you can't," Solon said, retying the satin ribbon of his robe into a sailor's knot. "Not for long, anyway."

Eureka looked down at Dad in the canoe. Before he'd died they'd grown apart. It was Rhoda, and then it was high school, and then it was the fact that she'd grown apart from everyone after Diana's death. She'd always assumed she and Dad would have time to reconnect.

"After Diana died, the sunrise amazed me," she said.

"You used to watch it with her?" Ander asked.

Eureka shook her head. "We used to sleep until noon. But I couldn't believe the sun had the audacity to rise after she died. I remember at her funeral, I told that to my uncle, about the sunrise. He looked at me like I was crazy. But then, a few days later, I found Dad in the kitchen, frying eggs. He didn't think anyone was home, but he'd gone through an entire carton. I watched him crack one into a pan, stare at it as it cooked, then flip it onto a plate. They formed a stack, like they were pancakes. Then he tossed the whole plate in the trash."

"Why didn't he eat them?" William asked.

"*It still works,* he said, like he couldn't believe it," Eureka said. "Then he walked out of the kitchen."

Eureka was supposed to go on, to say that Dad had taught her how to tell a joke, how to whistle through a sugarcane husk, how not to punch like a girl. He'd taught her how to fold a cloth napkin into an origami swan, how to tell if a crawfish was fresh, how to two-step, how to play a G chord on the guitar. He'd cooked her special meals before her races, researching the right balance of protein and carbohydrates to give her the most energy. He had shown her that unconditional love was possible, because he had loved two women who hadn't made loving them easy, who took for granted that his love was always there. He'd taught Eureka one thing Diana never could have: how not to run away when it felt impossible to stay. He'd taught her to persevere.

But Eureka kept all that to herself. She gathered her memories around her like a secret shield, the shadow of a shadow in a flooded valley of death.

Solon poured another broken glass of wine and rose from the cockfighting chair. A cigarette dangled from his lips. "When a loved one dies in an untimely manner," he said, "one feels as if the universe owes one something. Good luck, invincibility, a line of credit with the man upstairs."

"You're so cynical," Cat said. "What if it's the other way around and the universe has already blessed you with the time you had together?"

"Ah, but if I'd never loved Byblis, I wouldn't miss her."

"But you *did* love her," Ander said to Solon. "Why can't you cherish the time you had, even if it couldn't be forever?"

"You see, this is the problem with conversation," Solon said with a sigh, and looked at Ander. "All we ever do is talk about ourselves. Let us stop before we bore each other, well, to tears." He turned to Eureka. "Are you ready to say goodbye?"

"Dad's supposed to be with us," William said. "Can't I use my quirk to make him come back?"

"I wish you could," Eureka said.

Solon unmoored the canoe, then pointed the vessel toward an opening in the darkness. "He will float through there and drift gently out to the sea."

"I want to go with him." Claire reached for the canoe.

"As do I," Solon said. "But we still have work to do."

"Wait!" Eureka pulled the canoe with Dad's body toward her a final time. She withdrew the slender orichalcum chest from the inner pocket of his jean jacket. She held it up in the candlelight. The green glow within it pulsed.

"There it is," Solon murmured.

Ander had already returned the spear and anchor to his backpack. Eureka claimed the heirloom Dad had never meant to leave her. She tucked the chest under her arm. Solon leaned in close, inhaling ferociously. When Ander leaned in, too, Eureka sensed she should keep the chest with her, in her bag with *The Book of Love*.

She pressed her lips against her father's cheek. He'd always hated goodbyes. She nodded at Ander, who poured a dark green bottle of pungent alcohol onto the wood crates beneath Dad. Eureka reached for the gossipwitches' torch, still lit, resting among the stalagmites. She tipped the flame over the alcohol. The fire caught.

Clare stared ahead numbly. William turned away and sobbed. Eureka gave the canoe the smallest push, and Dad entered the wet darkness, joined the rhythm of the current. She wished him peace and soft light in a heaven without tears.

16

THE FILLING

Late that night Eureka awoke in the dim stillness of the cave's spare chamber, her mind haunted by the fading ghost of a nightmare. She'd been back in the avalanche of wasted dead. Instead of scrambling atop decaying bodies, this time, Eureka drowned in them. She struggled to dig herself out, but she was too deep in bones and blood and slime. It sluiced over her, warm and rank, until she couldn't even see the rain. Until she knew the dead would bury her alive.

"You *think* you have all that you need!" Solon's voice boomed over the waterfall.

She rubbed her eyes and smelled death on her hands. After Dad's funeral, she'd washed them in the cave's salty spring and filed her nails with a porous stone until there was no place else for the blood she'd spilled to lodge. But she still smelled Seyma on her hands. She knew she always would.

"You're wrong," Solon said.

Eureka tilted her good ear toward the sound and waited for a response.

But Filiz and the Poet had gone home, and everyone else was asleep: William and Claire shared a blanket at the foot of Eureka's bed. Cat was passed out on her side next to Eureka, singing in her sleep as she had always done, since their earliest sleepovers. Tonight she softly slurred the bridge from Crystal Gayle's "Don't It Make My Brown Eyes Blue."

On Eureka's other side, Ander slept on his stomach, his face buried in a pillow. Even in his dreams he disappeared. She laid her head close to his for a moment. She inhaled his scent and felt the warm power of his breath. Dim light displayed faint lines around his eyes and silver-blond hairs around his temple. Had they been there that morning? Eureka didn't know. When you spent so much time looking at someone it was hard to measure how they changed.

Yesterday, the idea that love aged Ander appalled Eureka. But it wouldn't matter now—Ander couldn't possibly love her anymore. No one could. She wouldn't let them. Freedom from love meant freedom to focus on getting to the Marais, damming her flood, finishing Atlas—and liberating Brooks.

What would Brooks think of what Eureka had done to Seyma? For the first time, she was glad that he was gone.

"I know," Solon's voice insisted. "I will deliver the last piece, but it's complicated. Delicate."

Eureka rose from her blanket and edged toward the hanging rug separating the guest room from the salon. The gossipwitches' torch burned low, balanced between two stalagmites. Its amethyst stones provided inexhaustible and intelligent fuel: the flame adjusted itself during the day, burning brightest just before bedtime, soft as candlelight when everyone retired.

A voice answered Solon:

"I turned my back on you."

A shiver went down Eureka's spine. It was her father's voice.

Eureka flew into the salon, expecting to find Dad sitting at the broken table, cracking an egg into a bowl and smiling, eager to explain the stunt he'd pulled.

The room was empty. The waterfall roared.

"Solon?" Eureka called.

A dim light glowed from the staircase that led to the cave's lower level. Solon's cloistered workshop lay below.

"I turned my back on you," the voice repeated, drifting up the stairs. It sounded so much like Dad's that Eureka stumbled as she hurried toward it.

At the base of the stairs, Solon sat on a spun silk rug under a hanging glass lantern. Someone sat across from him, his face turned away from Eureka. He was hard to make out clearly in the shadowy light, but Eureka knew it wasn't Dad. He looked as young as Solon, with a shaved head, broad shoulders, and a narrow waist. He was naked.

As Eureka reached the bottom stair, the boy's head turned toward her, and her breath caught in her throat. Something about the strange boy reminded her of—

"Dad?"

Tears glistened in the corner of Solon's eyes. "He fixed Ovid. Until now I wasn't sure it would work. There was gossip, of course, but one can never trust a witch. And anyone else who might remember is either dead or in the Sleeping World." He wiped his eyes. "Your father fixed it. Come and see."

Solon took Eureka's hand. She sat next to him on the rug, across from the naked boy. When she saw it more clearly, she realized it wasn't human—it was a gleaming machine crafted in the shape of a very fit boy.

"Amazing, isn't it?" Solon asked.

Eureka's eyes roved over the machine's anatomically impressive body, but when she looked at the robot's face, she found it hard to breathe. It was youthful, like an ancient Greek statue—but its features were unmistakably those of her father.

Heavy-lidded eyes gazed at her with paternal love. A hint of stubble stood along its chin. The robot smiled, and the crease along its nose was the one that Dad had passed down to Eureka and the twins.

"Eureka, meet Ovid, limited-edition orichalcum robot

from Atlantis," Solon said. "Ovid, meet Eureka, the one who's going to take you home."

Eureka blinked at Solon, then at the robot, who extended its hand. She shook it, amazed to find it pliant like a real hand, with a firm, confident grasp.

"Why does it look like my father?" Eureka whispered.

"Because it holds your father's ghost," Solon said. "Ovid is a ghost robot, one of nine orichalcum siblings crafted before Atlantis sank. Eight still slumber in the Sleeping World, but Ovid got away. Selene stole it before she fled the palace, and it has lived in this cave ever since. If Atlas knew his precious robot was here, he would do anything to get it back."

For the second time Eureka considered telling Solon about her encounter with Atlas at the Tearline pond. But it felt like a betrayal of Brooks. If Solon knew Eureka had secretly met Atlas, he wouldn't let her out of his sight. And she had promised to find Brooks again soon. Their triangle was delicate—Atlas wanted Eureka's tears, Eureka wanted Brooks back, Brooks surely wanted freedom. It was best to keep things among the three of them for now.

"I turned my back on you." The robot spoke in Dad's voice.

Eureka pulled back her hand, horrified. Then, slowly, she touched the robot's cheek—supple as human flesh—and watched its face brighten with Dad's smile.

"I have looked after Ovid for many years," Solon said. "I

always knew it was invaluable, but I could never fathom what made it run."

Eureka circled the robot and found nothing familiar about its body. From the back, it looked like a sculpture in a fancy French Quarter antique store. Only Ovid's face seemed possessed of Dad. She sat down facing Ovid. "How does it work?"

"Most modern robots are wired to function on a binary system," Solon said. "Ones and zeroes. But Ovid is a trinary being, meaning it operates in threes. It's very Atlantean. Everything is threes with them. Three seasons. Three sides to a story. Did you know they invented the love triangle?"

Eureka couldn't take her eyes off Dad's expression on the robot's face.

"Ovid is a soldier," Solon continued. "Like all things made of orichalcum, it is meant to be indentured to one master. You will find it very useful."

Eureka glanced at Solon. "Does it know where the Marais is?"

"Yes, it does."

"And it's going to take me there? And help me defeat Atlas?"

"That has long been the plan."

"When?"

"Soon."

She got to her feet. "Tonight?"

Solon pulled her back down. "The time is almost right,

but Ovid will not go prematurely. It is . . . special. Its orichal-cum is but a shell for what—or rather, who—fills it with purpose. Today, your father became the first ghost to fill it."

"The Filling," Eureka said. Solon had mentioned it last night. She sensed it was something terrible. Why was Dad involved?

"The Filling is Atlas's master plan. It is what the Seedbearers are—and the rest of the world should be—so afraid of."

"Tell me."

Solon walked to the wall where a bottle of prosecco rested in an ice bucket in a stone recess. He poured himself a glass, drained it, and poured himself another. Then he lit a cigarette and took a long drag.

"The world into which Atlantis rises will be a muddy, un-recognizable slop. After the flood, everything will need re-building. And rebuilding requires workers. But workers have been known to revolt. To avoid that, Atlas plans to use the dead to build his empire by housing ghosts from the Waking World in invincible, weaponized bodies he controls. Imagine a billion souls' hopes and dreams and energies and visions, all of their intelligence and experience combined. This is how Atlas will conquer the world."

Eureka stared into the waterfall. "If Atlas wants a world of ghosts, doesn't he have to kill everyone first?"

Solon stared sadly at Eureka. "Atlas won't have to."

"Because I'm doing it for him," Eureka said. "My storm is going to poison the entire Waking World? How soon?"

"Most will die before the full moon."

"Then who am I trying to save?"

"Everyone. But you must take their lives before you save them."

"I don't understand."

"Eureka," Ovid said in Dad's familiar bayou drawl.

"You will have questions," Solon said. "First, let us hear what your father has to say."

"That is not my father. It's a monster Atlas made."

"Every ghost gets a dying message," Solon said. "Until they adjust to inhabiting the robot, this death letter forms the entirety of the ghost's language. Think of your father as a little baby ghost who needs time and nurturing to grow to his full potential. Now, listen."

A metallic tear glistened in the corner of Ovid's eye as it began to speak. "When you were born I was afraid of how much I loved you. You've always seemed so free. Your mother was the same way, not scared of anything, never needing any help."

"I need you," Eureka whispered.

"It was hard when your mom died." The robot paused, its lower lip jutting out the way Dad's did when he was thinking. "It was hard before that, too. I knew you were mad at me, even though you didn't. I was afraid you'd leave me, too. So I protected myself, added people to my life like armor against loneliness. I married Rhoda; we had the twins. I don't know how it happened, but I turned my back on you. Sometimes when you try not to repeat your mistakes, you forget that the original mistakes are still unfolding. I never planned to live forever and it wouldn't matter if I had. Man plans, God cancels. I want you to know I love you. I believe in you." His orichalcum eyes gazed into hers. "Ander makes you happy. I wish I could take back what Diana said about him."

Today I met the boy who's going to break Eureka's heart.

"I don't believe it anymore," Dad said. "So you tell him to take care of you. Don't make the same mistakes I did. Learn from mine and make your own and tell your children what you did wrong so they can do even better than you. Don't turn your back on what you love because you're scared. I hope we'll meet again in Heaven." The robot made the sign of the cross. "Make things right, Eureka. Stare your mistakes straight in the eye. If anyone can, it's you."

Eureka flung herself into Ovid's arms and embraced it. Its body felt nothing like Dad's, and that made her miss him more than she had since he died. She grew disgusted with herself for allowing one of Atlas's machines to make her feel.

When she pulled away the robot's face looked different. She couldn't see Dad anywhere. The orichalcum features seemed to be rearranging themselves in a deep tangle of movement. It was a horrifying sight. Eyes spread. Cheeks slackened. The nose hooked at the bridge.

"What's happening?" Eureka asked Solon.

"Another ghost is surfacing," Solon said. "Now that your

father opened Ovid, it will draw all the newly dead within a certain radius to it. Think of it as a vortex of local ghosts."

"My dad is trapped inside with other dead people?" Eureka thought of her nightmare and drew her arms around her chest.

"Not dead people," Solon said. "Ghosts. Souls. Big difference. The biggest difference there is."

"What about Heaven?" Eureka believed in Heaven, and that her parents were there now.

"Since your tears began the Rising, all the souls who perish in the Waking World are trapped in a new limbo. Before you cried, they would have made their way, like the souls that died before them, wherever they were destined to go."

"But now?" Eureka asked.

"They are being held for the Filling. They cannot flow into Atlas's other robots until those robots rise with the rest of Atlantis. And if Atlantis doesn't rise before the full moon, the dead's deterioration will be too great. The souls won't make it into the machines, or to Heaven—if there is such a place—or anywhere else, for that matter."

"That's what you meant about the wasted dead," Eureka said.

Solon nodded. "Your tears have already killed many. In order for their souls not to rot and waste away, Atlantis must rise in the next seven days. All ghosts must flow into the machines. Your mission will be to find some method of release."

"Release into what?" Eureka asked.

"A better fate than eternal enslavement by the Evil One."

As the features on the robot's face fixed into place, Eureka began to sweat. Solon didn't have to tell her who the other ghost was inside Ovid. She recognized Seyma, the woman she had murdered, wrinkling the robot's skin.

"Filiz!" Seyma's ghost began her death message in a language Eureka was surprised to understand. "Do not let the Tearline girl deceive you. She is the world's worst dream come true." The old woman's voice softened. "A blind man could see how much I love you, Filiz. Why you never saw it, I don't know."

Then the robot closed its orichalcum eyes. Seyma was gone.

"Ovid is programmed with some sort of translation device," Solon said. "It knows what the listener will understand."

"My father's ghost and the ghost of the woman who murdered him are together inside this machine? How does that work?"

"The mind boggles," Solon said. "An unfathomable number of ghosts can populate Ovid's body, propelling its thoughts and deeds like the atoms of a wave. They will make Ovid brilliant, and immortal—and conflicted, I assume. World wars could rage inside a single orichalcum body . . . if some clever ghost were to organize a resistance." Solon paused and drummed fingers against his chin. "Actually, that sounds like fun."

"How many ghosts are in it now?" Eureka touched her yellow ribbon. "There was a girl we passed on the way to the Bitter Cloud. I wanted to bury her. . . ."

"So far it seems only two ghosts are imprinted. Ovid's acquiring radius is quite small at the beginning, but will grow with each ghost that fills the machine. It will be a grand rite of passage when Ovid acquires its third ghost. Then this miraculous trinary robot will be fully operational, ready for the world, such as it is."

"That's when I go to the Marais," Eureka realized.

"In good time. Remember, someone else still has to die before Ovid is ready to guide you. Before that grisly occurrence, I suggest you go upstairs and get some rest." Solon smiled into the waterfall. "I wonder who the lucky bastard will be."

17

TRYSTS

Cat was gone.

Eureka returned upstairs to find a pallet of empty blankets where she'd last seen her friend. She checked the kitchen, all six candlelit alcoves in Solon's salon, the tiny bathroom off the staircase. Cat had fled the Bitter Cloud.

Eureka had known Cat long enough to guess where she had gone. The Poet had pointed out his rooftop from Solon's veranda the night they arrived. It was just across the Tearline pond. For the first time, Eureka regretted not telling the others she'd seen Atlas the night before. Now Cat had crossed the witches' glaze without knowing he was near. If Atlas found her, he would look like Brooks to her. Cat had no idea how much there was to fear.

Eureka snatched her purple bag. She considered taking the witches' torch, but it would make her too visible in the dark. At the doorway of the guest room she paused to watch the twins and Ander sleep. William whimpered, nestling closer to Claire, who swatted him, then changed her dream-mind and embraced him.

Part of Eureka would feel safer if Ander went with her, but after Seyma's death, Eureka no longer knew how to be around him. And she didn't want the twins to wake up alone. Besides, if she did encounter Brooks and Atlas tonight, she couldn't risk Ander's trying to kill them.

She aimed to be back before sunrise, before any of them woke up.

Silently, she climbed the stairs to the veranda. Rain pinged off her thunderstone as she looked over the rail. She scanned the rocks for Cat. For Brooks.

The water had risen ten or twenty feet since that morning. On the far side of the pond, mouthlike black openings marked the Celan caves. One of those caves had swallowed Cat. Unless Atlas had found her first.

After circling the veranda's perimeter, Eureka discovered a place where she could safely jump to the rocks below. She was lowering herself over the rail when a hand grabbed her shoulder and pulled her back.

"Where are you going?" Ander asked.

Their shoulders touched. She wanted to hold him, to be held.

"Cat's gone," she said. "I think she's with the Poet."

"We have to tell Solon."

"No. I'm going after her. Go back downstairs."

"Are you crazy? I'm not letting you go out there, especially not alone."

"Cat could die," she said. "If . . ."

"Say it," Ander said. "Say what you think might happen to her. I know he's out there, Eureka. We both know it. What I don't know is why you're so eager to walk into his trap."

He wanted her to deny it, to touch the smooth line of his cheekbone where it angled toward his jaw, and beg him to come with her. She wanted all of that, too—but she couldn't want it.

"I can't lose you," he said.

"You watched me kill someone today. You know what my tears are doing to the world. You act like Cupid shot us with arrows and we're supposed to forget that everything is falling apart. We're in hell, and if I don't stop it, it's only going to get worse."

"If you could love yourself the way I love you, you would be invincible."

He was wrong. Love wasn't going to defeat Atlas. Ruthlessness and rage would.

"If you could turn off your feelings for me the way I've turned off my feelings for you, you'd never age a day." Eureka hoisted herself over the rail and leapt to the rocks below. Her ankles throbbed dully from the drop.

Ander sucked in his breath. When he exhaled into the rain it shot sideways across the pond and generated a single angry wave.

"You can stop caring for me"—he began to hoist himself over the rail—"but you can't stop me from caring for you."

"Eureka," a silky voice called from everywhere and nowhere. For an instant the limits of the witches' glaze glowed purple in the darkness. Through the steady patter of rain on rock, Eureka heard the low drone of buzzing bees.

"Who's there?" Ander paused. "Eureka, wait."

A figure wearing a long caftan stepped from the shadows. Esme's painted lips and eyelids looked like portions of the night. Raindrops pattered against the petals of her dress. Her fingers traced her crystal teardrop necklace, making little swirls.

"I can show you the way to your friend."

"You know where Cat is?" Eureka asked.

"Don't go with her!" Ander called as Eureka approached the witch. He had landed on the rocks and moved toward her.

"I can help you lose him." Esme nodded at Ander. "I heard your little lovers' quarrel. Didn't you know shallow worries like those have been washed away?" Her pointer finger beckoned Eureka closer. "It is time for deep women to rise."

Rain slid down Eureka's shoulders. "Where are we going?"

"To the Glimmering, of course," Esme said. "Step through the glaze within the glaze and be free."

Eureka glanced back at Ander. He was only a few feet

away. She took Esme's icy hand and stepped through one invisible glaze into another.

"Eureka!" Ander shouted, and she knew he could no longer see her. He rushed forward as Esme winked and pulled Eureka aside on the path. Ander spun in a circle.

"Come back!"

They didn't. They walked through the mountains in the rain.

For several minutes, Eureka wanted to return to him, to race back to the Bitter Cloud and bring Ander with her wherever she went. She didn't want to be so cruel.

But more than that, she wanted to want nothing but to destroy Atlas.

She touched her thunderstone, the yellow satin ribbon, and the blue lapis lazuli locket that hung from the long bronze chain. The thunderstone was an emblem of Eureka's power, the yellow ribbon was her symbol of hope, and the locket represented her purpose: to get to the Marais, the swampy noplace beyond her reach, to undo the Filling, to make Diana proud.

Eureka wondered what Esme's crystal necklace meant to her. Had it been a gift from someone she loved? Did she love? Sometimes the witch looked like a beautiful, intimidating older girl; other times, like now, she looked like an alien queen from another galaxy. Eureka wondered whether Esme's life had turned out the way she'd hoped it might. Or was she broken, like Eureka, masking pain with swarming bees and shimmering amethyst makeup and clothing made of orchid petals?

"What is the Glimmering?" Eureka asked.

Esme cupped one palm to the sky. She studied the rain gathering in it. "It is where your friend and her date have gone looking for freshwater—and where you shall discover your history. The truth is in the Glimmering."

"What do you know about my history?" Eureka asked, then: "There's freshwater nearby?"

Esme spread her fingers to let the water that had collected in her palm filter through. Where the water hit the earth, orchid stems wriggled from the muddy soil and laced themselves around the witch's ankles, blooming amethyst buds.

Esme leaned toward Eureka. "The Glimmering looks like water, but it isn't for drinking. It is a mirror that reveals a soul's identity through the deep recesses of its history." The buds at Esme's feet yawned into blossoms at her knees. She smiled. "Mortals can face many things, but they cannot face their true identities. A single glance in our Glimmering has been enough to drive everyone insane so far."

"Are we really all that bad?"

"And worse!" Esme smiled. "Mortals spend lifetimes admiring their good through ordinary mirrors. The Glimmering shows that which you are too weak and afraid to see." The witch stepped closer, bringing with her a waft of fragrant, honey-scented air. "It's very rare for anyone to make it back alive. Though of course"—she tapped Eureka's thunderstone with an amethyst fingernail—"there are exceptions."

"Is Cat there now?"

Esme's grin darkened. "Perhaps your friend's reflection in the Glimmering will mature her . . . into the grave."

Eureka grabbed the witch's shoulders. "Where is it?"

Esme's laughter rose from somewhere in the earth, the black heart of a volcano. Bees stung Eureka's hands. Rain fell on the rising welts, its salt amplifying every throbbing sting.

"Show me where it is!"

Like a ballerina at the barre, Esme raised her arm along her midsection, draped it over her face, then lifted it high above her head before it opened, like a flower. Her long, painted pointer finger gestured into darkness. Then the darkness shifted and a shimmering amethyst-colored haze lit a faint path in the night.

"If you hurry, maybe you can catch her."

Eureka swatted through bees and ran. The witch's silky giggle rang in her deaf ear as she tore over the muddy slush along the path. She didn't think of looking back.

Up ahead the gossipwitch's haze lit a quick-flowing stream the storm had cut into the earth. Eureka would have to cross the stream to follow the glow. She found the narrowest crossing and tested the water's depth with her foot. The bank sloped down several feet—after that, she couldn't tell. Eureka swallowed, touched her thunderstone, and waded in.

She inhaled sharply at the cold constricting her legs. She reached for the low branch of a hazelnut tree to steady herself as she moved forward. The water rose to her chest, not deep enough to use her thunderstone shield, not shallow enough for her to move confidently. The current was strong, rushing against her, urging her to join its flow, like a crowded high school hallway.

She slipped and lost her grip on the branch. She tried to put her feet down, but the current moved too fast. Her thunderstone floated along the surface as she swam hard for the far bank.

Sharp rocks struck her underwater. Something bit her lower back. A huge loggerhead turtle had clamped its jaw around her hip. The pain was excruciating. Eureka thought of Madame Blavatsky and her turtles and wondered if Madame B had come back from the dead to chide her for all the ways she'd failed her destiny. The turtle's eyes were wide, yellow green, determined. Eureka made a fist and pounded the turtle's head until its jaw slackened and it dropped off into the swirling stream.

She wasn't far from the bank, but she was in pain and knew her back was bleeding. She imagined Cat striding happily to an inviting, deadly spring. That horror helped her thrust her body forward, until at last her fingers scratched the muddy edges of the bank. The soggy earth she clung to crumbled into the stream, sending her flowing farther from the now distant purple glow.

Her body struck a tree trunk. She wrapped her arms around it before the current pulled her away. She steadied herself. She lunged at the bank again. This time she grabbed slimy roots that held fast enough for her to pull herself up. At last she heaved herself out.

She collapsed on the bank in the rain, and considered never moving again. Then the amethyst glow grew dimmer. Eureka sprang up and ran toward it. She rounded the corner of a muddy path. She climbed a staircase of steep boulders lit by Esme's glow.

Just when she began to fear that this was an evil prank, that this path led to a cliff overlooking rocks that stood like spears, the glow fell on a large, round pond. Rain fell on its surface, but the Glimmering was as smooth as a mirror. A spring bubbled gently in its center. Slender conical mountains rose beyond it. Doves cooed in nearby trees.

The pond was surrounded by a bright amethyst ring of flowers. Tall, purple-lobed, gossipwitch orchids. Purple flamingos struck curious poses as they stalked the enchanted border of the enchanted pond.

Eureka turned her good ear toward a happy moan she recognized from many after-party rides home with Cat. Her friend leaned against the trunk of a pine tree near the Glimmering, wrapped in the Poet's arms.

Something drew Eureka's gaze above Cat and the Poet, to the limbs of the tree they leaned against. A shadow shifted on a branch. Eureka didn't need moonlight to recognize Brooks. How long had he been up there, watching Cat, waiting . . . for what?

For Eureka, of course. She knew Atlas's plans now. She knew her role was to undo the Filling. She knew where his precious robot was. All this gave her power she didn't yet know how to use.

Hang on, Brooks, she yearned to say. *Just hang on a little longer.*

His legs dangled over a thick pine arm. He knew Eureka saw him. Very slowly, he drew his pointer finger to his lips.

"Dare I suggest a skinny-dip before we fill the jugs?" Cat said to the Poet. Leaning in the wet grass at their feet were four clay drinking vessels they must have brought from the Poet's cave.

"What is 'skinny-dip?'" the Poet asked.

"Allow me to demonstrate." Cat crossed her arms and began to remove her sweater.

"Cat!" Eureka called. "Stop!"

"Eureka?" For a moment a smile lit Cat's face. Then it disappeared. Eureka realized that Cat would have been happy to see the girl Eureka used to be—but not the murderer standing before her now. "What are you doing here?"

Eureka thought about the way she'd just treated Ander. What did she think she was holding on to? What good would it do to say she'd been worried about Cat? Anger flashed in her eyes. She was mad at herself, and at Atlas, but Cat was in her line of fire.

"This isn't a sexcapade with a bayou boy."

"Really?" Cat's face darkened. "I could have sworn this was Lafayette and we were in the alley by the daiquiri store. How stupid do you think I am? That's an actual question. I left my family to run away with you and some nut job you barely know. Then you, the girl I thought was my best friend, turn out to be the real nut job I barely know."

"Cat, we have to go."

"You act like you don't even care about all the horrible things happening."

"I care. That's why I'm here."

"But you can't cry about it, right? You have a great excuse to pretend that nothing matters, so you don't have to feel it. I left everything, lost everything, just like you. Guess what? I found freshwater. You're not the only person in the world who can help."

"Stay away from that water. It's dangerous. It isn't even water."

"Don't say anything else." Cat stopped Eureka. "I don't want to discover what new way you've found to underestimate me."

Eureka tried to pull her friend farther from the water. "I'll explain once we get far away from here."

"Go home." Cat snapped her arm free. It was the closest either of them had come to admitting that they weren't just temporarily at odds. Their real homes were gone. Eureka had destroyed them. This place, this night, that evil ten feet up in the tree, was all they had.

"Please come with me, Cat."

The purple light had disappeared. Eureka wondered if she'd imagined her encounter with Esme. The spring bubbled innocently.

"Girls"—the Poet raised one of the jugs—"let's all just rock the boat, there is nothing to be afraid of. See. . . ."

"Don't!" Eureka called after him. "Your reflection—"

The Poet turned to face the water. He stood at the Glimmering's edge. He lowered the jug toward the surface—then he stopped. He shook his head like he was trying to erase the vision before him. He dropped the jug.

Ten feet away and holding Cat back, Eureka couldn't see what the Poet saw in his reflection. He cried out something in his native tongue. His legs wobbled unsteadily. He reached into his cargo pockets and withdrew a can of spray paint.

"What's he doing?" Cat said.

Eureka held her tighter as the Poet sprayed a cloud of black paint above the Glimmering. He wanted to paint over what he saw, to change the canvas. But he couldn't. And he couldn't turn away. His cloud-lit profile revealed a boy in agony, but strangely, the Poet's hands reached forward, grasping for something ahead of him.

Esme's words returned to Eureka: *Mortals can face many*

things, but they cannot face their true identities. She glanced back at the pine tree, at the still shadow she knew was watching.

"He'll fall in," Cat said.

"No matter what happens," Eureka said to Cat, "promise you'll stay away from that water."

The Poet reached for his reflection in the pond, entranced. Then he tumbled into the water without a splash.

"Poet!" Cat shouted, dragging Eureka a few steps toward the water.

Eureka shivered as water spooled around the place where the boy had fallen. His arm shot out, straining toward the sky, still clutching the can of black spray paint.

"He's messing with us," Cat said, relieved. "Isn't he?"

When the can fell from the Poet's fingers, Eureka saw that the water was viscous, almost tar-like.

"Don't go down there, Cat."

"He needs help—" Cat said, but she didn't move.

"The witch warned me. That water is enchanted. Its reflection is lethal. It shows the darkest parts of people."

The Poet's elbow dipped beneath the Glimmering, as if something gripped it from below. Then his wrist was level with the surface. Cat screamed; Eureka held on. By the time the Poet's fingers disappeared beneath the Glimmering, the fight had left Cat's body. She slumped forward, dropped to her knees.

"He was kind to me when I needed a friend. He wouldn't

hurt a soul. . . ." Cat trailed off, looked at Eureka, then looked away.

Eureka knew they were both thinking the same thing: if the Poet's reflection had killed him, what kind of horror would Eureka see if she looked inside?

The Glimmering was still for a moment. Then three iridescent bubbles rose above its surface. One at a time they popped, leaving the faintest amethyst-colored shimmer in the air.

18

FEVER TO TELL

"She's not there."

An hour later Ander's frantic voice traveled up the waterfall from Solon's workshop. Eureka had finally dragged Cat back to the Bitter Cloud, where her friend collapsed on her pallet, pushing Eureka away when she tried to comfort her, crying silent tears until she slept.

Cat had wanted to stop at the Celans' caves to tell them about the Poet, but it was too dangerous to risk. The Celans already had Seyma's death to avenge. There was no telling how they would respond to losing one of their young.

"Not at the pond," Ander said. "Not with the Celans. I've looked everywhere. She just . . . disappeared."

"What do you want me to do about it?" Solon asked.

Eureka moved toward the stairs leading to his workshop. Now that Solon knew she'd snuck out, both boys would be furious with her. She had to tell them she was back.

"Come with me," Ander cried. "Search for her. Atlas is out there. I know it."

"All the more reason for you and me to stay home. We're no match for him."

"And Eureka is?"

"Let's hope so," Solon said. "If you were to meet Atlas in these mountains—"

"Maybe he's already done the worst thing he can do to me," Ander muttered.

Eureka paused at the top of the stairs. Embers of a fire glowed below.

"What do you mean?" Solon asked.

"There's something I should show you," Ander said.

Eureka peered over the staircase railing. Solon straddled a low-backed leather chair, drinking prosecco out of his broken glass and smoking a cigarette. Ander stood with his back to Solon. He looked thinner. Eureka was used to him holding his shoulders straight, but tonight they slumped as he lifted his shirt, revealing the muscles on his bare torso—and two deep gashes in his flesh.

Solon whistled under his breath. "Does Eureka know?"

"She has enough to worry about," Ander said. He sounded intensely lonely.

Eureka knew about the gashes—she'd discovered them the first time she kissed Ander—but she didn't know what they meant. There had been so much else to process the night her fingers found those strange slits in his skin. The intoxicating taste of his lips, the storm her tears had begun, Brooks lost in the bay, and the last, most haunting translation of *The Book of Love.*

"There's this, too." Ander held a long piece of white coral shaped like an arrowhead. "It was inside me. I pulled it from the wound."

Solon placed his glass on the floor with a soft clink, his cigarette dangling from his lips. He examined the coral, whipping his finger away when he touched its sharp point. "How long have you had this?"

"Since the day before the storm began." Ander flinched slightly when Solon's fingers probed his back. "Eureka went sailing with Brooks. I knew she wasn't safe, so I followed her in the water. I saw the twins fall overboard"—he closed his eyes—"and her dive after them. But before I could do anything to help, something tore into me."

"Go on." Solon ashed his cigarette.

"It wasn't invisible, but it wasn't visible, either. It was a wave moving independently from the other waves, a sovereign force of darkness. I tried to fight it, but I didn't know *how* to fight such a thing. I pity Brooks, now that I know what he endured."

"The coral dagger carves a gateway for Atlas to enter Waking World bodies. It is so sharp because it is dead." Solon leaned back in his chair. "I've never known Atlas to inhabit two earthly bodies at once, let alone a Seedbearer body. He grows bolder all the time. Or perhaps he isn't working alone."

Who else would he work with? Eureka wanted to ask. She sensed from the fear that flashed across Ander's face that he knew whom Solon meant.

Solon handed the coral back to Ander. "Hold on to this. We will need it."

"Am I possessed?"

"How would I know?" Solon asked. "Do you feel possessed?"

Ander shook his head. His arm twisted behind him to trace the gills. "But they won't heal."

Solon took a drag from his cigarette and said, "Worst-case scenario is your possessor lies dormant within you for now."

Ander nodded miserably.

"On the bright side," Solon said, "you should be able to breathe underwater. You could swim away and save Eureka the trouble of pretending she doesn't love you." Solon swirled the golden liquid in his glass. "Of course, there *is* the Glimmering."

Eureka felt like an arctic wind had crossed the cave. She'd known the moment Esme spoke about her history that she would have to face the Glimmering, that it was part of her preparation for Atlantis. She would do it alone. She didn't want any of the others going near it again.

Ander leaned closer, hanging on Solon's words.

"It looks like an ordinary pond," the elder Seedbearer explained, "but it's the masterwork of the gossipwitches. One's reflection in the Glimmering is said to reveal who one 'truly' is, as ridiculous as that sounds. You could try it. I don't believe in identity, reality, or truth, so there's no reason for me to take the narcissistic peek. Which is ironic, because I'm extremely narcissistic."

"How do I get there?"

"It isn't far—south of the Celans' caves, through a series of what used to be valleys before your girlfriend grew a conscience. Rapids likely roar there now. A gossipwitch could escort you, but"—his face twitched worriedly—"their help is costly, as you know."

"You think I should go, even if it—"

"Burns your face off?" Solon finished Ander's thought and stared sadly into his empty glass. "That depends. How badly do you need to know?"

X

The sky outside the Bitter Cloud was rusty gray, signaling dawn. Ander had spent his life watching Eureka from a distance—but that morning she was the voyeur.

She lagged behind, stalking him like a coyote stalks a deer.

He moved quickly over dark rocks, through stands of dying trees. The orichalcum spear's sheath gleamed in a belt loop of his black jeans.

He looked different at a distance. When they were close, chemistry got in the way, making Eureka's body buzz, clouding her vision so that all she saw was the boy she wanted. But out in the wild diluvian dawn, Ander was his own person.

She was so focused on her subject that Eureka hardly noticed the path they followed. It was different from the path Esme had illuminated that night. When Ander arrived at the Glimmering, Eureka crouched behind a boulder as the sky lightened in the east. The wind was cold, its chill bone deep. As always, Ander stayed dry in the rain.

Her arms wanted to hold him. Her lips wanted to kiss him. Her heart wanted . . . to be another kind of heart. She thought the person capable of yearning and love had died with Seyma and Dad. But the physical need lingered, undeniable.

She looked for Brooks's body in the pine tree. She didn't see him there, or anywhere.

Ander's eyes looked sunken. She sensed the fear in him, like a hunter senses it in prey. He paced the shore, ran his fingers through his hair. He inhaled deeply and pressed his hand against his heart. He stood where the water lapped the shore, closed his eyes, and hung his head.

"This is for you, Eureka," he said.

She stepped out from behind the rock. "Wait."

He was at her side in an instant. He studied her lips, her dusting of freckles, the widow's peak in her hairline, her shoulders and fingertips, as if they'd been separated for months. He touched her cheek. She leaned into him for a moment—blissful instinct—then forced herself away.

"You shouldn't be here," both said at the same time.

How similar their preservation instincts were, their tendency for sadness. Eureka had never met anyone as intense as Ander—and even that was familiar. People in New Iberia often said Eureka was "intense," meaning it as an insult. Eureka didn't think it was.

"If my family finds you . . . if Atlas does," Ander said.

Eureka looked around, her gaze hovering on the empty pine tree. "I have to know the truth."

Ander faced the Glimmering. Rain glanced off the air around his skin. Now that she was up close, Eureka admired the ridges of Ander's cordon.

"Me too," he said.

"When Brooks was taken," Eureka said, "he became so different. I see now that it was obvious." Bitter rain struck her lips. She hated that she'd done nothing to help Brooks, that he struggled alone. Was she making the same mistake with Ander, afraid to confront a frightening change in him?

"You don't know me well enough to know if I'm different," Ander said.

Eureka watched a cloud drape his face in shadows. It

was true. He had guarded his identity closely. Yet he knew so much about her.

"You know yourself," she said.

Ander grew impatient. "If I'm possessed, I can't be around you anymore. I won't let him use me to kill you. I would go into the far distance and never see you again."

Then Ander would be free from his feelings for her. He wouldn't grow old like Solon had when he'd been in love with Byblis. Wasn't that what she wanted? She tried to picture carrying on without him, toward Brooks and Atlas and the impossible dream of untangling them and redeeming herself. Would it be better for Ander if he left her now?

"Where would I go?" Ander moaned softly, closing his eyes. "I wouldn't know what to do if I weren't next to you. That's who I am."

"You can't rely on someone else to define you. Especially not me."

"You talk like we're strangers," he said. "But I know who you are."

"Tell me." He had touched her most vulnerable reflex. Eureka immediately regretted her words.

"You're the girl who described falling in love more truly than anyone ever has. Remember? Love at first sight that shatters your world's skin. Not fearing someone's flaws and dreams and passions." He took her in his arms and held her tightly. "The unbreakable bond of reciprocal love. I'll never stop caring for you, Eureka. You think all you feel is sadness. You don't know what your happiness could do."

Ander believed there were more sides to Eureka than she would allow herself to see. She thought about the way Esme had tapped the thunderstone when she said there were exceptions to the Glimmering's deadly rule. Eureka approached the pond, slipped her necklace over her head. She held the stone over the water.

"What are you doing?" Ander asked.

The Glimmering answered. Lacy bands of water formed from its depths and drew up around the surface, like a deck of liquid cards being shuffled. A mauve fog spread out above the Glimmering, then gathered into a cloud of concentrated purple in the center, inches from the softly gurgling spring. The cloud stretched into a spire of purple vapor, which imploded and vanished into the center of the pond.

The Glimmering had stilled into a shining mirror.

"I don't think we should do this," Ander said.

"You mean you don't think *I* should do this."

"You could die."

"I need to know who I am before I go to the Marais. The witch told me. My history is in here."

She expected him to protest. Instead, Ander took her hand. The gesture moved her in a way she hadn't expected. The two of them lined the toes of their shoes up with the edge of the water. Eureka's heart was pounding.

They leaned over the Glimmering.

The surface filled with color and she saw the outline of a girl's body. She saw a stunning white gown where her jeans and blue button-down shirt should have been reflected. She took a breath and lifted her gaze slowly, toward the reflection of her face.

It was not Eureka's face. The girl looking up from the Glimmering had dark hair and big, searching black eyes. She had dark skin, high cheekbones, a broad, confident smile. Her lips parted when Eureka's lips did; she tilted her chin at the same angle as Eureka's chin.

Maya Cayce, Eureka's nemesis from Evangeline, the girl who'd stolen her journal, who'd tried to steal Brooks, stared back at her. Eureka gaped. How could it be? In her reflection, her lips curled into a smile. The image burned into her. It would be there forever, locked in the amber of her soul.

"I don't understand," Ander said blankly.

"What does it mean?" Eureka murmured. "How can it be her?"

"How can it be who?" Ander sounded dazed and haunted. Eureka pointed at her reflection, but she saw that Ander's eyes were fixed to the space where his reflection . . . *should* have been.

No one was there. Nothing looked back at Ander but the lead-colored sky.

19

EVICTED

"The trick is to be calm and illogical, just like him," Solon was saying to the twins when Eureka and Ander returned to the Bitter Cloud later that morning.

They sat before the broken fire pit in the center of the salon. Candles dwindled in stalagmite candelabra. Glass shards littered the floor. No one had thought to clean up after the raid. The twins faced Ovid, who sat cross-legged on a green and gold Turkish rug. His posture was lifelike, his features uniquely appealing, but his eyes were as dead as stones. Claire and William lay on their stomachs, examining the robot's gleaming toes.

"Solon, no—" Eureka said. The robot was neutral now, but she knew how quickly he could morph into the ghosts he carried. Hadn't the twins been through enough without having to see Dad's dead face in the machine?

She wondered whether the Poet's ghost inhabited the robot, whether the acquiring radius Solon had mentioned now reached the Glimmering.

"Don't worry, he's asleep." Solon stood behind Eureka, placed his index and middle fingers along the right corner of her jaw, like he was checking her pulse. Then he twisted his fingers clockwise and whispered: "For when you need to know."

He was showing her how to power down the robot. She noticed the subtle infinity-shaped indentation on the inside of Ovid's jaw.

"We need to talk to you," she said. "We just came from the Glimmering."

Solon's eyebrows shot up. "Did your vanity survive?"

"What's the Glimmering?" Claire asked as she climbed on Ovid's shoulders the way she used to climb on Dad's.

"I saw something in there," Eureka said to Solon.

"Her hissstory," a soft, feminine voice sang.

Eureka turned and saw no one. Then bees appeared, a few at a time, until they were swarming the eye sockets of the skulls on Solon's walls.

The gossipwitches entered the salon in swaying caftans. They arranged themselves in the shape of a triangle, with Esme at the point closest to Eureka.

"Well, good morning, Ovid," Esme said. "I see your crap-shoot tinkering finally paid off, Solon. Tell me, how did you bypass the valve filled with vermilion sands? Or didn't you? Oh—did someone die?"

"It was the children's father, since you're sending condolences," Solon said.

"All witches are orphans," Esme said to Claire. Eureka wondered if it was possible that the witch was being kind. She turned to Eureka. "Did you enjoy the Glimmering?"

"Do not lie," the old witch snorted. "We have underwater eyes. We saw everything you saw." She looked at Ander. "And did *not* see."

"What did she say?" Solon pointed at the old witch. He spun toward Ander and let out a noise somewhere between guffaw and cough. "Exactly what didn't you see?"

"I—I don't know," Ander stammered. "We need to talk."

"You do not belong," the old witch said. "Get it? You're *nothing*!"

The middle witch said something behind her hand to the old witch. They looked at Eureka and laughed.

"You know what my reflection means," Eureka said to Esme.

The witch smiled and tilted her head, considering her reply as she looked at the twins, at Ander. "Some truths are best kept secret from loved ones."

Then Esme shrugged and laughed, and Solon laughed and

lit another cigarette, and Eureka saw everything clearly and completely: no one had any idea what was going on. If there was a system or a meaning to the magic around them, no one knew what it was. Eureka would have to take matters into her own hands.

A shadow shifted in the back of the cave and Eureka heard a sniff. Cat poked her head out from behind the tapestry separating the guest room. Eureka knew they were still in a fight, that things between them would never be the same, but her body moved to be with Cat before her mind could stop her.

"What are they doing here?" Cat asked.

The witches flicked their tongues and turned to Solon. "We did not receive our payment yesterday," Esme said. "We require triple wings today."

"Triple wings." Solon laughed. "It can't be done. The bugs have bugged out."

"What did you say?" Esme's forked tongue hissed. Her bees paused in their busy circles to tremble in the air.

"I was raided yesterday," Solon said. "I lost nearly everything. The butterfly room, the hatchery—gone." He pulled a small velvet pouch from his robe pocket. "I can offer you this. Two grams of orchid petals in your favorite color."

"This trifle does not aid us in our mission," the middle witch said.

The old witch glared at Solon through a monocle, her

amber eye huge and distorted behind the glass. "We cannot go home without more wings!"

Esme raised her hand to quiet the others. "We will take the robot."

Solon let out a sudden laugh that became a ragged smoker's cough. "Ovid is not collateral."

"Everything is collateral," the old witch said. "Innocence, afterlives, even nightmares."

"Tell it to the judge." Cat had slipped away from Eureka to stand in front of Esme. " 'Cause the robot stays with us."

The girl-witch raised an eyebrow. She seemed to be preparing to do something terrifying. But Eureka had driven Cat to karate lessons. She'd watched Cat's fists make both of mean Carrie Marchaux's eyes black. She recognized Cat's expression when she was about to whale on someone.

Cat's left leg snapped up. Her bare foot connected with the witch's jaw. Esme's neck twisted to the side and four shiny white teeth shot from her mouth. They clattered across the floor like loose mosaic tiles. The blood that dribbled from the witch's lips matched her amethyst gown. She wiped the corner of her mouth.

"That was for the Poet," Cat said.

Esme smiled a wicked, toothless smile. She flicked her forked tongue, and every bee in the cave swarmed around her head. She flicked her tongue again. The bees dispersed, flowing as a team over the cave floor, retrieving each of her teeth. She threw her head back and opened her mouth wide. The bees entered her mouth and placed the teeth back in the blood-wet grooves in her gums. She turned to her companions and giggled.

"If the girl gets this incensed over a silly boy, imagine when she finds out that her whole family"—Esme turned to Cat, spitting purple blood as she hissed the words—"is rotting on the putrid New Shores of Arkansas."

Cat tackled Esme. Bees stung her arms and face, but she didn't seem to notice. She had the witch in a choke hold, until Esme snapped her neck free. Cat tore at the gossipwitch's hair as bees crawled up her hands, her fingers trolling the back of Esme's head. Then she paused as disgust filled her face. "What the—"

"Control your impudent friend, Eureka!" Esme shouted, and struggled to untangle herself from Cat. "Or you will all regret it."

Cat thrust the witch's head down toward her chest.

Where the back of Esme's skull should have been was an amethyst-colored void, at the center of which a single monarch butterfly flew furiously in place.

This explained the gossipwitches' endless appetite for winged creatures. This was how they flew.

Cat plucked the butterfly from the void in Esme's head. Its wings beat just once more between her fingers; then the insect curled up and died.

Esme roared and flung Cat off her. The other gossip-witches gaped in horror at the back of her empty head. They touched the backs of their own heads, checking to make sure everything was still intact.

Bees flocked to Esme's fist, coating it like a glove. She towered over Cat, grabbed the back of her head, and punched the base of Cat's skull with her bee-bound fist.

Pain exploded in Cat's eyes. She screamed a brutal scream.

Eureka shoved Esme aside and swatted at the bees on Cat's scalp, but they wouldn't fly away. She tried to pick them out of Cat's hair. They stung her hands and would not budge. They were a part of the base of Cat's skull now, swarming the back of her head, stinging and re-stinging endlessly.

Esme staggered backward to rejoin the other witches. She was out of breath. "If you will carry Ovid as far as the threshold, we will take him from there."

"The only thing you're getting is out of here," Eureka said.

"Be gone!" Solon said, taking courage from Eureka's stand. "I've wanted to say that to you bitches for so long."

"You're not thinking, Solon," the middle witch said. She and the old witch were supporting Esme, who looked faint. "Remember what happens when you can't afford our glaze. . . ."

"Nothing lasts forever," Solon said, and winked at Eureka.

"All your little enemies will find you," the old witch said. "The big one will find you, too."

"Solon," Ander said, "if you let them drop the glaze—"

"Are the bad people coming back?" William leaned on Eureka. She hated that she could feel his rib cage through his shirt.

"Don't cry," she whispered automatically as she tended to Cat's scalp. "I won't let anything happen to you."

It was too late. William's tears fell on her shoulders, on her cheeks. Their innocence was startling, a sparkling jewel in the black rift. She changed her mind.

"Cry," she said. "Cry it all out on me."

William did.

"We will give you until midnight to change your mind," the old witch said. "Then the glaze is gone."

Solon stamped out his cigarette. He walked to where Cat whimpered woozily in Eureka's arms. He kissed Cat's cheek.

"As you wish." Rage surged beneath the surface of Esme's weakened voice. The other two witches flicked their tongues and four bees slowly returned to orbit their heads. The rest remained with Cat.

Carrying their crippled companion, the old and older gossipwitches lumbered back through the long, dark hall of skulls.

20

YET TROUBLE CAME

Around dusk, Eureka and Ander stood at the edge of the veranda and looked down at the Tearline pond. Solon had retreated to his workshop with Ovid, and the twins and Cat were resting in the guest room. Cat said the throb in her skull had dwindled to the level of a migraine. She barely felt the constant stings anymore; that pain was easier to bear than knowing what had happened to her family.

"Maybe it was just gossip," Ander had said, but they all sensed that the witches spoke the truth.

They had divvied up the last of the food—two small apples, a few gulps of water, the dregs of a box of muesli. After Eureka ate, hunger churned in her more fiercely than before. Her body was weak, her mind cloudy. She had not slept since waking from her nightmare of drowning in the wasted dead. Six nights remained until the full moon—if they even survived that long.

The rain had fallen for so long she didn't feel it anymore. It had become as regular as air. She leaned over the veranda's railing, touched Ander's back so that he leaned over, too. Two blurry shapes looked up from the surface of the pond.

"You didn't disappear just because you weren't there in the Glimmering," she said. "And I . . ."

"You're not the face you saw, either?" Ander asked.

"I went to high school with that girl," Eureka said. "Maya Cayce. We hated each other. We competed over everything. When we were young we used to be friends. Why would I see her in my reflection?"

"Somewhere all of this makes sense." Ander's fingers lightly traced her neck. "The question is: do we survive the journey there?"

Eureka turned from the reflection to the real. Her hands slid up Ander's chest, her fingers twined around his neck— and she knew she shouldn't. Her hands had murdered yesterday. They were out of food. The glaze would be gone by midnight.

"I wish we could stop everything and stand here forever."

"Love can't be stopped, any more than time," Ander said softly.

"You're talking like love and time aren't connected," Eureka said. "For you, they're the same thing."

"Some people measure time by how they fill it. Childhood is time, high school is time." He touched her lips with a fingertip. "You have always been my time."

"I would puke," a voice said behind Ander, "but it might attract starving locals."

Someone stepped from the shadows of the cherry tree. The witches must have dropped their glaze early. He had found them.

"Brooks," Eureka said.

"Atlas." Ander lurched forward. So did Brooks. Eureka was caught in the middle, both of their bodies against hers.

They would fight now. They would try to kill each other.

"Get out of here," Eureka said quickly to Brooks.

"I think he's the one who should get out," Brooks said to Ander.

Ander's lip curled in disgust. "You're going to lose."

Brooks's face became a gruesome flash of rage. "I've already won."

Ander drew the long orichalcum spear from its sheath at his hip. "Not if I slaughter that body before your world can rise."

"Ander, no!" Eureka spun so that her body shielded Brooks. For a moment she felt the familiar heat of his chest. "I won't let you."

"Yes, please, Eureka, save me," Brooks said. Then he lunged forward with all his might and sent Eureka tumbling. When Ander bent to check on her, Brooks rammed him hard. He grappled for the spear.

Ander's back arched over the veranda's rail. He couldn't right himself. He grabbed hold of Brooks's forearm and took him down with him. Eureka tried to stop them, but they were already gone.

She ran to the edge of the veranda. The spear had slipped from Ander's hands and out of Brooks's reach, too. The boys clutched each other and swung desperate fists as they tumbled through the air, each blow missing its mark, forced into truce by chaos and gravity. Then they splashed through the surface of the Tearline pond.

During the stillness that followed, Eureka couldn't help imagining that both boys had disappeared from her life forever, that love was gone, that it was easier that way.

But the boys' heads surfaced. They spun in the water until they spotted each other. Twenty feet of tears separated them. Brooks dipped back underwater and became a black blur. He swam toward Ander with ferocious grace.

Ander's body rose in the water, which quickly turned red around him. Then he was dragged beneath the surface.

All was eerily quiet again. Eureka paced the veranda for an hour-long minute before she remembered both boys had gills that allowed them to breathe underwater.

She dove in.

Water engulfed her. The thunderstone shield bloomed around her. She couldn't see them. She plunged a few feet deeper, moving toward the opposite shore.

She sensed movement below her and slipped to the bottom

227

of the shield. Brooks had Ander pinned to the floor of the pond and was tearing at his chest with his mouth, as if he were trying to eat Ander's heart. The pain on Ander's face was so severe that Eureka feared he would lose consciousness.

She dove toward the boys, swimming as hard as she could. She drew within five feet of them, balled her hands into fists to use against Brooks. This wasn't her best friend; it couldn't be. Then she remembered the shield. There was no way to reach Ander as long as it protected her. Did she have time to race to the surface, throw off her thunderstone, and swim back here again? As Eureka paused, Ander turned his head and exhaled.

A powerful wave sent Eureka tumbling backward, spinning end over end. She and her shield spun horizontally in the water, trapped within a swirling vortex. She felt herself lift up.

Higher and higher she spun, catching dizzy flashes of Brooks and Ander. All three of them moved in different orbits, caught in an underwater whirlwind made of Ander's Zephyr.

The light above Eureka grew closer, more intense, until . . .

She shot out of the water, spinning upward. Her thunderstone shield evaporated. The whirlwind had surfaced to become an enormous tornado. Beneath her, Ander reached for Brooks. Blood flowed from his chest and entered its own orbit, splattering Brooks as he spun by.

Then Eureka was out of the wind spout, hurtling through the air, toward the nearby cliff that stood above the pond. As she fell from the sky, she was amazed by the sight of an enormous sloping rainbow that stretched beyond the horizon.

She heard a guttural cry and looked over her shoulder. Brooks was flying far into the distance, still a hostage of Ander's Zephyr. She didn't see Ander anywhere.

Eureka landed on a rock with a deep and painful thud. Her bones throbbed as she rolled to her side and cradled herself for a moment, shivering in the rain. She touched her thunderstone and Diana's locket and the yellow ribbon, and she breathed. Eventually she struggled to her knees.

She didn't know where she was, or where Ander or Brooks had ended up, but from the rock, she could see most of the Celan valley. It looked like a picture of the surface of the moon. She saw the orchid-ringed Glimmering to the south. She saw a thousand silver circles dotting the landscape, bodies of water born of her tears. She saw the white caps of far mountains, the elbow-shaped Tearline pond in the valley between the caves, and, not fifty feet away, Solon's veranda.

She climbed toward it. The center of the veranda was where the rainbow ended. Ruby blended into vivid orange, then into gold, then into a verdant ivy green, then indigo, and, finally, into the toxic-lovely purple Eureka had come to associate with the gossipwitches. The rainbow stretched into a night now black as coal. Neither sunlight nor moonlight had made it.

Looking closer, Eureka saw four upright silhouettes inside

the rainbow, floating toward the veranda. A buzz made Eureka think the gossipwitches had arrived, but she heard no laughter, saw no flash of orchid. And this buzzing was different, more like a rasp than the contented song of bees.

The four approaching figures were motionless—except for their heaving torsos. Eureka realized that the buzzing in the wind was the sound of labored breathing.

Seedbearers.

Each one was intensely focused on keeping another's body aloft. They worked their breath as if they were wings beating for one another.

Eureka was finally close enough to see a figure at the base of the rainbow, alone in the dark on the veranda. He looked like someone's great-grandfather. The rainbow streamed from his mouth like an endless puff of smoke. His back was arched uncomfortably, as if the rainbow began somewhere deep inside him. He wore a silk robe and a strange black mask.

The old man breathing the rainbow into the sky was Solon.

But it couldn't be. His body looked ancient. The skin on his hands and his chest was mottled with age. His back was stooped. How had Solon aged a century in the space of an afternoon? When he explained the Seedbearers' aging process, he'd said feeling nothing had kept him young for decades. What—or who—had revived Solon's feelings, his capacity for love?

As Eureka hiked over rocks and approached the back of the veranda, the first silhouette stepped out of the rainbow.

It was a boy about her age, wearing a baggy, mud-splattered suit. The suit was familiar, though the body wearing it looked vastly different from the last time she had seen it. The boy faced her and narrowed his eyes.

Albion had killed Rhoda, abused the twins. He was the mind behind Diana's murder. He looked eighteen instead of sixty, but Eureka was certain it was him.

Three more Seedbearers stepped out of the rainbow. Chora. Critias. Starling. All of them were young. They looked like teenagers dressed in their grandparents' clothes.

Eureka hauled herself over the rail. She was sore and bleeding. Solon had brought the Seedbearers here on purpose. Why? The rainbow broke off at his lips. What remained hung in the air in colored particles, then drifted to the ground like psychedelic leaves.

The hooded mask he wore looked as pliant as cotton, but was made of tightly woven black chain mail, so thin that up close it was transparent. Beneath the mask, Solon looked a million years old.

"Don't be alarmed," Solon said, his voice muffled. "It's merely a mask over a mask over a mask."

"What's going on?" Eureka asked.

"My masterpiece." Solon looked into the night sky, now darker and more dismal without the glorious light. "Those colored rays of breath pave a Seedbearer highway that connects us anywhere in the world."

"Why would you do this?"

He patted her cheek. "Let's greet our guests." Through the mask, Solon's smiling eyes surveyed the figures before him. "Eureka, I think you've had the pleasure of meeting these four tubes of crap."

The Seedbearers stepped forward, as bewildered as Eureka.

"Hello, cousins!" Solon bellowed merrily.

"It took three-quarters of a century," Chora said, "but the fool has finally come around. To what do we owe the pleasure, Solon?"

Solon's laughter echoed behind his mask.

"Take off that ridiculous mask." Albion's voice was startling in its youthful timbre.

"Your bitterness seems to be treating you well," Solon said.

"We have grown strong on hatred and revulsion," Albion said. "Whereas poor Solon walks like an autumn leaf in its last throes. Don't tell me you've fallen in love again?"

"It has always seemed to me that hate is a form of love," Solon said. "Try hating someone you don't care about. Impossible."

"You betrayed us, and now you are pathetic," Chora said. "Our business is with Ander. Where is he?" She glanced around. Eureka did, too, fearful of what had happened to Ander, to Brooks's body, to Atlas.

"Ah, there they are!" Starling grinned. Her long braid was

now a lustrous blond. "The little streaks of piss we should have killed when we had the chance."

Cat and the twins emerged onto the veranda. Cat's head was still abuzz with bees.

"Go back!" Eureka ran toward them.

"Speaking of Ander," Solon mused, pausing to cough into the sleeve of his robe, "I've been wondering just how does he stay so young? I've never seen a boy more swallowed whole by love—yet since he arrived at the Bitter Cloud he hasn't looked a day over eighteen. Don't you think that's odd, Albion?"

Ever since Eureka had learned what love did to a Seedbearer, she'd found new evidence of age on Ander every hour. But now, observing Solon's shocking old age and the other Seedbearers' return to youth, Eureka saw how extreme the changes in them were.

Did that mean Ander didn't really love her?

"Where is Ander?" Chora repeated. "And will you please take off that ridiculous mask. My God," she said, getting an idea. "Do you require oxygen to breathe?"

"He always was a heavy smoker," Starling said.

"A Seedbearer with emphysema," Critias said. "What an idiot."

"It's true my lungs are as black as the blues," Solon said, "but I wear this mask for quite a different purpose. It is loaded with artemisia." His finger hovered over a silver dot on the

233

side of his mask. "To activate it, all I have to do is press this button."

"He's lying," Chora said, but her fearful voice betrayed her.

Solon grinned behind his mask. "Don't believe me? Shall I demonstrate?"

"What are you doing?" Eureka cried. "You'll kill Ander, too."

Albion's head snapped toward her. His eyebrows lifted. "Going to weep again?" He drew near, holding a vial the same shape as the lachrymatory Ander had used, but a far less intricate one made of dull steel.

Eureka wasn't going to cry. She slapped at the lachrymatory in Albion's hand and grabbed him by his throat. She tightened her grip. The Seedbearer wheezed. He tried to push her off, but Eureka was stronger.

Albion looked different from the last time they faced each other, but Eureka had changed even more. She saw that he feared her. She snarled at him, dark rage in her eyes.

William began to cry. "Don't kill anyone else, Reka. . . ."

From the corner of her eye, Eureka saw William standing with Cat and Claire, sad and skinny and filthy. He wasn't the same boy who used to catapult into her bed every morning, spilling action figures across her sheets while she picked clumps of dried maple syrup from his hair. Eureka loosened her grip.

"Albion?" Solon snapped his fingers. "The show's this way. I'd pay attention if I were you. I used to agree with you. I used to think we had a reason to stop her." He turned to Eureka. "But nothing can stop her. Least of all us."

Chora stepped slowly toward Solon. "The game has changed. It's not what we would have wanted, but we can still use her tears to improve our position. If you were to come back to us . . ."

"Take the mask off, Cousin," Critias said.

Solon's finger moved toward the silver button on the side of his mask. Eureka imagined the poison filling Ander's lungs in the distance. She imagined his shock becoming defiance as he gagged, his magnificent breath going out of him. The painful resignation as his body stilled. His soul rising. She wondered what his last thought would be.

She thought of the way his voice always sounded like a whisper. And the scissoring motions his fingers made when he ran them through his hair. The way his hand fit inside hers. The shade of blue his eyes took on when she walked by, even if he'd just seen her a moment before. How he kissed her as if his life depended on it. The person she became when she kissed him back.

Solon placed his hand over his heart. Then he grinned and pressed the button. "Bombs away."

Poisonous gas, as green as the aurora borealis, glided over his face.

21

ILLUSIONMENT

The artemisia spooled over Solon's face, shrouding his wrinkled brow, then his eyes, then his cheeks. The last thing to disappear behind the vapor was an extraordinary smile.

The Seedbearers circled him. Starling chewed her nails. Chora gulped as if drowning. Albion's face wore the expression of someone about to be beaten. Critias's cheek shone with the trail of a single tear as he turned to the others. "Do we have any parting words?"

Solon's body stiffened and fell forward. He crashed to the veranda like a felled tree. Eureka rolled him onto his back and tore at the chain mail near his neck until her fingers burned. The mask was as welded to Solon as he had been devoted to his final mission.

"Is he dead?" Cat asked.

Eureka rested her head against his chest. Still as ice. The smooth silk of Solon's bathrobe was wet against her cheek. She waited for breath.

A single labored wheeze came from Solon's chest. Eureka grasped his shoulders. She wanted his face to reveal the truth of things—why he had done this, what Ander's fate was, what would become of Eureka and her quest to save the world—but his expression behind the mask was cloudy.

Maybe it was a lie. Maybe artemisia didn't kill Seedbearers vicariously. Maybe Ander was still alive underwater and would ride a wave over the rail of the veranda, so she could hold him like she had in her bedroom in Lafayette, when love was new.

Maybe the next time she saw Brooks he would just be Brooks, and what possessed him would be gone like a disease someone found a cure for.

Maybe she hadn't flooded the world with her tears. Maybe she had nothing to do with it. Maybe it was another rumor spun by girls leaning into water fountains.

Maybe her parents and Madame Blavatsky and Rhoda and the Poet were alive and could inspire and frustrate and love her still.

Maybe the nightmare of these past months really *was* a nightmare, an indulgence of her wild imagination, and soon she would wake up, put on her running shoes, race the sun as it rose along the misty bayou, before Brooks swung by to pick her up for school, a steamy cinnamon latte waiting for her in the cup holder.

Solon's body convulsed. He gripped his neck and strained for air. He punched once, twice, three times against the side of the mask. There was a hiss, and then a jigsaw crack split the mask down its center. It fell in two pieces on either side of Solon's face. Acid-green artemisia fumes met their death in the rain. Eureka inhaled a whiff of licorice-scented air—then the vapor was gone.

Solon's eyes were closed. Scraggly gray stubble had sprouted into a thick beard that crept down his neck like lichen. His close-cropped hair was now the color of a snow leopard and his skin was extravagantly wrinkled, mottled with the freckles of old age.

"Solon," Eureka whispered.

His eyes flashed open. His lips wavered toward a smile. With a trembling hand he reached inside the pocket of his robe and withdrew a gray envelope. He pressed it into Eureka's hand. It felt silky and strange.

"I wanted a good death," Solon whispered. He looked around, like he was deciding whether this one qualified. Then he closed his eyes and was gone.

"It was good," Eureka said.

A deep, guttural scream grabbed her attention. Albion was staggering toward her. He lumbered forward, off-kilter, like a drunk.

"You're coming with us," he wheezed, and lunged for

Eureka, stumbling over Solon's legs, falling onto the body of his dead cousin. He writhed. His fingers tore at his neck. Phlegm dribbled from the sides of his mouth.

Behind Albion, Critias doubled over, wheezing. Chora and Starling were already on the ground. Painful gasps and coughs echoed off the rocks. Eureka, Cat, and the twins held each other as the Seedbearers' breathing slowed. Albion strained to reach Eureka's ankle. It was his last act.

All of them were dead.

Which meant Ander was dead. Eureka clutched her head.

She thought of Ovid. He was downstairs, close enough to acquire these new ghosts. Dad and Seyma . . . and now Solon, and the other Seedbearers. Were they all together now?

Was Ander there?

She faced the water. Where was he? How had he spent his final breaths? Her mind rewound to the first moment they had spoken when he slammed into her car, the weird and lovely way he'd caught her tear. How had they gotten from there to here? Eureka wished she'd done everything differently. She wished she could have said goodbye.

She ached for the release that only tears could bring. She knew she couldn't, knew she wouldn't, but as much as she tried to be as unfeeling as Ovid, Eureka was a human girl trapped inside a human body. Heat welled in her eyes.

A great splash erupted near the edge of the pond. A spout of water crested above the veranda's rail. A blond head appeared in its center.

Ander spilled himself out of the water, which fell back into the pond. He was bleeding and straining to breathe. How much time did he have left?

Eureka flung her arms around his neck. He spun her around like her weight was a wonderful surprise. Their lips were centimeters apart when Eureka pulled away. She'd been so sure she'd lost him. She put a hand against his chest, wanting to feel his heartbeat, the rise and fall of his chest.

"Is he here?" Ander asked.

"Who?"

"Atlas! Did you see which way he went?"

Eureka shook her head. She opened her mouth but couldn't find the words to say he had only moments left to live.

"Why are you looking at me like that?"

Eureka stepped aside to reveal his family.

Ander raked his fingers through his hair. He leaned down and held his hand in front of Albion's face.

"Am I a ghost?"

Eureka touched the tips of Ander's hair. It felt so good, so alive, that she caressed his scalp, his brow, his cheek, his neck. He turned his head into her hand.

"No," she said. She wondered whether Ander knew what she knew about Ovid and the Filling.

"I don't understand. When one Seedbearer dies—"

"All of them die."

"But I'm still here," Ander whispered. "How?"

Eureka remembered the envelope Solon had given her.

She'd stuffed it in the pocket of her jeans. She pulled it out, lifted its flap. Inside was the lachrymatory containing her tears, wrapped in a piece of paper covered in lovely cursive.

Eureka quickly slipped the vial inside her pocket. She unfolded the paper and read aloud:

> *"To Whom It May Concern (Eureka):*
> *"Am I dead yet?*
> *"Good.*
> *"There is a fine bottle of brandy in the pocket of the farthest silk robe in my closet. You will know it from its antique bamboo hanger. Once you are safely ensconced inside, crack it open, and gather round you all those who remain and care. Or perhaps just those who remain. Then you shall know a portion of the truth."*

Eureka looked up as Cat, William, and Claire stepped over Seedbearers to draw closer.

"What else does he say?" William asked.

Eureka read on:

> *"I'm serious. Go inside.*
> *"Eureka, lest you became paralyzed by indecision: You won't waste Ander's final moments rifling through a closet full of silly silk robes, hunting for booze like a lucky bum who swung in through the window. The boy could live to taste a million of your kisses, barring*

catastrophes out of my control. I'll explain everything in
a moment."

"We should honor his request," Ander said. He kicked Albion aside and lifted Solon from the ground.

They descended the stairs into Solon's salon. Ander laid Solon's body on the rug next to his chair, where he could be near the waterfall. He went downstairs to retrieve the brandy. William brought out the witches' torch for light, and Eureka sat atop the broken dining table and read aloud:

> *"Are you still mad at me? You should have seen your face when you realized what I'd done. Yes, I wrote this letter before I saw your face, but I know how angry you will be and were. I'm exploding time and tense in my last testament!*
>
> *"I'm not unvain enough to say it didn't bother me to grow old in the dusk of my existence. I didn't wish to care for you all so deeply, but I did.*
>
> *"Brave, bold Claire—may you grow up and remain fearless.*
>
> *"Enigmatic William—hold on to your mystery.*
>
> *"Cat, you nuclear bomb, in another life, I'll seduce you.*
>
> *"Ander. Survivor. You are the only man I've ever admired.*
>
> *"And Eureka. Of course, my feeling began with you. You draw emotion from the stoniest souls.*

"I summoned the Seedbearers, to kill them and to kill myself using the artemisia in the orichalcum chest. But what about Ander? you'll be wondering. The truth is beautiful: Ander was raised by Seedbearers, but he is not a Seedbearer. He was born to an irresponsible mortal family in California with a weakness for joining cults. They were persuaded to give him over to the Seedbearers backstage at an auditorium in Stockton. And so he was raised to believe he was bound by Seedbearer laws. They needed an age-appropriate decoy, someone to blend into the background of your youth.

"But he was never one of us! And so . . .

"He lives!

"For some time I have suspected that something wasn't right about him—or rather, that something wasn't wrong—but I couldn't be sure until the witches revealed that he saw nothing in the Glimmering.

"The witches only care about returning home to Atlantis, so their Glimmering only reveals one's reflected Atlantean identity. Because Ander has no true lineage connecting him to the Sleeping World, he has no reflection in its mirror. The Glimmering would have killed him if your thunderstone had not protected you both.

"Ander does not belong in Atlantis, bless him. Not belonging is the greatest gift. Always remember that.

"Once I discovered my death would not kill Ander—that, indeed, my death would help you by removing the

Seedbearers from the equation—I had no choice but to take the ancient plunge all my heroes have taken. Two stones, one bird, as the Poet might say. I hope I shall see him soon."

"I don't understand," Ander interrupted. "If I'm not a Seedbearer, how can my breath do the same things the others' can?"

"The Poet told me this story," Cat said, "about quirk thieves who sneak into hospital nurseries and study babies' magic. Maybe the Seedbearers chose you because they knew they could make your quirk blend with the things they wanted you to do."

While the others speculated, Eureka studied the rest of Solon's letter. After the first page, the paper stock changed . . . to parchment—the same parchment in *The Book of Love.* Here was the same cryptic writing Eureka had hired Madame Blavatsky to translate. Here were the missing pages from *The Book of Love.*

Enclosed are pages from your book. I'm sorry I couldn't tell you sooner; I've had them all along. Years ago, I made a vow to Byblis never to share their contents. They were her deepest shame. But I think she would have wanted you to see them and know the truth.

The gossipwitches can be employed as translators.

Use this envelope to find them. Make a deal. You're smarter than they are.

You may not like what you discover. That's the nature of discovery. Byblis was never the same after she learned the truth of her history. I can't guess how you will handle the news, but you deserve to know.

I was never meant to be your guide. A leader is a dealer in hope. This explains my failure, and it explains why you, Eureka, must triumph.

From the other side,
Solon

P.S. The witches hold more than an understanding of your text. There is something else I bartered to them years ago. It is yours. Get it back. And then get going. You have all you need to travel to the Marais. From there, it's up to you. Atlas will be waiting. Hurry but don't rush. You know what I mean.

P.P.S. Do not neglect to bring Ovid! You'll need him more than you can know. If you don't kill each other, you might become great friends. He possesses unsuspected depths. . . .

22

MOTHER TONGUE

"No, they don't hurt," Ander was saying to Cat when Eureka finished reading.

He had lifted his shirt to reveal his gills. The twins were mesmerized, gathered around him, examining his skin. When Cat leaned down, the bees on the back of her head buzzed and crawled. Every few moments she winced as one stung her.

No one but Eureka saw the envelope in her hands pulse with a light as purple as the gossipwitches' caftans. Eureka blinked and the light was gone.

"I went to the Glimmering to see what they meant . . . ," she heard Ander say.

Then the envelope pulsed with light again. This time Eureka saw that the top flap fluttered like a wing. She opened her palm. The envelope fluttered a second time, then rose above her hand in the air. It was not *like* a wing—the envelope was *made* of wings. Two large gray moths had embraced to carry Solon's letter. They'd been still until now, when they slowly separated, as if waking from an enchanted sleep. They pulsed with amethyst light, then swooped toward the entrance of the cave.

Eureka looked to see if the others had noticed. They were still absorbed by Ander's gills. "Solon thinks Atlas tried to possess me but I fended him off."

Eureka sensed the moths wanted her to follow them. She tucked the letter and the torn pages of *The Book of Love* into her pocket next to the lachrymatory. She reached for her purple bag, which hung on a hook-shaped stalagmite near the door. She lifted the eternal torch from another stalagmite where William had rested it and crept silently away, like she had in the old days with Madame Blavatsky's lovebird Polaris.

"What was it like to have no reflection?" William asked Ander as the moths led Eureka into the skull-lined hall.

"What did Eureka see in the Glimmering?" Cat's voice trailed down the hallway, and Maya Cayce's reflection flashed through Eureka's mind. *Somewhere all of this makes sense,* Ander had said. She hurried away from the memory of her reflection, from Cat's question, and from her loved ones.

"Eureka?" Ander's voice called.

They would try to stop her from going to the witches. But

Solon had never been so clear about her needing to do something. She would go to the witches to retrieve what was hers.

She ran after the moths, skulls grinning as she passed them in the dark. Outside, rain blasted her, cold and ferocious, slashing sideways like a wall of whips. The sun was rising, lightening a low section of the dark gray sky.

Something was different. Behind her, the glazeless entrance to Solon's cave was visible to the outside world. The depression in the rock looked so mundane, so obvious, so bereft of magic unfolding within.

The moths pulsed, calling Eureka with their glowing purple light when she thought she'd lost them in the rain. She followed them up a series of slopes that looked like gargantuan anthills, rounded a corner, and found even higher mountains.

In the distance, on top of the tallest peak balanced an immense rectangular rock. Dark crevices suggested doors and windows. A flat landing marked the entrance to the witches' home.

"How do I get up there?" Eureka asked the moths.

They hung in the sky, glowing, disappearing into fog, glowing. She touched her thunderstone, her locket, the ribbon, and began to climb.

Mud oozed between her fingers as she picked her way up the rock. When the cliff grew sheer and Eureka didn't know how she could continue, the guiding moths wove around her hands, gesturing whether the surest route up was a few inches to the left or right. Loose rocks plummeted as Eureka climbed above them. The peak was so treacherous she wondered if it had ever been approached by anything that couldn't fly.

At last Eureka stood before a doorway. It was made of a thousand dark gray moth wings woven together, fluttering, alive, in the shape of one majestic pair.

"Do I knock?" she asked the guiding moths. They flitted against the door until it absorbed them. Eureka could no longer distinguish them from the other wings.

The door parted, softly severing a vast web of tiny connections, revealing a dazzling room inside.

The walls were made of amethyst; the floor was strewn with orchid petals. Twenty or so gossipwitches lounged around a purple fire. Three of them shared a giant, swaying moth-wing bower. One hung upside down from a brilliant purple pole, her caftan draped over her face.

The witches smoked a long, reedy pipe that curled to a spiral tip. Bright green, licorice-scented fumes swirled in the air above the pipes' embers. They were smoking artemisia, but unlike the Seedbearers, the gossipwitches seemed to thrive on the drug. They laughed as tipsy bees bumped clumsily around their heads.

Eureka spotted Esme on the far side of the room. She looked revived, as if the secret void in her head had never been exposed, her butterfly never crushed between Cat's fingers. Eureka tensed with rage and fear that Cat would never recover as completely.

Esme whispered in another youthful witch's ear, her hands cupped over her mouth, exuding glee over some secret. The way the witches giggled reminded Eureka of girls at Evangeline, girls she would never see again.

When Esme looked up at Eureka, her crystal teardrop necklace gleamed in the shallow of her collarbone. Suddenly Eureka knew what it was, why it had always drawn her eye.

"Your necklace," Eureka said, feeling light-headed from the fumes.

Esme twirled the charm on its silver chain. "This old thing? Solon gave it to me ages ago. Don't tell me he wants it back. Unless he changed his mind about the robot?"

"Solon is dead."

Esme slid one hand onto her hip and walked directly through the fire to Eureka. "Isn't it a pity," she lisped through her forked tongue.

"That necklace wasn't his to trade. It belongs to me."

Eureka had come for more than the necklace, but since she had nothing to offer in return, she'd decided to make one demand at a time.

The witches whispered to each other, forked tongues flicking over their teeth. The sound became a single wet hiss that snaked its scaly way into Eureka's bad ear.

Then the hissing stopped. Pouring rain flowed into the silence.

"You may have your family heirloom back." Esme slipped her hands behind her neck and unfastened the chain.

Eureka nodded stoically, though she wanted to cheer. She reached for the chain, but Esme swung the teardrop crystal inches from Eureka's hand. Then the gossipwitch jerked it back and cupped it in her own palm. She whispered into Eureka's bad ear, her replenished stock of bees grazing Eureka's cheek.

"You will owe us something in exchange."

"The necklace is mine. I owe you nothing."

"Perhaps you're right. But you will still deliver what we want. Fear not, you want it, too." She smiled. "May I fasten the clasp for you?"

Esme wrapped her long fingers around Eureka's neck. She smelled like honey and licorice. Her touch was like the soft fuzz of a bee, or a rose just before you're pricked.

"There," Esme breathed.

Eureka felt a burst of heat and heard something sizzle. Blue light flashed as the orichalcum chain holding the crystal teardrop entwined around the bronze chain of her mother's locket. The pendants shifted, ground against each other, like ghosts within a robot. After a moment, the teardrop crystal, the thunderstone, the lapis lazuli locket, even the faded yellow ribbon had converged to form a single, sparkling pendant.

It looked like a very large diamond in the shape of a tear. But inside its smooth, flat surface was a flicker of yellow—from the ribbon—then blue—from the lapis lazuli locket—then steely gray—from the thunderstone, refracting inside the crystal in the purple firelight.

"It fits," Esme said.

"But my thunderstone," Eureka said. "Will it still work?"

The skin where the pendant touched her chest was hot. It singed her fingers when she touched it.

Esme's expression was sphinxlike. She pulled a vial of purple salve from her pocket and pressed it into Eureka's hand. "For your friend. The bees will never leave her, but if I am right about her character—and I do loathe being wrong— she will grow to cherish them. This will disappear the pain. Do you have any more requests? Any other services you would like us to provide?"

Eureka produced *The Book of Love*'s missing pages. "Can you read this?"

"Of course," Esme said. "It is written in our mother tongue, read best with closed eyes."

Behind Esme, the old witch with the monocle patted a purple pillow. "Make yourself at home," she hissed.

Eureka sat. She wanted to get the translation and hurry back down the mountain, back to the Bitter Cloud. But the fire was warm and the pillow was comfortable, and suddenly her hand held a mug of something steaming. She brought it cautiously near her face. It smelled like grape soda spiked with anise alcohol.

"No, thank you." Diana had read Eureka fairy tales. She knew not to drink.

"Please imbibe." The witch beside her pushed the cup to Eureka's lips. "You will need a tad of Dutch courage."

All around the lair, witches raised matching mugs, then drained them in a gulp.

The witch tipped the cup. Eureka winced and swallowed.

The brew tasted so unexpectedly wonderful—like caramel hot chocolate thickened with cream—and Eureka was so unfathomably thirsty, and that first swallow filled her body with such long-awaited warmth that she couldn't stop. She guzzled the rest before she knew what she had done. The witches beamed as she wiped her lips.

"What a joy to see the old language again," Esme sang, flipping through the pages Eureka had given her with her eyes closed. "Shall I begin at the beginning, which is never a beginning but is always in the middle of something already begun?"

"I already know some of the story," Eureka said. "I had a translator at home."

"Home?" Esme lifted her chin. Her eyes were still closed, amethyst lids glittering.

"In Louisiana, where I lived . . . before I cried." She thought of Madame Blavatsky's crimson lipstick, her tobacco-scented patchwork cloak and flock of lovebirds, her compassion when Eureka needed it most. "My translator was very good."

Esme's painted lips pulled skeptically on her spiral pipe. Artemisia embers glowed. She opened her eyes. "One would have to be from our home, from Atlantis, in order to read this text. Are you sure this translator did not feed you lies?"

Eureka shook her head. "She knew things she couldn't

have known. She could read this, I'm certain of it. I believe my mother could, too."

"You mean to suggest that someone has been dipping our pure tongue in the filthy creeks of your world?"

"I don't know about that—"

"What *do* you know?" Esme interrupted.

Eureka closed her eyes and remembered the exhilaration she'd felt when she first learned her ancestor's story. "I know Selene loved Leander. I know they had to flee Atlantis to be together. I know they boarded a ship the night before Selene was supposed to marry Atlas. I know Delphine was scorned when Leander chose Selene." She paused to survey the gossip-witches, who had never seemed so serious, so still. They were hanging on her words the way Eureka had hung on Madame Blavatsky's, as if she were telling the old tale for the first time. "And I know the last thing Selene saw when she sailed away were gossipwitches, who spoke the curse of her Tearline."

"*Her* Tearline?" Esme repeated with a strange lilt.

"Yes, they prophesied that someday, one of Selene's descendants would cause the rise of Atlantis. It would be a girl born on a day that doesn't exist, a motherless child and childless mother whose emotions brew like a storm her whole life until she couldn't withstand them anymore. And she wept." Eureka swallowed. "And flooded the world with her tears. That's me. I'm her."

"So you don't know the most important part." With great

care Esme smoothed the missing pages, held them up to the amethyst light. "Do you remember where you left off with your imposter translator?"

"I remember." Eureka unzipped her bag and pulled out the plastic-sheathed book. She turned to a wrinkled page flagged with a green Abyssinian lovebird feather. She pointed at the bottom corner, where the text tapered off. "Selene and Leander were separated in a shipwreck. They never saw each other again, but Selene said"—Eureka paused to remember her exact words—" 'The witches' prophecy is the only lasting remnant of our love.' "

"Your translator guessed correctly. We witches clearly are the stars of this story, but there is one other . . . lasting remnant about which you should know." Esme held the parchment up to the light again, closed her eyes, and uttered Selene's missing words:

"For many restless years I have kept the final chapter of my story locked inside my heart. I painted a romance using only bright colors. I sought to leave out the darkness, but as the colors of my life begin to fade, I must allow the narratory darkness in.

"I must face what happened with the child . . .

"The last time I kissed Leander, we were sailing from the only home we'd ever known. The ghost robot Ovid steered our ship. We had stolen it to help us. It was still empty, devoid of souls. We hoped Ovid's absence might slow the Filling, that once we reached our destination, it might reveal how to defeat Atlas.

"Leander's caress soothed me when skies darkened; his embrace reassured me when they wept a chilling rain. He kissed me nine times, and with each tender touch of his lips, my lover changed:

"First came the lines around his smile.
Then his blond hair grew white.
His skin became papery, loose.
His embrace slackened weakly around my body.
His whisper became hoarse.
The need in his eyes dimmed.
His kiss lost its urgent lust.
His frame stooped in my arms.

"After his last, weary kiss, he pointed to the woven basket he had carried onboard. I assumed it contained a nuptial cake, perhaps some ambrosial wine to toast our love.

" 'What's mine is yours,' he said.

"I lifted the basket's lid and heard the babe's first cry.

" 'This is my daughter,' he said. 'She does not have a name.'

"When he had bid Delphine farewell, she presented the child—the child they shared. Leander could not bear to leave the infant with an evil mother, so he grabbed her and he ran. As he did so, Delphine cursed him:

"He would age rapidly if he loved anyone but her.

"I asked him jealous questions about the baby, about his love *for Delphine, but he struggled to remember. His mind had become as feeble as his body.*

"The child cooed in her bassinet. I feared her. What would she do, when she was older and felt betrayed? I looked at the sea and knew she would do worse things than her mother.

"I lost my love in that storm—Leander was so decrepit by the time a thick bolt of lightning split our ship, I knew he must have perished in the wreck that followed.

"But his daughter survived.

"When I awoke on a windswept abandoned shore, I found Ovid submerged in wet sand—and the baby in her bassinet, at the edge of soft ocean waves. I thought of killing her, leaving her to die—but she had his eyes. She was all I had left of my love.

"In the early years the robot, the girl, and I spent together, I almost forgot who her real mother was. She was my treasure, my life.

"Over time, the girl grew to be like her mother.

"For seventeen years I kept her hidden, until one day I returned from bathing to find her disappeared. Ovid knew which path she'd taken, but something told me not to follow. Like a flame suddenly extinguished, she was gone, and I was cold and alone.

"I never saw her again. I had never given her a name."

Esme put the parchment on her lap. She opened her eyes.

"I don't understand," Eureka said.

"I shall put it plainly for you: the years have forged a

false history of your lineage. Selene was a pretty girl and a decent horticulturist, but she was not your matriarch. You are descended from the grandmother of all dark sorcery. The Tearline springs from Delphine."

Eureka opened her mouth to speak but found no words.

"Her tears of scorn and heartbreak sank Atlantis," Esme said. "Yours will raise it."

"No, that's not what happened."

"Because you don't want it to be what happened?" Esme asked. "If the hero does not match the story, it is the hero, not the story, who must be rewritten."

Eureka's temples throbbed. "But I didn't cry from scorn and—"

"Heartbreak?" Esme asked. "Are you certain?"

"You're lying," Eureka said.

"I lie as frequently and as convincingly as I can. But then there is the matter of the Glimmering, which reveals only that which is truer than the truth. Do you happen to recall your reflection?"

The memory of that cold, cruel face flashed before Eureka's eyes and she knew that the girl in the reflection wasn't Maya Cayce. Her gaze had been wiser, darker, deeper. Her smile icier than that of even the most frigid high school queen. Eureka had been looking at Delphine. Her body tensed. She imagined squeezing Esme's cheeks until no laughter could escape her pretty, painted mouth.

She blinked, surprised by the violence of her fantasy.

Esme smiled. "Delphine is who you come from, why you are the way you are. Dark-hearted. Mind as deadly as a nest of vipers. You are capable of great and terrible things, but you must free yourself of the bonds of love and kindness holding you back. Come with us. We will show you the way to the Marais. Then you will show us the way to Atlantis—"

"No." Eureka rose and stepped backward.

"You'll change your mind." Esme followed Eureka to the doorway. She stroked the twisted end of her pipe. "Funny, isn't it? Everyone thinks the bad guy is Atlas. . . ."

"Even Atlas thinks the bad guy is Atlas!" a witch in the background howled.

"When, actually"—Esme leaned forward to whisper in Eureka's bad ear—"it's you."

23

OVID'S METAMORPHOSES

Eureka could barely see Ander through the rain as he ran from the entrance to the Bitter Cloud and caught her in his arms.

"Where have you been?"

Everything was different about him. His hair was wet, his clothes soaked and stuck to his skin. His eyes were a pure, crystal-clear blue, where they used to be clouded by a lovely melancholy.

Was this how Ander wore joy? He looked fantastic, but far removed from the brooding, unreachable boy she'd fallen for back home.

That boy would have hated that she'd run off to an artemisia-drenched witches' lair. This boy's embrace said: *All that matters is you're here.*

The truth had done this to Ander. He knew who he was—or who he wasn't—and it looked good on him.

"I have something for you," Ander said.

"Ander, wait"—any word not confessing her secret was a lie—"before you—"

He shook his head. "This can't wait."

His arms curved around her back and pulled her body against his. He tipped her backward and pressed his lips to hers. The salty rain flooded between their lips. This was what heartbreak tasted like.

Eureka felt like an imposter. She couldn't breathe and she didn't want to. What if she could die while kissing him, allow his love to suffocate her? Then he'd never know who she really was, she would never have to face the grand lie she had become, and the rest of the half-drowned world could go on paying for her pride.

She touched the corners of his eyes where she'd found wrinkles days ago. "Your face."

"Do I look different?" Ander asked.

His eyes creased when he smiled. His hair was a thousand shades of flaxen gold. But Ander wasn't an old man any more than Eureka was an old lady. They were teenagers. They were growing up and changing all the time and it couldn't be stopped or slowed.

"You look like you," she said.

He smiled. "You look like you, too."

What did he see when he looked at her? Was her darkness swelling as visible as the shadows lifting from him?

He reached for the teardrop crystal that had absorbed her other pendants. He gasped and quickly drew his hand away, as if he'd touched a flame.

"From the gossipwitches?"

She nodded. "The locket, the thunderstone, and the ribbon are inside."

"I can't tell you how free I feel," Ander whispered. "There's no more risk in caring for each other. We can be together. We can go to the Marais. You can defeat Atlas. I can be with you the whole time. We can do this, together." He touched her lips. His eyes swam over her face. "I love you, Eureka."

Eureka closed her eyes. Ander loved a girl he thought he knew. He loved that girl very much. He had said it was the only thing he was sure of. But he could never love the person she truly was, a descendant of darkness, more evil than the most evil force Ander could imagine.

"That's great," she said.

"I have to kiss you again." He drew her close, but her heart wasn't in it. Her heart could never be in something so right, so good.

A violent rapping interrupted their kiss. Eureka jumped away from Ander and spun around. A shadowy figure leaned against the entrance to the Bitter Cloud holding an umbrella over its head.

Her heart quickened. Was it Brooks? She yearned to see him again—even though she knew he was bound to evil. Or maybe she yearned to see him *because* he was bound to evil.

"Who's there?" Ander put his body between Eureka and the figure.

"Only me."

"Solon?" Eureka wiped rain from her eyes and discerned Ovid's lithe frame. The robot's left hand had sprouted an orichalcum umbrella. Its face bore the loving, aged features that the lost Seedbearer had worn at his death.

" 'O a kiss, long as my exile, sweet as my revenge,' " the robot said in Solon's voice. "That's Coriolanus. Shakespeare already knew what you are learning, Eureka: the soldier can return from war but he can never go home." The robot tipped its umbrella toward the Bitter Cloud. "Let's talk inside. I'm waterproof, so rain makes me lonely."

Ovid collapsed the umbrella as they entered the cave through the hall of skulls. Water streamed past their feet, the flood flowing toward the salon. The Bitter Cloud was desolate now and filling with salt water, nothing like the fascinating chamber of curiosities it had been when they arrived. The air was cold and dank.

Claire was throwing fistfuls of colored mosaic tiles in the air. William used his quirk to retrieve them before they hit the rising water.

"Eureka's back!"

The twins splashed through deep puddles as they ran to her. William made it into her arms, but Claire stopped short of the robot and looked at it distrustfully.

She hunched her shoulders. "Why does Ovid look weird?"

"It looks like Solon," William said into Eureka's shoulder. "It's scary."

Cat sat in Solon's cockfighting chair with her eyes closed. Eureka poured some of the witches' salve into her hands and massaged it over the bees, which now crawled all over her friend's scalp. Cat flinched at first, then gazed up at Eureka. Tears dotted her eyes.

"Are they gone?" she asked, patting her hair.

"No."

"It doesn't hurt anymore."

"Good."

Eureka helped Cat to her feet. Cat's heels sank into a puddle—then both of her feet lifted off the floor. It lasted just a second. Cat looked down at her feet, then at Eureka, then down again. She held out her arms and furrowed her brow and made herself levitate, this time for longer, a full foot off the floor.

She touched her bee braids and giggled a laugh that didn't sound like Cat. "That bitch turned me into a witch." She gazed at Eureka with wide eyes. "You know, this is the first thing in a long time that actually feels *right*?"

"Sit down." Solon's voice spoke through the robot. "Watch closely. Prepare to have your minds blown."

They gathered around the fire pit with the waterfall tumbling and the skulls eavesdropping, just as they had when Solon welcomed them to the Bitter Cloud. Ovid presided in Solon's place, holding his old, empty broken glass.

Solon's features wavered, then twisted gruesomely, like the robot's face was made of clay. William whimpered in Eureka's lap. Then Ovid's nose tapered. Its lips swelled. Its cheeks grew longer.

"Poet?" Cat leaned forward shakily.

The Poet within the robot seemed to size up Cat's new do approvingly, then he twisted out of recognition as another face filled the orichalcum void.

Seyma's features sharpened and squashed as if someone had pressed her face against a sheet of glass. She grimaced and was pulled away, replaced by the thin, old lips of Starling, then, more rapidly, by the dark grimace of Critias, the wizened ruthlessness of Chora, and, finally, by the cold hatred in Albion's eyes. He struggled to speak through the robot, but couldn't. Eureka got the gist of what he wanted to say.

At last, their father surfaced.

"Daddy—" Claire cried in the voice she used when she was having a nightmare.

Dad was gone, replaced by Solon.

"You will encounter all of them eventually," Solon's voice said. "For now, while they are learning to be ghosts, I control a great percentage of the robot's drive. I will sow seeds of resistance from inside, but as the others mature they will have their own agenda. We must make our move soon, while I can still be your primary guide."

Eureka rose. "Let's go."

"Sit," he said. "First I must show you the way." Again Ovid's features softened. This time, they became a screen on which a waterfall appeared. A projection of white water streamed down the robot's forehead. In the center of its face a strange bubble vibrated. It took Eureka a moment to recognize it was her thunderstone shield. A small version of Ovid appeared beneath the shield, its body arced in a gorgeous dive as it balanced the shield on its shoulders.

At the end of the waterfall, Ovid's screenlike face became bright white and bubbly. Soon, the bubbles cleared and the water turned a deep turquoise. Then Ovid was swimming, a strong and rapid breaststroke, the shield strapped to its back with an orichalcum band.

A version of Eureka was inside the version of the shield. It was like watching a movie of herself in a dream. Someone sat beside her, but the image was too small to see who it was.

The vision faded from Ovid's blank face. Solon's sculpted features returned.

So the waterfall was how Eureka would get to the Marais. She looked down at her crystal teardrop and prayed her thunderstone still worked.

"Ovid is adept at open-sea swimming," Solon's voice said,

"but within these caves the currents are capricious. The angles of the tunnel-like flumes that lead to the outside world are deadly sharp. Your journey will be smoother once you clear them."

"How do I do that?" Eureka asked.

"How do *we* do that," Ander corrected her. "You must time your departure between three and four in the morning, when the moon draws the tides high, and the flumes' currents flow toward the egress of the caves. You already practiced how to enter the waterfall when you fetched the orchid. Do it again. Filiz will join you; I always promised I would take her with me. All others who wish to accompany you must run with you into the fall. And then, like love itself, Ovid will lead you where you need to go."

Again the robot's features shifted into their bland, attractive, neutral state. It closed its eyes. It whispered: "Rest."

During the long electric moment that followed Eureka became sure of three things:

She could not take her loved ones with her. They would not let her go alone. She was going to have to ditch them.

24

FLIGHT

Wind spun Eureka's hair as she staggered to the edge of the veranda. She tried to find Diana's star, but there was no sign of a universe beyond the rain.

Since Diana had died, it was like an organ had been removed; Eureka's body didn't work the way it had before. How could Diana, the sparkling woman Eureka had treasured, have descended from darkness?

And yet Diana *had* abandoned her family. She'd slapped her daughter so roughly it turned Eureka's emotions inward for a decade, until they nearly killed her. Diana held deadly secrets behind her brilliant smile.

Selfish. Heartless. Narcissistic. When her parents divorced, Eureka heard people in New Iberia call Diana these things.

Eureka had dismissed it as bayou gossip. She'd convinced herself these attributes belonged to the accusers, that they projected their failings onto Diana's absence.

Eureka considered that the woman she aspired to be was also the woman who manipulated, lied, then disappeared. Diana had been a ghost in Eureka's life, filling her with feelings while telling her not to feel. She had raised a daughter who ran cross-country, treasured the twins, fell in love too easily—and was a murderer. Once you put murder on your résumé, no one saw anything else. Eureka was as full of dark contradictions as Diana. She was moments away from abandoning everyone she loved, leaving them to unknown, watery fates.

Ander and the others had been sleeping when she left. She'd never seen him so peaceful. She'd pressed her lips to his for just an instant before she'd gone.

The Tearline pond was rising. She could reach over the ledge and touch it. Soon she would be in the Marais. She would have to face Atlas, stop the Filling, and rescue Brooks at the same time. Solon said she would know what to do when she got there, but Eureka couldn't fathom it yet.

Her fingers danced along the water's surface. After Diana died and Eureka swallowed those pills, when all that was left was a panicked, catatonic void, Brooks was the only person she could be near. He hadn't wanted her to snap out of anything. He'd loved her as she was.

But even Brooks must have a limit. Even if she saved him, even if she brought him back, could he love this darkest side of her?

Lightning flashed. It would keep raining. The water would keep rising. Soon her tears would swallow the Bitter Cloud.

Eureka had to move. She couldn't wait for the tides to be right. She had to get to Ovid, to disappear before the others woke.

Hands on her shoulders made Eureka jump.

"Go back inside, Ander."

"If I see him, I'll be sure to tell him that." Warm breath tickled Eureka's neck. She turned and gazed into eyes brown and bottomless.

Brooks.

Atlas.

His touch was familiar, yet somehow older than their bodies. His eyes flashed with something bright and mesmerizing she'd never seen before. It pulled her closer.

How could a monster's arms feel so good? Why did the thrill of his chest against hers make her pulse with excitement? She should pull away. She should run.

He lowered his head and kissed her. Shock immobilized her as his lips parted hers. His hands rolled through the waves of her hair, then over the waves of her hips. Their lips locked again and again. It wasn't like any kiss she'd ever had before. Her body throbbed. She felt like she'd been drugged.

"We can't—"

"Don't be afraid," Brooks said. Atlas said. "It's only me now."

"What do you mean?"

"I got rid of him. It's over." His eyes shone like they had when Brooks visited her in the psych ward after she'd swallowed those pills, when he'd brought her pecan pralines and she'd told him, melodramatically, that it was the end of the world. She'd never forget his response: no big deal, he'd promised; after the end of the world, Brooks would be there to give her a ride home.

"How did you do it?" Eureka masked the suspicion in her voice.

A raindrop glittered on his eyelashes. She brushed it away instinctively.

"You don't have to worry about that anymore. You don't have to worry about anything. I know what he wants. I know his weakness." He caressed the back of her head. "I can help you beat him, Eureka, as soon as we get to the Marais."

The water on the veranda was up to their ankles. She lifted his T-shirt to examine his back. The dual set of deep red slashes had faded to pale scars. Did that mean Atlas was gone? She turned him around and brushed the hair from his forehead. The ring-shaped wound was less glaring, but it was there.

A smart girl would assume Brooks was lying. . . .

A smarter girl would keep that assumption to herself.

Even Atlas thought he was the bad guy, the gossipwitches had said. That meant Atlas didn't know Eureka's true lineage. He didn't appreciate her darkness.

"Someday I'll tell you the story of how we met and how we parted." He turned away and the wound on his forehead glowed. "I will never forgive myself for the things he made me do. What happened with the twins—I can't—"

"Let's not talk about it." Eureka wasn't so heartless that she could think of William and Claire, whom she would soon abandon.

When he faced her, she felt how much she had missed Brooks like a punch in the stomach. Then she saw something behind his eyes—a ragged, foreign mania—and she was certain the boy before her was lying.

"You believe me, don't you?"

"Yes," she whispered. She would make him believe she did. She would get close enough to Atlas to learn how to win. She would stop the flood. She would save Brooks. She flung her arms around him. "Don't ever go away again."

She felt him stiffen in her embrace. When she pulled away, he was beaming.

"I'm going with you to the Marais." He eyed the crystal teardrop dangling from the orichalcum chain. "We don't have a lot of time." His fingers reached for the pendant.

Eureka leaned away from him. Her facade and Brooks's

facade could bump up against each other's—hands and eyes and lips and lies—but the necklace was hers.

"This trip must be only you and me," he said. "It's not safe for the twins or Cat or—"

"You and me. That's how I want it."

Brooks's eyes lit up like they did when he saw her round a corner at Evangeline, or when she got dressed up for the honors dinner and broke a high heel stepping from the car.

A giggle filled the air, curved the rain. Eureka looked up, expecting to see gossipwitches gliding toward her through the clouds. Instead, one vast pair of wings, aglow in soft amethyst, beat gently overhead.

The wings were shaped like a butterfly's. They beat with graceful strength and lowered in the sky until they were thirty feet above Eureka's head. Then she saw a creature's graceful silver body between the huge wings. It had a long neck, four hooves, a thrashing white tail.

The horse was stunning. It had stockings of white on its front legs and a white star between its eyes. It neighed, raised its neck, and extended its shimmering M-shaped wings. They spanned a hundred feet on either side and were composed of a multitude of tiny flying things—bees, moths, fireflies, and black-and-white-striped baby hoopoe birds—beating their own wings in unison. Iridescent violet seams near the horse's shoulders bound the wings—cruelly, beautifully—to its body.

A rustling came from the center of the horse's left wing.

Slender fingers wriggled through the layers of wings, followed by a palm, which glided forward as if parting a curtain. Esme's face filled the gap.

"What do you think of our Pegasus?"

"Pegasus Two!" an unseen witch shouted from the top side of the wing.

"Yes, yes, we created one before. He was sacrificed to progress, like Icarus, or Atari," Esme said. "We will call this one Peggy to distinguish." She reached into a silver satchel strapped to the base of the horse's neck and tossed down a ladder made of moths. "A stolen horse is not our preferred way to travel, but when Solon ran out of wings . . . No matter. We will be home soon and everything will be as it should long have been."

Brooks reached for the ladder. The moths reorganized, drawing together, then tapering to stretch a little lower. He stepped onto the lowest rung, turned, and extended a hand to Eureka.

"You always said you wanted to fly away. Here's your hallelujah by and by."

The words were from her favorite hymn. She'd sung it with Brooks in oak boughs when they were kids, the bayou below snaking into the distance until it disappeared. "I'll Fly Away" gave Eureka hope. Atlas wouldn't have known about it. He was using Brooks's memories to bait her, as Solon said he would. If there were memories to steal, there was still a Brooks inside, somewhere, to save.

"I don't know—"

Could she fly away from the twins, Cat, and Ander? Would they drown if Eureka left with Brooks?

Brooks smiled. "You know."

She didn't have Ovid, and she couldn't go back for it now. Could she trust that the gossipwitches wanted to get home badly enough to take her to the Marais? Was this voyage what Esme had said she owed them?

Thunder cracked overhead. Eureka ducked. Brooks was still holding out his hand.

"Come on," he urged.

Maybe he was lying about everything else, but he was right about Eureka. She knew she had to go. She knew her loved ones couldn't come with her. She knew there wasn't any time. She knew she had to save the world. And she knew that the only way to get there was with the one she had to destroy. She took his hand.

"Eureka!"

Ander sloshed across the flooded veranda as her feet lifted from the stone.

Water streamed from her running shoes. She dangled a few feet in the air. The hurt in Ander's eyes pierced her.

Rain soaked his shirt, flattened his blond hair across his forehead. He looked so ordinary and beautiful that Eureka thought if things were different, if every single thing were different, she could fall in love with him from scratch.

"Wait!" she shouted up at the gossipwitches.

Eureka heard what sounded like a whip. The ladder bounced as Peggy's wings flattened overhead. The silver horse neighed in protest.

"There's no time for this!" Brooks shouted at Esme.

"There is time for a single goodbye," Esme said from the gap in Peggy's wing. "We will wait."

"What are you doing?" Ander shouted.

"I'm sorry!" Eureka called over the drone of a million wings. Her heart raced wildly. She imagined it bursting from her chest, sending fragments of chaotic love onto the two boys she was caught between. "I have to go."

"We were going to go together," Ander said.

"If you knew the things I know, you wouldn't want to go with me. You'd be glad I was leaving. So be glad."

"I love you. Nothing else matters." Ander blinked. "Don't go with him, Eureka. He's *not* Brooks."

Brooks laughed. "She's already chosen. Try to be a man about it."

"Eureka!" Ander didn't look at Brooks. His turquoise eyes were trained on her for the last time.

"Eureka," Brooks whispered in her good ear.

"Eureka!" the middle gossipwitch shouted from above. "It's time to make a choice. Close your eyes and say goodbye to someone. Do not burden our beast of burden with the burden of your beastly heart."

Eureka met Esme's eyes and nodded. "Let's go."

A million pairs of wings beat in unison. Peggy climbed in the sky.

"Ander!" she shouted.

He stared up at her, hope in his eyes.

"Take care of the twins," she said. "And Cat. Tell them . . . tell them all I love them."

He shook his head. "Don't do this."

I love you, too. She couldn't bring herself to say it. Instead, she would take it with her, packed inside her heart. She would take all of them with her in her heart. She didn't deserve them, but she would take them. Cat's life-affirming humor. Claire's strength. William's tenderness. Dad's devotion. Rhoda's stubbornness. Madame Blavatsky's intuition. Diana's passion. Ander's love. They had given Eureka their gifts and she would take them with her wherever she went.

"Goodbye," she called through the rain as she flew away.

25

THE MARAIS

Eureka watched the world shrink beneath her. Peggy climbed a thousand feet and leveled off below wispy dregs of clouds. Eureka and Brooks rode her bareback, gripping her glossy silver mane. Two dozen gossipwitches rode atop the horse's wings. They held the beating fabric like children on a sled.

Below, rivers burst from their banks. Red mud spurted across the land like blood from a wound. Where towns had stood a week ago, buildings sagged and highways buckled, sideswiped by water. Flash lakes drowned former valleys. Forests rotted black. As they flew south, great white waves tumbled into altered shoreline, leaving miles of mud in wakes that once were neighborhoods. Houses floated down streets, searching for their owners.

Eureka vomited over the side of the horse and watched it arc toward the ravaged earth. There had been nothing in her stomach but acid. Now there was even less.

"Are you okay?" Brooks asked. Atlas asked.

She rested her cheek on Peggy's velvety neck. She stared ahead until her eyes found the horizon. She imagined every devastated thing below sliding over that horizon like a waterfall. She imagined the entire broken world flowing into fire at the end of everything.

Brooks leaned in to her good ear. "Say something."

"I didn't think it could be worse than my imagination."

"You'll fix it."

"The world is dead. I killed it."

"Bring it back." He sounded like the old Brooks, like someone who believed Eureka could do anything, especially the impossible. She was angry with herself for letting down her guard. She wouldn't do it again. She had to be careful, confiding in the enemy.

"How did you find them?" Eureka nodded in the witches' direction.

"I didn't," Brooks said. "They found me. When I freed myself, it was like I was waking from a coma. She"—he nodded at Esme, who lay like a sunbather on Peggy's wings—"was standing over me when I opened my eyes. She offered me a ride. I said I had to find you first. She laughed and said, 'Mount the mare, stud.' Then they brought me to you." He looked around. "I never thought we'd top the time we hitched to Bonnaroo in that convertible van. But we've topped it."

That trip was one of Eureka's fondest memories. The driver had started in L.A., in one of those homes-of-the-stars tour buses. There were brochures in the seat pockets with maps of the Hollywood Hills. He picked up hitchers across the country, until all the seats were filled. They spent the trip squinting into the rolling hills of Tennessee, pretending to see movie stars hiding behind poplar trees. It was another thing Atlas couldn't have known without Brooks.

Esme flicked an amethyst whip against Peggy's wing. The beast banked west. They were flying over water now. All land had disappeared.

"You don't want to hear this," Brooks said, "but I learned things from Atlas."

"Like what?"

"The story of Atlantis is the longest cliff-hanger in history, but someone will finish it. . . ." As his voice trailed off in the rain, Eureka thought of Selene's words in *The Book of Love*:

Where we'll end . . . well, who can know the ending until they have written the last word? Everything might change in the last word.

It was Selene's life story, but everyone talked about their life as if it were a story: leaving out the boring parts, exaggerating the interesting sections, crafting a tale as if everything had inevitably led to this very moment on this very day, saying these very words.

Somehow, Eureka would finish this story. Future tellers of the tale could embellish what they wanted, but no Tearline girl would enter the scene after she exited. Delphine was alpha; Eureka was omega.

It was nearly dawn, the end of another sleepless night, five days until the full moon. Thunder cracked. Peggy raised her wings. Eureka couldn't see the gossipwitches' faces, but she could hear their jubilation and see where their leaping feet touched down on the wings.

"We're getting close." Brooks leaned over Peggy and gazed at the surging ocean waves.

Eureka didn't recognize the white-tipped water; it looked nothing like the oceans she'd sailed, swum, flown over in planes, or navigated from within her thunderstone.

In the distance, waves thrashed the shores of a desolate strip of marshland coated in an undulating black sheet. Peggy neighed and dipped her head. She began her descent.

As they drew closer, Eureka saw that the black sheet was made of billions of brine flies that had claimed the marsh as their home.

Eureka touched her pendant. Its warmth was welcome now in the chilling rain. She imagined that Diana's scrawled *Marais* had become a cursive sparkle in the diamond. Could Atlantis lie beneath this undistinguished streak of mud?

"We're nearly there," Brooks said. Atlas said. He turned his lips against her neck and whispered: "Cry for me."

"What?"

"It's the only way inside."

"No—"

"Still holding on to Mom's advice?" he asked, darkening as he spoke. "Wouldn't you say that ship has sailed? How does it feel to fail your dead mother's one request? How does it feel to fail the person who sacrificed her life in a war the world is really waging against you?"

She couldn't let Atlas trick her. She had to trick him. But the third tear still had to fall. That was why she'd come to the Marais. Atlantis had to rise so those she'd killed would not be wasted dead. Their souls had to go into the Filling. After that, Eureka's and Atlas's plans diverged. He thought the souls of her world would do his work, but she would find a way to set them free.

She felt for the pocket of her jeans. Her fingers traced the outline of the silver lachrymatory through the fabric. Solon had left it to her when he died. He'd known what she had to do. Eureka called on the bright strength of the ones she'd left behind. She called on the darkness within her.

"You're a pretty good villain, Atlas."

He raised an eyebrow at the sound of his name, but he did not deny it. The game was over. "Pretty good?"

"Everybody has a weakness."

"And what is mine?"

"Naïveté," Eureka said. "You don't know what every girl knows, from New Iberia to Vladivostok: *we* make the best bad guys. Guys never stand a chance."

Eureka unscrewed the lachrymatory and pitched it over Peggy's wings. The orichalcum vial tumbled through a sea of clouds. Her tears poured out, glittering like diamonds. A swell of heat against her chest startled her. Her hand flew to the crystal teardrop and was burned.

Her throat tightened. Her chest heaved. She wasn't going to cry—but she felt the way she had when she shed the tears the lachrymatory contained. She felt those same tears form again, as if every tear had a ghost that could return.

The ground shuddered so hard it made the air above it shudder, too. Peggy bucked and whinnied. And then:

The rain stopped.

Clouds stretched apart like cotton. Round rays of sun shone through. Eureka let them punch her shoulders, her lungs, and her heart, telling her brain to get happy.

"We are home!" the witches shrieked. "Look!"

The sun lit a long crack in the marsh below. The crack widened into a gorge and then, at its center, a small green dot appeared—

And began to grow.

The tree stretched skyward first. Its trunk shot up like it had been launched from the core of the earth. Eureka heard its creaking groan, and more . . . in *both* her ears. Birds singing, wind rustling, waves tumbling ashore—a wall of rich, reverberating stereo.

"I can hear again."

"Of course," Atlas said. "A wave of Atlantean origins took

your hearing, now my kingdom restores it. There is yet more restoration in store."

"That wave took my mother, too."

"Indeed," Atlas said cryptically.

By then the tree was a hundred feet tall and as thick as the ancient redwoods in the California town where Eureka had been born. The tree branched out. Sinewy limbs spun from its trunk, twisting wildly until its boughs overlapped in long and tangled fingers. Leaves sprang, wide and thick and glossy green. Jonquil-like white flowers exploded from their buds. *Narcissus,* Ander would say. Eureka's ears heard each moment of this wild growth, as if eavesdropping on a sparkling conversation.

New trees sprang up around the first. Then a silver road encircled the sudden forest, which wasn't a forest, but a magnificent urban park in the center of a rising city. Blindingly pristine gold- and silver-roofed buildings ascended from the marsh, stretching in all directions to form a perfectly circular capital. A ring-shaped river bordered the city; its swift current moved counterclockwise. On the far bank of the river was another mile-wide ring of land, this one verdant green and blooming with fruit trees and terraced grapevines. The agricultural band was encircled by another, clockwise-current river. At its edges, a final ring of land rose into towering purple bluffs. Beyond the mountains, the ocean lapping its rocks stretched into a blurry blue horizon.

Atlantis, the Sleeping World, had awoken.

"What now, bad girl?" Atlas asked.

"Get off! Get off!" the witches shouted. "We are going home to our mountain!"

Esme snapped her whip at Peggy, who reared in the sky. Eureka slipped backward. Her hands grabbed at Peggy's mane, but not quickly enough. The horse threw Atlas and Eureka from her back.

They fell toward Atlantis. Eureka saw Atlas's panic flash in Brooks's eyes and it reminded her of something . . . but she fell so fast, she soon lost the boy and the body and the enemy and the memory.

She fell and fell, as she'd fallen through the waterfall in the Bitter Cloud. Back then she had landed in water and her thunderstone had shielded her. Ander had been swimming toward her. No one would save her now.

She landed on a green leaf the size of a mattress. She wasn't dead yet. She let out an amazed laugh; then she slid off the leaf and was falling again.

Branches battered her limbs. She grabbed at a thick one. Her arms wrapped around it, as, incredibly, the branch wrapped around her. Its embrace held her still. Its bark was the texture of a tortoise's shell.

Eureka shook bark and leaves from her wet hair. She wiped blood from a scratch on her forehead. She felt for her necklace. Still hot, still there. The lachrymatory was gone.

Atlas was also gone.

All around Eureka, lush trees continued to grow from the marsh, until they matched the height of the first tree. She was in the center of a canopy of trees in the center of a park in the center of a city in the center of what might be the only land left on earth.

Strange birds sang strange songs that Eureka heard in both ears. Vines snaked up the tree trunk so quickly, she jerked her arms away, lest they become portions of the forest. The trees smelled like eucalyptus and pecans and fresh-cut grass, but in every other way they were unrecognizable. They were broader and taller and more brilliantly green than any tree she'd ever seen. She climbed across another bough. It swayed under her weight, but the wood felt steady, strong.

"You're losing, Cuttlefish." Atlas jumped from a branch above her to one below. He climbed downward, and when he reached the tree's lowest bough he turned slowly, winked at Eureka, and jumped.

He landed face-first in the thick-sprouting grass. After that he didn't move.

Another trick. She was meant to follow him, to fear for Brooks's well-being—and be trapped.

But she was already trapped. She was in Atlantis with her enemy. She was supposed to be here. This was a step along the path to redeeming herself. She couldn't stay in this tree forever. She was going to have to go down and face him.

She descended the branches. The longer she looked at Brooks's back, the more fearful she became. The body on the ground was the porch that led to the cathedral of her best friend's soul.

Her feet touched Atlantean earth. She grabbed Brooks's shoulders, rolled him over. She laid her head against his chest and waited for it to rise.

26

DISPOSSESSED

It wasn't the first time Brooks had fallen.

A wave of déjà vu swept through Eureka as she laid her head against his chest:

They were nine years old. It was the summer before Eureka's parents divorced, so she'd still had a whole and buoyant heart, a matching smile. She didn't know that loss was alive in the world, a thief always about to slam you and steal everything you had.

That summer, Eureka and Brooks had spent sunsets high in the grand pecan tree in Sugar's backyard, past the city limits of New Iberia. Brooks had a bowl cut and light-up Power Rangers sneakers. Eureka had skinned knees and a gap between her front teeth. She'd been shredding her way through the endless smocked dresses Diana kept pulling from the attic.

It happened on a Sunday afternoon. Maybe it explained why Sundays always made Eureka lonely. Brooks had been playing with the lyrics of her favorite Tom T. Hall song, "That's How I Got to Memphis." Eureka had been trying to harmonize with him. She'd grown annoyed with his improvisations and shoved him. He'd lost his balance, tumbled backward. One minute he was singing with her, and the next—

She'd tried to catch him. He fell for an eternity, his brown eyes locked on hers. His face grew smaller; his limbs stilled. He landed on his back, roughly, his left leg twisted beneath him.

Eureka still heard her scream in her mind. She'd leapt from the branch to the ground. She'd knelt beside him on skinned knees. First, she'd tried to pry his eyelids open, because Brooks's smile was mostly in his eyes and she needed to see it. She'd said his name.

When he didn't stir or answer, she prayed.

Hail Mary, full of grace . . .

She said it over and over, till the words were tangled and held no meaning. Then she remembered something she'd seen on TV. She pressed her mouth against his. . . .

Brooks's arms encircled her and he kissed her, long and deep. His gleeful eyes popped open. "Gotcha."

She slapped him.

"Why did you do that?" She wiped her lips on the back of her hand, studied the shine their kiss made below her knuckles.

Brooks rubbed his cheek. "So you'd know I wasn't mad at you."

"Maybe now I'm mad at you."

"Maybe you're not." He grinned.

In those days, it was impossible to stay mad at Brooks. He'd limped back to the tree, and as he'd ascended its branches, he'd sung new, worse lyrics to the song:

> *If you shove somebody enough, you'll tumble*
> *wherever they go—*
> *That's how I got to Memphis, that's how I got to*
> *Memphis.*

They never talked about the kiss again.

※

Now, on the foreign forest floor, Eureka buried her face in his chest. His body seemed at peace. She wondered whether Atlas had finally gone away and left behind the body of her best friend.

She raised her head and studied the galaxy of freckles on Brooks's cheeks. She brushed hair from his eyes. She felt the scar of his wound. His skin was warm. Were his lips?

She kissed him lightly, hoping like a little girl to revive him, hoping like a little girl to pretend.

She might keep her lips against his forever, penance for

having been stupid enough to leave with Atlas, stupid enough to drag Brooks's body here, stupid enough to abandon everyone else she loved.

He stirred.

"Brooks?" She gulped and said, "Atlas?"

His eyes were closed. He didn't seem to be conscious—but she had felt something shift. She studied him. His chest was still, his eyelids motionless.

There it was again.

Eureka's fingers vibrated where they touched his shoulders. A gale swept over Brooks. A warm, buzzy feeling spread to her arms, the back of her neck. She pulled her hands from Brooks's shoulders as an incandescence rose from his chest and hovered above his body.

Whose essence was this—Brooks's or Atlas's? Both of them had shared the body, like the ghost sharing Ovid. Eureka couldn't see the essence so much as she could sense it. She passed a trembling hand through it.

Cold.

Footsteps sounded on dewy grass. A boy about her age stood over her. She'd never seen him before, yet he was familiar.

Of course—she had seen him depicted in the illustrations of *The Book of Love.*

Atlas wasn't handsome, but there was something alluring about him. His smile was assured. He wore brilliant, finely tailored clothing in shapes and pieces Eureka didn't have words to describe. They glittered gold and red, as if made of rubies. His reddish-brown hair was curly and wild. His fair skin was lightly freckled, and his eyes were soft copper—but haunted, vacant. They looked past her, into a distance only they could see.

She stood up and matched his height. He'd been with her for so long, but this was the first moment they'd met.

"Atlas."

He didn't even look at her.

The incandescence above Brooks's body swirled toward the boy, and she knew it had not been her best friend's soul. It was Atlas, discarding Brooks's body in order to reclaim his own. But where was Brooks's soul? Atlas closed his eyes and absorbed the incandescence into his chest.

After a moment, when he opened his eyes, they had changed into a deep, penetrating brown, like the center of a redwood tree—far different from the irises he'd had before. Eureka knew she was standing before the most powerful person she had ever met.

She knelt beside Brooks again. His chest was no longer warm. What would happen if she wept now? Could her tears reflood Atlantis and send all of them back underwater? What would happen to the wasted dead?

Atlas tilted his head. "Save your tears."

His voice was rich and deep and strangely accented. Eureka understood him—and she understood he wasn't speaking English. He knelt over Brooks, too.

"I didn't know he was handsome. I can never tell if the inside matches the outside. You know what I mean."

"Don't talk about Brooks," she said. She wasn't speaking English, either. Intuition for the distant language must flow through her Tearline. The Atlantean tongue rolled fluidly from her, with the tiniest breath of translation in her mind.

"I don't believe we've properly met. My name is—"

"I know who you are."

"And I know who you are, but introductions aren't simply polite, they are law in my country, my world." He took her hand and helped her rise. "You must be my friend, Eureka. Only I am allowed enemies."

"We'll never be friends. You murdered the best one I had."

Atlas's lips turned downward as he glanced briefly at Brooks. "Do you know why I did it?"

"He was just a vessel to you," she said, "a way to get what you wanted."

"And what do I want?" Atlas stared into her eyes and waited.

"I know about the Filling."

"Forget the Filling. I want you."

"You want my tears."

"I will admit it," Atlas said. "At first you were just another Tearline girl to me. But then I got to know you. You're really very fascinating. What a strange, dark, and twisted heart you have. And what a face! Contrasts beguile me. The more time I spent inside that body"—he sighed, nodded at Brooks—

"the more I relished being near you. Then you disappeared with . . ."

"Ander," Eureka said.

"*Never* say that name in my kingdom!" Atlas shouted.

"Because of Leander," Eureka murmured. "Your brother who stole—"

Atlas grabbed Eureka's throat. "*Everything from me. Understand?*" His grip loosened. He composed himself with a breath. "He is flushed from both our lives now. We will not think of him again."

Eureka looked away. She would try not to think of Ander. It would make her mission easier, even though it was impossible.

"When you were gone," Atlas said, "the ghost of your beauty haunted me."

"You want one thing from me—"

"I want always to be near you. And I get what I want."

"You haven't gotten what you wanted in a long time."

"I didn't have to bring you here," Atlas said. "I saw your tears fill the lachrymatory. I could have taken it and left you rotting in those mountains. Think about that." He paused and gazed into the treetops thousands of feet above. "We were getting on so well," he whispered in her no-longer-bad ear. "Remember our kiss? I knew you knew it was me all along, just as I imagine you knew I knew you knew. Neither one of us is dumb, so why don't we stop pretending?".

He reached for her with a warm, strong hand. Eureka whipped away, mind whirring. She needed to resume pretending, to never stop, if she was going to survive. She had to trick him and she didn't know how.

"Are you wishing you had shot me when you had the chance?" Atlas asked, grinning. "Don't worry, there will be yet more chances for you to end my life—and to prove your love by sparing it."

"Give me the gun and I'll disprove it now," she said. "You know why I didn't shoot."

"Oh yes." Atlas gestured toward Brooks. "Because of this corpse."

The trees beyond Atlas rustled as ten girls in thigh-high boots and short red dresses with orichalcum breastplates stepped out from behind them. Their helmets shifted colors in the sun and hid their faces.

"Hello, girls," Atlas said, and turned to Eureka. "My Crimson Devils. They will see to your every need."

"Her bed is ready," one of the girls said.

"Take her to it."

"Brooks!" Eureka reached for his dead body.

"You loved him," Atlas said. "You really loved him best of all. I know it. But you shall love again. Better, stronger"—he caressed Eureka's cheek—"deeper. As only a girl can do."

"What should we do with the body?" one of the girls asked, nudging Brooks's chest with her boot.

Atlas thought a moment. "Have my ostriches had breakfast?"

Eureka tried to scream, but a harness fell over her face. A

metal bar snapped between her teeth. Someone tightened the harness from behind as green artemisia vapor swirled before her eyes.

Just before she lost consciousness, Atlas held her close. "I'm glad you're here, Eureka. Now everything can begin."

27

THE LIGHTNING CLOAK

Eureka awoke chained to a bed.

Her bed.

Four cherrywood bedposts rose above her on the antique queen she'd slept in before she cried. The thrift-store rocking chair swaying in the corner used to be her favorite homework spot. An Evangeline-green sweatshirt hung over its arm. Eureka's eyes throbbed from the haze of artemisia as her blurry reflection came into focus in her grandmother's old mirrored chest of drawers across from the bed.

Wide metal cuffs bound her wrists to the upper corners of the bed, her ankles to the lower corners, and her waist across the center. When she tried to jerk free, something sharp cut into her palms and the tops of her feet. The cuffs were barbed with spikes. Blood pooled over the cuff on her right wrist, then trickled down her arm.

"How does it work?" A husky voice startled her.

A teenage girl stood at her bedside, bent over Eureka's left hand like a manicurist. A laurel wreath adorned her amber hair. Her crimson dress plunged into a deep V ending just below her tattooed navel. She wore Eureka's crystal teardrop necklace.

"Give me back my necklace." The strange Atlantean words hurt as they left Eureka's parched throat. She tried to kick the girl with her knees. Metal spikes bit her waist. Blood bloomed through her shirt.

A snicker came from Eureka's other side. Another girl in another crimson dress. Her laurel wreath capped a smooth black bob, and her cold aquamarine eyes were focused on Eureka's right hand.

Crimson Devils, Atlas had called his guards.

"Where's Atlas?" Eureka said. *Where is Brooks's corpse?* she wanted to ask. She was used to the idea that the two boys occupied the same body. But she had watched her friend die, and only the enemy remained. A raging desire to kill Atlas flooded her.

"Watch," the second girl told the first.

Eureka felt a sting of heat, like the girl was injecting her fingertips with hot glue. A shimmery blue substance coated her fingers. Eureka touched the pad of her thumb to her forefinger and a jolt zipped through her, like the time she'd stuck her finger in an outlet when she was six.

"Don't." The dark-haired girl pried Eureka's fingers apart, smoothing more blue over Eureka's thumb. "It's going to hurt, but by sunrise, we'll have everything we ever wanted. He promised. Didn't he promise, Aida?"

"We're not to talk to her, Gem," Aida said.

"Sunrise." Eureka repeated the four-syllable Atlantean word. She tried to turn her head toward the window to gauge the time, but a crimson dress blocked her view.

"If he learns you were talking to his—"

"He won't." Gem glared at her companion.

"Then stop talking to her." Aida turned toward a desk on the left side of the room, which stood precisely where Eureka's identical desk stood back home.

"I want to see Atlas." Eureka squirmed against her bonds.

What was happening at sunrise? How could she destroy these girls and free herself before then? She closed her eyes and channeled the Incredible Hulk, master of transforming rage into strength. She willed the mirrored chest of drawers to become a thousand whirling glass daggers, slicing flesh, splashing crimson onto crimson. But then what? How would she find Atlas?

In Lafayette, escape had been her bedroom window, then the arms of the oak tree just beyond it. But when Gem shifted and Eureka could see out the window, no oak tree reached for her. Sun shone in. The light felt tired, evening's last rays.

They were very high up, a thousand stories above the ground. Gold and silver rooftops shimmered distantly below, and beyond them rings of water and land led to the ocean, which flowed into a horizon at the edge of whatever was left of the world.

"Tell me what happens at sunrise," Eureka said.

Gem was next to Aida at the desk. "Let me do the heartplate."

As Gem reached across the surface of the desk something strange happened to her hand. It blurred, like it had passed behind a pane of frosted glass. The blurring lasted only a moment. Gem's hand sharpened again and she was holding a silky piece of material, the same shimmery blue as whatever was on Eureka's fingers. Eureka thought she saw a lightning bolt flash across its center.

"Unbutton her shirt," Gem said.

Cold air braced Eureka's skin as Aida's fingers worked their way down her shirt. Then a feeling like nostalgia settled over her as the blue square was laid across her chest. Warm and heavy, it reminded Eureka of how she felt watching videos of Diana on her laptop.

Her breath came shallowly as Gem smoothed the heartplate over her chest. Aida ran a finger from Eureka's right temple, across her forehead, to her left temple, and Eureka understood that while she had been unconscious, the girls had affixed a band of the blue substance to her head.

"The ghostsmith counsels subjects before charging the cloak," Gem said.

"You've never met the ghostsmith," Aida said. "Besides, this is for Atlas. No wasting time. He wants the lachrymatories filled." She applied pressure to the inside corners of Eureka's eyes. Two blurry silver outlines fixed just below Eureka's vision. The lachrymatories. She was supposed to cry into them.

"It won't work," Eureka said.

"It always works," Gem said. She moved to the wall, where Eureka's painting of the weeping Saint Catherine of Siena hung in a cobwebbed corner. She flipped a switch Eureka couldn't see.

Pain crashed into Eureka. She was engulfed by absolute darkness. She arched her back. She tasted blood. The pain doubled, then redoubled.

When the pain was total and familiar, bright points of light entered her vision, meteors showering the sky of her eyelids. One point of light drew closer. Burning heat filled her pores. Then Eureka was inside the light.

She saw a faded floral-print suitcase by a door. Lamplight flickered somewhere. Her nostrils flared at the odor of broken pickle jars—that scent always brought her back to the night her parents split up. She saw Diana's feet in their gray and pink galoshes, her hair wet with rain, her eyes dry with determination. The front door opened. Thunder outside was so real it rattled Eureka's bones. The suitcase was in Diana's hand.

"Mom! Wait!" Eureka felt the back of her eyes burning. "Don't you love me enough to stay?" Never before had she voiced the question that plagued her all the time. She tried to pull away. It was just a memory. A memory of tears building before she'd known better.

It was so real. Diana leaving. Eureka left behind . . .

"No!"

The white light was whipped away. The searing pain cooled to a third-degree burn. Eureka shook like an earthquake, rattling the metal cuffs binding her to the bed. The afterimage of Diana was still abandoning her eyes.

A tall figure stood in the doorway of Eureka's replica bedroom. He wore a long silver smock and a grease-smeared orichalcum welding mask.

"The ghostsmith," Gem whispered.

Footsteps approached the bed. Silver-gloved hands plucked the lachrymatories from Eureka's eyes. At least she had not cried. The ghostsmith slipped them inside a silver pocket in his smock.

He removed the heartplate from Eureka's chest without a word. He pulled the blue material from Eureka's fingers and forehead. She bore the pain silently and studied the gleaming surface of the ghostsmith's mask. She wanted to see the face behind the orichalcum.

The ghostsmith deftly wove the fragments of blue material into a single long strand, a wide, blue glittering band. Then he

302

wrapped it seven times around his wrist and used his other hand to knot it. A lightning bolt flashed through the fabric. Eureka wondered what it had looked like on her skin.

"Come close, girls," a peppery voice echoed from inside the mask.

Gem and Aida had been trying to slip silently out the door. They turned and drew slowly toward the ghostsmith.

"Atlas ordered this done?" the ghostsmith asked.

Eureka discerned the faintest lisp.

"Yes," Aida said. "He—"

"You will pay for his mistake."

"But—" Aida began to tremble as the ghostsmith removed his mask.

A long, lustrous mane of black hair tumbled from it, revealing pale skin decorated by a dazzling constellation of freckles. Round black eyes peered from a dense curtain of lashes.

The ghostsmith was a teenage girl.

The ghostsmith was Delphine—Eureka's very-great-grandmother, source of the Tearline and Eureka's darkness.

The ghostsmith dipped forward and kissed Aida on the cheek. When her lips met Aida's skin a spark passed between them. A burning odor stung Eureka's nostrils and the girl's eyes filled with tears. Aida fell to the ground. She began to weep. She rolled back and forth, lost in sudden sorrow, a black hole opened with a kiss.

Aida's shaking gradually lessened. Her sobs quieted. Her

final cry broke off midway, leaving a feeling of unfinished desperation in the room. She rolled onto her face. The stolen teardrop necklace clinked when it hit the floor.

Delphine's red lips loomed close to the other Devil. Gem turned toward the hall and ran. The ghostsmith darted after her, had the girl back inside the room in an instant. Her gloved hand clamped around Gem's neck.

Gem's lips quivered. "Please."

Inches separated their skin. Delphine puckered her lips, then paused. "You have worked for me before."

"Yes," Gem whispered.

"Did I like you?"

"You did."

"That is why Atlas chose you to betray me."

The girl said nothing. Delphine swooped to the ground, lifted Aida's corpse, and pushed it roughly into Gem's arms.

"Show Atlas what happens when he crosses me."

Gem staggered under Aida's weight and fled down the hall.

Eureka and the ghostsmith were alone. She turned toward the bed.

"Hello." Delphine's voice was softer. She'd switched from Atlantean to English. She avoided Eureka's gaze, looking instead at the bedposts, the desk, the rocking chair. "This must be distracting."

One swipe of Delphine's hand along the wall made the familiar furniture vanish. The room was gray and bare. The bed Eureka lay on was now a cot.

"He commissions convincing holograms," Delphine said, "but Atlas does not appreciate the horror of nostalgia. No one wise looks back at what they were." She poured water from a pitcher into a goblet that glistened like a star. "Are you thirsty?"

Eureka wanted a drink badly, but she jerked her chin away. Water spilled down her chest.

Delphine put the goblet down. "Do you know who I am?"

Eureka looked into Delphine's dark eyes and, for a moment, saw her mother. For just a moment, she wanted to be held.

"You're the villain," she said.

Delphine smiled. "I am certainly that, and so are you. We're a team now. I'm sorry about the lightning cloak. When I designed it"—she stroked the blue band on her wrist—"I never anticipated it might be used on you."

"What is it?" Eureka sensed she wasn't finished with the lightning cloak. The more she understood, the more she could withstand.

"It is woven of my agony, so pure and deep that it connects to all agony inside everyone it touches. What you felt was my pain seeking your pain in the astral light. Had I not interceded, you would have felt every shred of misery you've ever known and ever would know in the future. Call it a mother's intuition that I got here in time." Delphine touched Eureka's cheek with her gloved hand. "Pain is power. Over time I have absorbed it from many thousands of agonized souls."

"What about Aida?"

"Another soul put out of her misery, another bump to my arsenal of pain," Delphine said. "She was also a message to Atlas. We send each other little notes throughout the day."

"Take me to him," Eureka said.

" 'Take me' is such a submissive phrase," Delphine said, trying too hard to mask her jealousy. "Is that really what you want? Because I can give you anything, Eureka."

"Why would you help me?"

"Because"—Delphine seemed stunned—"we're family." She slipped her gloves off and clasped Eureka's hand with long, cold fingers. "Because I love—"

"What I want is impossible."

Delphine sat on the edge of the bed and recovered from Eureka's interruption. She flashed a lovely smile. "There's no such thing."

Eureka could have asked for the safe retrieval of the twins and Cat and Ander—but if that were what she truly wanted, she would never have abandoned them. She wasn't their protector anymore. Maybe Delphine was right about not looking back at what you used to be.

"All you have to do is ask," Delphine said.

Eureka would call her bluff. "I want my best friend."

You really loved him best of all, Atlas had said. Had he been right?

"Then you shall have him," Delphine said.

"He's dead."

306

Delphine lowered her lips toward Eureka's, the way she'd done to Aida. But no spark flashed between them, only the warmth of red lips on Eureka's right cheek, then her left. Diana used to kiss her like that.

She heard a series of metallic snaps as the barbed cuffs were released from around her wrists, then her waist, then her ankles. Delphine slipped an arm under Eureka's neck and raised her from the bed. "Only the ghostsmith decides who is dead."

28

THE GHOSTSMITH

Delphine led Eureka through a tunnel made of jewel-toned coral reef. They emerged from a sand dune on an empty beach and left matching trails of footprints as they strode toward the sea. The sun was pink and low.

By sunrise, Gem had said. That was how long Eureka had to defeat Atlas.

Farther down the shore, dark purple rocks rose into jagged mountains.

"Isn't that where you were born?" Eureka asked Delphine. "You were raised in the mountains by the gossipwitches."

By now, Esme and the others must have made it back. Eureka imagined Peggy alighting on one of the crags, a dozen delighted witches sliding off her wings. After all these years and all they'd seen, would their return home satisfy them?

Delphine stared into the blue horizon. "Says who?"

"Selene. *The Book of Love*." Eureka felt for her bag and realized it was gone, of course, stolen by the Devils along with her crystal teardrop. She was bereft of all the things that used to strengthen her.

It was better that way. Rage strengthened her, the way other people's pain strengthened Delphine.

"Snuff out that dim fairy tale," Delphine said. "Our future burns too bright."

Ahead, a soaring wave climbed the water. It curled like a swimming giant's arm toward the shore. Eureka braced herself for the wipeout, but where the mighty beast was about to break—where the wave's foaming lip was inches from shore—it defied gravity and the tides and whatever moon still spun in the sky. It hung, on the verge, as if captured in a photograph.

"What is that?" Eureka asked.

"It is my waveshop."

"You build waves there?" Eureka had come to associate rogue waves with Seedbearers, but maybe Delphine had been behind the wave that killed Diana.

Delphine tossed her head. "Occasionally. Architecturally." She gestured at the suspended wave like it was a building she'd designed. "I specialize in the dead and dying. That is why I am called the ghostsmith. My range is wide, as all things yearn to die."

She led Eureka along the shore until they faced the

suspended wave's barrel. Its trough looked dim and cavern-ous, like a room with a sand floor and curving water walls. A pale oval of daylight shone through the opposite end.

"I have waited an eternity to bring you here," Delphine said.

Eureka wondered what she meant, what lie Eureka rep-resented to Delphine. She thought about Delphine absorbing pain from everyone she'd ever tortured. She knew pain made its own time. After Diana died, minutes had outstretched millennia.

"Come inside," Delphine said. "See where I do my most essential work."

Eureka studied the wave, seeking the trap.

"Don't worry," Delphine said. "This wave looks on its last legs, as if it is about to rejoin the sea that bore it. But I can keep it up forever. You'll see once you're inside."

The wave's motion had somehow been arrested, but when Eureka touched the wall of water, she bruised her fingers on the unexpected rush that churned within it. She drew closer to Delphine and entered the suspended wave. The ocean wrapped around them like a shell around two black pearls.

Music played from somewhere. Eureka was chilled to recognize it—Madame Blavatsky's bird Polaris had sung the same tune outside her window in Lafayette.

Damp sand lit up beneath Eureka's feet as she walked far-ther into the oblong space the wave had carved. By the time she reached the center of the waveshop, the ground shone with brilliant golden light.

They were not alone. Four teen boys had their backs toward Eureka. They were naked, and the impulse to stare at them was strong. Each of their backs bore scars from lacerations. The slight silver sheen of their skin was familiar. These were ghost robots, like Ovid, vessels for Atlas's Filling.

Two of the machines used shovels to chuck a crumbly gray substance from a small slag heap into a glowing pit at the far end of the suspended wave. The other two robots were locked in debate. They weren't speaking English or Atlantean. They didn't seem to be speaking the same language even as themselves. A single robot made one point in what Eureka thought was Dutch, switched to Spanish to second-guess himself, then concluded in what sounded like Cantonese. The others responded in languages she guessed were Arabic, Russian, Portuguese, and a dozen more unrecognizable tongues. They spoke in tones Eureka was used to hearing just before a fight at Wade's Hole. She glanced at Delphine, who held a fragile smile on her lips.

She remembered Dad's ghost battling Seyma's ghost and, later, the Seedbearers' ghosts inside Ovid. It had been chaos: multiple identities struggling to claim one robotic body. Solon had said these machines were built to accommodate many millions of dead souls. Eureka wondered how many ghosts were already inside each of these silver boys.

One of the debating robots held what looked like a sheet of water. It was a map—or a reflection of a map. It hovered between his hands like paper and appeared to be composed solely of different shades of blue.

He pointed at the center and said in a Cockney accent, "Eurasia by sunrise, innit?"

Eureka's eyes adjusted to make sense of the map. Coastlines remained foreign, but the turquoise shape of the Turkish mountains she and Ander had climbed to reach the Bitter Cloud appeared in the center. She allowed herself to think of her loved ones for a moment. If Eurasia was still in question, could they have survived the Rising?

"Ander," she whispered.

One of the robots whipped around. Its lean orichalcum face bore the stern expression of a middle-aged woman—but only for an instant. It quickly morphed into the gaunt, furious features of a young man who was about to snap. It made a fist.

Eureka made one, too.

Delphine slid between them and placed cool hands on Eureka's shoulders. "Lucretius," she said in Atlantean, "this is my daughter."

Lucretius's features changed again, into those of an avuncular man. Silver whiskers sprouted from its chin. "Hello, Eureka."

"I am not her daughter."

"Don't be silly." Delphine's strong massage was like ice on the back of Eureka's neck. "I've told everyone about you."

"What are they doing?" Eureka gestured at the other two robots, which had not looked up from the glowing pit.

"I can't wait to show you," Delphine said, and drew Eureka closer.

"Wait." Beyond the glowing pit, close to where the suspended wave's lip hovered above the shore, five more robots slept on chaise longues beneath a wide umbrella.

"Those robots are still filling," Delphine said. "Soon they will be alive with the experiences of hundreds of millions of souls."

Eureka slid from Delphine's grip and climbed a slope of sand toward the sleeping robots. Ocean sounds rushed above her, but the waveshop's watery walls held still.

Wisps of light gathered around the robots' skin. She knew this aura was made of ghosts, that all the energy flowing into the machines came from someone she had killed.

"What happens when they're filled?"

"Then come the beatings," Delphine said.

Eureka eyed the scars on the backs of the waking robots poring over their maps.

"They don't wake from the Filling obedient," Delphine said. "Not with all those willful ghosts competing inside." She reached for a silver whip resting on a silver table near the sleeping robots. A blue jellyfish writhed at its tip. She passed the whip to Eureka. It was as light as a ghost.

"In my hand, this whip deals deep lashes of transformational pain. I train my robots to allow only their ghosts' efficient and useful attributes to rise to the surface. This enables my boys to perform many millions of tasks—with no threat of rebellion." Delphine paused, turned Eureka's face to hers. "This work is in your blood and in your tears. Do you understand?"

Eureka was repulsed and shamelessly intrigued. "What kinds of tasks?"

"Anything. Everything. Dry out the world you drowned, pave roads, plant crops, slaughter stragglers, cure diseases, erect a stunning empire that spans the globe." Delphine pointed at the robots' glowing auras. "See the possibilities flowing in."

Tiny images flashed around the machines: a hand writing a letter, a boot wedging a shovel into soil, a computer monitor filled with complicated code, a sprinter's legs crossing a golden meadow. Just as Eureka recognized each flash it disappeared inside its robot, which acknowledged the acquisition with a muscle flex or a facial twitch, as if it were having a nightmare.

One robot's eyes opened. Delphine placed two fingers in the infinity-shaped indentation on its neck and twisted clockwise, just as Solon had demonstrated at the Bitter Cloud.

"Go back to sleep, pet. Dream. . . ."

Eureka should have felt horrified, but there was something tempting about sparing a soul's most essential knowledge, memory, or experience—and lobotomizing the rest. She wished she could have done it to herself after Diana died.

It wasn't like Eureka recognized the dead flowing into the robots. She didn't see her brother's hands performing a magic trick or Cat solving a calculus equation in the robots' auras.

"After the beatings," Delphine explained with a smile, "I turn the ghost robots over to Atlas. Their dissemination across the drowned world has long been his vision. He will take care of the dirty work for us. All you and I have to do is wait."

"Wait for what?"

"The opportunity to turn everything against him."

Delphine led Eureka to a tall mirror in the center of the waveshop. It was made of softly undulating water. Eureka didn't want to look, but the temptation was too strong. Cold gripped her stomach when Delphine's stunning reflection appeared where Eureka's should have been. When she looked at the space before Delphine, Eureka's own face smiled darkly back.

"The world will be ours, Eureka." Her voice sounded precisely like Diana's. Eureka closed her eyes, leaning closer to her dark, seductive ancestor.

"You're going to get rid of Atlas?" she asked slowly.

"Depose, dispatch, destroy . . . I haven't yet decided which I like the sound of best. But—practical matters before poetry. You may know that one of my robots was stolen and never recovered. Tonight I make Ovid's replacement. Would you like to help?"

Eureka knew from *The Book of Love* that Selene and

Leander escaped Atlantis with Ovid and the baby girl stowed inside their ship. But that had been ages ago.

"If the robot can be replaced," she asked, "why wasn't it done long ago?"

For the first time Delphine looked upon her coldly. Eureka lost her breath.

"It cannot simply *be* replaced like a lover," Delphine said. "My robots require the darkest materials to come into being. But that wouldn't have been in your book, would it? Neither would our fate after the flood. Selene missed all that, too. You don't know what Woe was like, how we were stagnant beneath the ocean for millennia. Only our minds could move. Try to fathom the insanity that brews in one who must endure such impotence. Every Atlantean suffered, all because he dared to break my heart."

"Leander."

"Never say his name." Delphine repeated Atlas's rule. Eureka now wondered if it was actually the ghostsmith's rule. Was she the source of all Atlantean darkness?

Delphine smoothed her hair. She inhaled deeply. "There's not much time. The replacement must be ready in time to catch the final ghosts."

"How many souls are still alive?" Eureka asked.

"Seventy-three million, twelve thousand, eight hundred, and six," the robot Lucretius called.

"I must finish before sunrise." Delphine gestured toward

the opposite end of the wave, where no nuance of sunset remained in the sky. "When the morning light is centered there, our homeless ghosts will find their shelter."

She took a seat at an already spinning potter's wheel. Behind her, near the arching back of the wave, a tall golden loom displayed a half-woven square of shimmery blue fabric. Lightning flashed across it—more of Delphine's agony.

"Gilgamesh," Delphine called. "More orichalcum."

One of the shoveling robots reached inside the pit and retrieved a huge, glowing red mass. As he carried it to Delphine, it cooled in the misty air to the silver of orichalcum. He eased it onto Delphine's spinning wheel.

Her bare foot pumped the pedal, whirling the plate faster. The tempo of the song that had been playing throughout the waveshop sped up. It was melancholy and beautiful, all minor chords.

"This wheel generates the music that keeps the waveshop from crashing in on itself," Delphine said. "It must be wound frequently, like a clock."

As her hands glided through the fiery mass of orichalcum, it sizzled and softened into the consistency of clay. A muscular calf began to take shape.

"You're sculpting the robot," Eureka said.

Delphine nodded. "Do you know the nature of orichalcum?"

Eureka knew that the lachrymatory, the anchor, the chest

317

of artemisia, the spear and sheath that Ander had taken from the Seedbearers, and Ovid had been the only orichalcum in the Waking World. "I know it's precious."

"But you don't know why?" Delphine said.

"Things are precious when they're hard to come by," Eureka said.

This made Delphine smile. "Long ago, I began an experiment: Grind the flesh and bones of my conquests into fine powder. Add heat and a gelatinous enzyme from the Cnidaria—you call it a jellyfish—while it is still in the medusa stage. Much like the stare of my snake-maned friend, the medusa enzyme transforms ordinary corpse powder into the most durable and lovely element in the world." She caressed the orichalcum leg on her wheel. "And I transform that into whatever I please. I have mined orichalcum in this manner since before Atlantis sank. Atlas's empirical conquests used to provide the bodies. Now your tears have given me endless material to work with. By sunrise, all that will be left to do is convert the living into ghosts."

"What happens at sunrise?" Eureka asked casually, though she wanted to scream.

"The survivors are preparing arks. A community in Turkey has long anticipated a flood. Perhaps you know of them? The living are traveling there from around the world to board their ships. We can see them in the water map. This is convenient, because it gathers all the living souls in one place.

We must stage the final apocalypse before they disperse again across the seas."

Eureka met Delphine's eyes. They were so dark she could see her face reflected in them. "That's why Atlas wants more tears."

"Yes." Delphine gestured over her shoulder, lighting the space behind her. What looked like a cross between a medieval catapult and a futuristic rocket launcher sharpened into view. "The rest of my cannons are in Atlas's armory, but I keep an early model here." She rose from her wheel, lifted the cannon's hatch, and withdrew a palm-sized crystal globe. "A single crystal shell, armed with one of your tears, will do thirty-six times the damage of your world's nuclear bombs."

"But I'm not going to cry," Eureka said.

"Of course you are." Delphine returned the crystal globe to the cannon with care. "You're unsettled by Atlas's mistake with the lightning cloak. But no one will harm you—ever again." She caressed Eureka's hair. "We must all make sacrifices. Your tears are your contribution, though you may choose what makes them flow."

"No."

"Surely you have enough to cry about"—Delphine tilted her head—"losing your greatest love so recently? Remember, I know how you feel. I had my heart broken, too."

But had it been Delphine's broken heart that sank Atlantis—or pride and embarrassment and the pain of losing her child? Were their Tearline stories truly as parallel as Delphine wanted Eureka to believe they were? Had Delphine had a Cat, a father, and siblings who loved her as heedlessly as Eureka's did? Eureka didn't think so.

And Ander. He was nothing like Leander. He was a boy who hadn't deserved any of the shattering pain he'd known in his life. He'd loved Eureka because of his heart, not his destiny. The thought of him made Eureka turn inward, backward, to the moment she'd first seen him on the dusty road outside New Iberia. He had showed her love was possible, even after heart-erasing loss.

"You know where he is," Eureka said. If Ander and the twins and Cat could at least be spared . . .

"You must not worry yourself with what might have been," Delphine said, "only with what broke you. Love is crippling. Heartbreak gives us our legs."

"Then why are you with Atlas?" Eureka asked before she could stop herself.

"With Atlas?" Delphine asked. "What do you mean?"

"The way you talk about him, sending each other notes." Eureka paused. "Your tears have the same power as mine. They could fill the cannons, but he won't put you through the pain of shedding them. It's because he loves you. Doesn't he?"

Delphine doubled over laughing. It was a cold sound, a winter wind. "Atlas cannot love. His heart's not tuned that way."

"Then why—"

"Your problem is you feel ashamed," Delphine said. "I am more in love with my power than I could ever be with a boy. You, too, must embrace your darkness."

Eureka found herself nodding. She and Delphine envisioned different destinies for Eureka, but maybe, at least for a moment, their paths intersected.

Delphine wiped sea mist from her face. "Did you know I have had thirty-six Tearline daughters? I loved them all—cruel ones, bashful ones, dramatic ones, homely ones—but you are my favorite. The dark one. I knew it would be you who reunited us."

There was endless adoration in Delphine's voice that reminded Eureka of the way Diana used to talk to her. It had sometimes made Eureka shy away from Diana's love. It was the kind of love Eureka didn't think she would ever understand. Maybe Delphine had not been lying when she said she would do Eureka any favor.

"What you said before, about getting to decide who is truly dead . . ."

Delphine nodded. "The fate of your friend Brooks. Atlas told me about him."

"Could you bring him back?"

"Would it make you happy?"

"Then you could bring all these people back." Eureka pointed at the ghosts filling the machines. "You could stop turning corpses into weapons and bring them back to life."

Delphine frowned. "I suppose I could."

"How?" Eureka asked.

"If you're asking about the limits of my powers, I have yet to find them." Delphine clasped her hands beneath her chin. "But I believe you're asking what I *will* do. These ghosts have a higher purpose. I promise you won't miss them when they're gone. But"—she smiled—"our army can spare one. Even a strong one. Assuming he has not been pulverized. You shall have your Brooks, on one condition."

"Name it."

"You must never leave me." Delphine drew Eureka into a tight embrace. "I've waited too long to hold you. Say you'll never leave me." Then she whispered, "Call me Mother."

"What?"

"I can give you what you want."

Eureka glanced up at the suspended wave and saw in it the wave that had killed Diana, that wave that had stolen Brooks away. An instinct rushed into her: she didn't understand why, but she knew if she could get Brooks back, somehow she could fix things.

She pushed through her sickened heart into a black space where there had never been a Diana and no reason to feel a thing about using this word:

"Mother."

"Yes! Go on!"

Eureka swallowed. "I will never leave you."

"You've made me so . . . happy." Delphine's shoulders

shook as she pulled away. A single tear shone in the corner of the girl's left eye. "What's about to happen, what I'm about to do for you, Eureka, you must never tell anyone. It must be our special secret."

Eureka nodded.

Delphine took a step back and blinked. The tear left her eye and fell.

When it hit the sand, Eureka felt it deep inside her. She watched the earth split open as a single white narcissus flower sprang up from the sand. It grew rapidly, rising several feet, branching out into more flowers, countless blooms, until the plant was taller and wider than Eureka.

Then, slowly, the flower transformed into a figure. A body. A boy.

Brooks blinked, stunned to find himself before Eureka. His hair was long and untamable. He wore cutoffs, a green Tulane sweatshirt, his father's old Army baseball cap—the same clothes he'd worn the last day they'd sailed together at Cypremort Point. Goose bumps rose on his skin, and Eureka knew that he was real. He looked at his hands, up at the suspended wave, into Eureka's eyes. He touched his face. "I didn't know the dead could dream." He gazed at Delphine, who walked to stand beside them. "Maya?"

"You may call me the ghostsmith." Delphine bowed slightly.

Brooks gasped, and Eureka wondered how he had experienced Delphine from the other side. His eyes housed a darkness that made Eureka feel less alone.

"I decide who is dead and who is not," Delphine said. "And you are not."

Eureka threw her arms around Brooks. He smelled like the old Brooks and sounded like the old Brooks; he held her like no one could but Brooks. Even though she had been tricked before, she knew this was real.

"Eureka," he whispered in a voice that chilled her to her core. "It's my fault. I couldn't climb it, so he took over. Now there's no way out."

"Don't worry," she whispered back, confused by what he meant about climbing. "Now that you're here, I can do it. I have to."

She could feel him shake his head against her shoulder. "Whatever happens"—he pulled away to look her in the eye—"I love you. I should have said it long ago. It should have been the only thing I ever said."

"And I love—"

"You may play with him once the sun has risen." Delphine pressed a hand between their bodies. "I'll even let you use the whip. Until then we have work to do."

Eureka's eyes begged Brooks for more about what he knew and where he'd been, but a waterfall sprang up around him like a cage that hung in the air. She couldn't see him anymore.

"Eureka!"

Delphine returned to her potter's wheel and pretended she couldn't hear Brooks scream.

Eureka pressed her hands against the waterfall. It soaked her. Through it, she could feel Brooks's shoulder, then his face. She wondered why she couldn't feel his arms reaching back for her. "Stay with me."

"He's not going anywhere," Delphine said. "You can trust me. Now you must prove I can trust you."

"Delphine?" A crown of red hair hovered at the wave-shop's entrance. Atlas did not look happy.

29

THE LOVED ONE

"I assumed you would be working when Eureka arrived," Atlas said as he entered the waveshop. The golden light that Eureka's footsteps had lit turned red as he approached.

Delphine did not look up from her wheel. She pedaled slowly, lengthening each note of the strange music.

"You said you were not to be bothered." Atlas brushed Delphine's dark hair to one side and rested a hand on her shoulder.

When Delphine looked up at Eureka she was really looking through her. "You said you wouldn't hurt her."

"Show me one scratch on her body." Atlas approached Eureka and made a close circle around her, seeming not to notice the cuts on her wrist, her bloodied shirt where his spiked cuff had bound her waist. His breath was hot on her neck. His eyes moved across her skin like spiders. "She is in mint condition."

Eureka envisioned spinning on him, twisting his neck until his arteries popped and the fire in his eyes went cold. She saw the murder in vivid detail, from the strained gurgle coming from his throat to the pathetic thud of his dead body in the sand. But she craved more than Atlas's annihilation. She also had to steal the profits he had made from her tears. She had to undo the Filling, and she didn't yet know how.

"You used my lightning on her," Delphine said. "There are deeper wounds than scratches." Her focus returned to the orichalcum kneecap her long fingers were shaping. "She must come to the tears in her own way."

"She refused," Atlas said.

Tension swam between their words. It reminded Eureka of her parents' preliminary fights. The memory of Diana's leaving returned—the nightgown tickling her ankles . . . the storm outside and within . . . the slap forever on her cheek, haunting it.

"I continue to refuse," Eureka said.

Delphine reached for Atlas's hand, stopping him before he lunged at Eureka. She stroked the coarse red hairs on his forearm. "Give it time."

"Time." A note of sarcasm entered Atlas's voice as he gazed down the wave toward the dark eye of sky. "The one luxury we lack."

"I sense them building in her," Delphine said. "They will come before sunrise."

Atlas bowed his head. "I am chastised. No harm will come to her when she is with me from now on."

"She is with me from now on," Delphine corrected.

"You have your work to do," Atlas said. "Let me look after her tonight. I have something for her, a surprise."

From inside his waterfall prison, Brooks bellowed violently.

"Who's in the cage today?" Atlas asked with a nod.

Delphine's gaze checked Eureka's before she said, "A boy I want to play with later."

"You always have liked to make them seethe first," Atlas said. Eureka couldn't tell if he was jealous or amused.

"I will destroy you!" Brooks shouted, his voice muffled by the sound of the waterfall.

"Oh, he'll be fun." Atlas chuckled.

Eureka's teeth clenched. Atlas's laughter made her hands itch to kill. She weighed her options. Defend her friend now and lose—or bide her time?

Atlas stepped closer to Brooks, surveying the waterfall cage. Then his fist plunged into it. The barrier curved pliantly around his fist, likely allowing Atlas to strike Brooks in the stomach, though Eureka couldn't see her friend through the waterfall. When Brooks howled, Eureka felt his pain in her own gut, like a twin.

Then came a dull shatter, like a hammer against a block

of ice. She knew Brooks had tried to fight back, but his fist couldn't penetrate the water. His cage didn't work that way.

"Was that necessary?" Delphine asked, bored.

Eureka's arms wanted to enclose the waterfall, to cradle Brooks. But she could show no reaction or Atlas would guess who was inside.

He stood before her now with his mesmerizing redwood eyes and sharp white teeth. He fingered a lock of her wet hair. "I have a present for you, Eureka. An apology for your experience with the lightning. With Delphine's permission, I will take you to it."

"You have nothing I want."

"Perhaps no *thing*. Perhaps *someone*."

"What sickness are you up to?" Delphine looked up from her wheel. The music's pace quickened and Eureka became afraid.

Atlas shook his head and slipped an arm around Eureka's waist as he steered her toward the wave's exit. "I want to see the amazement on your face."

※

"Remarkable, isn't it?" Atlas paused at the midpoint of the second bridge they'd crossed since leaving the waveshop. At either entrance, two giant statues of his likeness drew long silver swords on each other.

When empty, both bridges stretched low across their wide

moats, but when tread upon, they rose into towering arches, offering spectacular views of the city ahead.

"I can give you a beautiful life, Eureka," Atlas said. "You always wanted something more extraordinary than the bayou—didn't you? If you help me, I will welcome you here. The cost is tiny, the reward endless."

The nearly full moon hung over the skyline of Atlantis, which glittered like a galaxy fashioned into buildings. They were shaped like roller coasters, with gem-colored swimming pools slanting down their roofs. Parks burst through the city's seams, astonishing flora growing so rapidly that the topography was ever changing. Commuter trains swam through the sky. Behind them, the Gossipwitch Mountains rose starkly.

"I have lived in a hundred other bodies," Atlas said, "seen a hundred other worlds. None came close to my Atlantis. Imagine if we had never sunk . . ."

Eureka leaned against the bridge's orichalcum railing. Now that she knew how the precious metal was mined, everything made from orichalcum looked like rotting flesh. "But you did sink."

"That is literally ancient history."

"Alternative history, you mean. Most people don't believe you ever existed."

Atlas forced a bitter laugh. "Most people no longer exist."

Looking into the moat below, Eureka saw Delphine's face in her reflection. "How did you forgive her?"

"What?"

"If Delphine had never cried that tear, you never would have sunk."

"Did she say something about me, about that?"

The time it took Eureka to think of an answer made Atlas squirm. "You must really love her, that's all I mean."

As Atlas's eyes probed Eureka's for information, she understood that his relationship with Delphine had nothing to do with love, and everything to do with fear. Maybe no one else could see it, but Delphine ruled the king.

They walked down the bridge in silence and were greeted by a gathering of Atlanteans. Twinkling city lights illuminated the Atlanteans' made-up faces, their exquisite jewelry and clothes. Atlas gave a gentle wave and the crowd broke into applause.

"Is this your queen, sir?" a woman's voice called out in Atlantean. A bright blue heptagonal hat shielded her features.

Atlas raised Eureka's hand high in the air. "Isn't she marvelous? Everything I deserve?" His false smile deepened, as if seeing Eureka through his subjects' eyes. "She could use a scrub, of course. And these clothes must be burned and never spoken of again. But where better to shop for replacements than in our city?"

As the crowd applauded, Atlas gestured toward a man at the front who was holding up a small black box.

"There he is! Smile for the royal holographer!" Atlas

slipped an arm around Eureka's waist and held her close. She could feel his rapid breathing. "Imagine your dead friend stands in my place, and smile."

The crowd cheered even louder at the first forced peek of Eureka's smile. The applause was deafening, but their expressions were vacant as they clapped. She loathed them. Did they not know about the Filling? She wanted all of them turned into ghosts. They were either idiots or as selfish as their king.

The mob circled around her as she and Atlas passed a cobbler, a market, and a hologram shop, each with lifelike wax statues of Atlas marking their doorsteps, advertising their wares.

"I bought my *sole* at Belinda's," a prerecorded Atlas panned through a speaker outside the cobbler's.

"Nothing turns me on like Atlantean ardorfruit," his voice blared through the speaker above an Atlas statue about to bite into a golden triangular-shaped fruit. "Tender. Tangy. Take some home tonight."

Atlas steered Eureka into a central triangle surrounded by grand and gleaming buildings. Flags of many shades of blue hung from a hundred eaves, cascading in the wind.

"They love me," Atlas told Eureka without a hint of irony. They mounted a stage that appeared to be floating. Half a dozen Devils lined its perimeter.

"What's the penalty if they don't?" Eureka asked.

"Delphine could never connect with the public like this."

Atlas glanced at Eureka, adding, "Her powers are remarkable, no one is arguing that, but without me, she's just a witch in a wave."

Eureka wondered whether he was lying for her sake or for his. Delphine wasn't here because she didn't have to be. She made Atlas do it for her. The king was a ghost, a puppet, like Delphine's other creations.

They stopped in the center of the stage and looked down at a hundred Atlanteans. These people didn't love him. No one did. Perhaps because it was so obvious he didn't love anyone back. Eureka wondered if he ever had. Delphine said his heart wasn't tuned that way. All of this mattered, but Eureka wasn't sure how.

The royal holographer passed his device through the air before Eureka's body, following her curves with his arm. Then he pulled a level and a great plume of silver smoke rose from his device. A huge hologram of Eureka popped into view in the middle of the audience, which parted, clapping and curtsying before her likeness.

"I give you," Atlas boomed into an invisible microphone, "your Tearline girl! Eureka sacrificed her heart to resurrect your world. And soon her tears will bring you more good fortune. By tomorrow, the so-called Waking World, which has oppressed you for thousands of years, will be vanquished. We will have ascended. One question remains." He turned to Eureka and kissed her hand with flair. "How to repay the girl who gave her heart so you could taste the sweetness of supremacy? Eureka, my treasure, this gift wasn't easy to come by, so I do hope you'll appreciate it."

He looked skyward. The crowds' eyes followed. Eureka tried to hold off as long as possible, but curiosity betrayed her and her chin lifted toward the night sky. Something large and green and formless lowered toward her. When it was twenty feet overhead, Eureka saw it was a fleet of green Abyssinian lovebirds. There were thousands of them, carrying what looked like a huge golden birdcage toward the stage.

Though she couldn't see beyond the birds, Eureka was gripped by the sudden premonition that Ander was inside the cage. She imagined the lightning cloak enfolding him, scrambling his mind with torturous memories, stripping his sadness of meaning. Her heart raced the way it had the first time they kissed.

The cage landed with a boom on the stage. Atlas clapped his hands three times. The birds scattered into the night. Inside the cage—

Stood Filiz.

"Well?" Atlas asked Eureka, his arms spread wide as if to receive her enormous gratitude. "My Devils picked her up along the inner moat this morning. We have all sorts of ways to torture trespassers, but I said, 'No, no, she must be a friend of Eureka's.'" He turned toward the crowd and yelled, "And any friend of Eureka's is a friend of mine!"

Filiz's hands were stuffed in the pockets of her tight black jeans. Her cheek was badly bruised, her T-shirt torn down the middle. Her chin was low, and her red hair hadn't been washed in many miles. Her eyes rose slowly. No words found Eureka.

"I'm having trouble reading you, darling." Atlas laughed for the audience's benefit. "Is this what gratitude looks like in the so-called Waking World? Here I stage a beautiful reunion between you and your loved one, whoever she is. She followed you all the way here, so she's clearly devoted. She has the most refined taste in hair color imaginable"—he waited for the crowd's laughter to rise and fall—"and yet you look upon her as if she were offal. Has Delphine hardened you so much already?"

Eureka moved toward the cage. "How did you get here?"

If Filiz was in Atlantis, maybe Eureka's loved ones were, too. No one should care enough about Eureka to follow her here, but she knew they did. Did Atlas have them imprisoned, too?

"Speak up, girl," Atlas said. "We'd all like to know."

Filiz swallowed, adjusted her black choker necklace. "My grandmother told tales of the Atlantean mountains where the gossipwitches live." She spoke Atlantean, too. "Her grandmother told her that her grandmother told her"—she paused, swallowed, gazed into Eureka's eyes—"that whoever visited those mountains would find the answer to life's greatest question."

"The Gossipwitch Mountains?" Atlas scoffed. "How

stupidly rumors warp over millennia! Those mountains are for the unclean and undesired. Forget the wisdom of your ignorant elders. You are fortunate to have trespassed upon civilization."

"I can see that now." Filiz's gaze bored into Eureka, who raised her eyebrows as if to ask, *Are they here?* Filiz nodded subtly and looked toward the mountains.

"Open the cage," Eureka demanded.

"Your tears will unlock her cage."

Eureka would never cry to save Filiz. Filiz knew it. Didn't Atlas?

Again Eureka recalled Delphine's words that Atlas's heart wasn't tuned for love. In fact, he seemed to completely misapprehend it. He couldn't see what others saw so clearly. Atlas thought love was his subjects' affected adoration.

A flash of self-consciousness crossed his face as Eureka studied him. He drew a torch from its holder at the edge of the stage. The gossipwitches' amethysts glowed at the base of its flame. Atlas thrust the torch inside the cage. Filiz screamed as tendrils of flame found her skin.

Atlas withdrew the torch and looked at Eureka. He tipped the flame. "Again?"

"Oh, how I wish I were in the mountains my elders spoke of," Filiz said, rubbing the burnt places on her arms, staring hard at Eureka.

Could she trust Filiz? The two of them shared a murderous recent history. Was this a trick?

"If you like being burned, please continue discussing the mountains." Atlas lifted the torch, preparing to strike Filiz again. Eureka stepped between them.

She slapped the torch from Atlas's hand and shoved him. He stumbled across the stage. After he righted himself, he glanced quickly at the audience and forced a laugh. "So feisty!"

Buoyed by laughter in the crowd, Atlas grinned and picked up the torch. This time, as he approached, Filiz snapped her fingers, igniting a flame in her hand twice as tall as the one Atlas held.

"Was she not searched for fire starters?" Atlas roared at his Devils.

Before the Devils could answer, Filiz hurled her fireball at Alas. Eureka grabbed Atlas by his hair and made him duck. If the fire grazed him, Filiz would die.

The fireball flew into the crowd and landed on a man's blue fur coat. Atlas reached through the bars of the cage and grabbed Filiz by the neck.

"I'll do it!" Eureka shouted. "Don't hurt her. I'll cry."

"Eureka," Filiz warned.

An approving roar sounded from the crowd. Atlas watched them for a moment, then released Filiz. He straightened, smiled, and nodded behind him. Two Devils approached Eureka. One of them handed her a lachrymatory made of silver, woven with blond human hair. Eureka thought of Aida, whom Delphine's pain had killed.

"Not here," Eureka said to Atlas as she took the lachrymatory.

"But, darling, they have come for the show," Atlas said.

"I'm not an actor. What I feel is real."

"Of course." Atlas masked his disappointment. "Give her every comfort she desires," he announced before the crowd, then lowered his voice for the Devils. "I don't care what you have to do. Fill the vial by sunrise."

30

CRIMSON KISS

Eureka had to reach the mountains.

Filiz had given her a signal: answers awaited her in the gossipwitches' lair. At least, Eureka *thought* that was the signal. Maybe Filiz had been lying. Maybe Eureka was taking a hint that hadn't been dropped.

It didn't matter. Getting to the mountains was the only plan she had.

Once she got there, she might have to face four people she had loved and left behind. It would eat up essential energy. But Eureka had become skilled at shutting down her heart. She would take what she needed from the witches, then move on.

First, she would have to lose the Devils ushering her

through the coral tunnel. Six of them, armed with orichalcum billy clubs and crossbows tucked into sheaths sewn into the back of their crimson dresses. These girls were stronger than they looked. Their biceps flexed; veins protruded from their forearms. If they returned her to Atlas's castle, it meant the lightning cloak for Eureka.

"She's dragging," one murmured. "Trying to slow us down."

"Hurry up." Another girl gripped Eureka's neck and jerked her to the side.

Red coral stung the center of Eureka's brain. She hadn't seen the wall coming.

One of the Devils made a retching noise, and Eureka watched as the girl wiped blood off her hand. Eureka understood, dimly, that the blood was her own.

Something told Eureka to jerk her upper body toward the girl, who responded with a practiced block that sent Eureka to the ground. The Devils were trained for combat.

Eureka spat blood. The girl's feet inched away from where it landed.

Two Devils lifted Eureka under her arms. They walked her through the tunnel, farther from the mountains. Eureka wondered about the depth of their combat experience. They'd been frozen beneath the ocean for many thousands of years in a realm where no one aged or died. What cause could they have fought for, what enemy could they have killed? What could these girls know about loss? Eureka wanted to teach them.

She remembered Delphine's lips on Aida's cheek. Pain seeking pain in the astral light. Pain was power, Delphine had said.

"I need to rest," Eureka said.

"Don't respond," a brunette Devil said.

"Water." Eureka reached for a red leather canteen around the girl's waist. "Please."

"Atlas said she'd trick us."

"A dehydrated person can't cry," Eureka said. "If you want to keep your job, give me a drink."

She'd made them nervous. As the brunette slowly unscrewed her canteen's lid, Eureka dipped toward the other, a slender blond girl wearing blue-tinted glasses.

Eureka didn't know what she was doing. She thought about Delphine and her broken heart. She thought about Diana and the wave that broke her body. She thought about her own agony flowing across every day that followed. She kissed the blond girl's cheek.

Zzzzt.

Sharp pain filled Eureka's body as a vision filled her mind: A younger version of the blond girl was being dragged across the threshold of a house by older, laughing Crimson Devils. Before she could say goodbye to her family, the girl was flung into the back of a silver wagon. Eureka heard a door slam and saw darkness and felt sobs.

Back in the tunnel, the blond girl screamed, and Eureka screamed, and it lasted only a moment, but when Eureka's vision cleared she saw the Devil on the floor, convulsing, dying.

Eureka's pain subsided slowly, like a temper. She spent an instant admiring Delphine for silently enduring this agony when she'd killed Aida. Eureka was dizzy and wanted to vomit.

The canteen fell to the ground. The brunette Devil glanced between Eureka and her convulsing friend. She took a step backward.

"You're next," Eureka said.

She paused, fearing the pain killing the second guard would cause.

Thwack.

Stars exploded before Eureka's eyes as an orichalcum club hit the back of her shoulders. Eureka spun around, her lips homing in on her attacker. She shoved another Devil aside—and froze.

It was happening again. Her hands barely touched the girl—she was only trying to move the Devil out of her way—but the pain came, and then another vision. A wall of fire. A baby screaming on the other side of it. Then Eureka was in the mind of the Crimson Devil as a young girl, the moment she gave up on saving her baby sister, the moment she turned away and ran from the blaze into the night.

The girl in her hands dropped to the ground. Eureka's hands groped for another. It didn't need to be a kiss. When

342

she was enraged, all of her skin could kill. She was her own lightning cloak.

The club struck her spine. She howled and grabbed behind her, finding flesh. New pain. New visions. A boy and a girl kissing, hotly, madly, breathing fast. Eureka didn't recognize either of them, but she felt the pain of heartbreak and betrayal on behalf of the girl in her grip. She heard the club hit the ground, and then felt the girl slide, lifeless, from her hands.

Her arms flailed again, this time grabbing two Devils at once. Her vision hadn't cleared enough for her to see them, but Eureka could feel them writhing and, more keenly, she could feel the wild telescoping of their deepest agonies:

Fat. Dull. Worthless. A mother's voice branded one girl's heart.

And then a different mother, lying dead in a cold room, tiny embers of a fire remaining in the hearth. Blood all over the sheets. All over the Crimson Devil sobbing at the woman's side.

Eureka reached for more flesh, more pain. A bottomless hunger for agony grew inside her. Her vision cleared. She was grasping at air, alone in the coral tunnel. Crimson dresses fanned around her feet. Had she killed them all so quickly? One, two, three, four, five—

"Don't move," a voice behind her called.

Eureka turned and something blade-sharp bit her gut.

Wetness. Heat spooling through the fingers clutching

343

her stomach. Everything red. An orichalcum arrow lodged in her flesh. She grimaced and yanked it out. Green vapors swirled from her open wound. The glowing arrow was artemisia-tipped.

The remaining Devil stood twenty feet away, her crossbow resting on her shoulder. As Eureka stumbled toward her, she loaded another arrow, aimed shakily, and fired. A green flash bloomed through the tunnel.

Eureka ducked. Or maybe she fell. She was on her knees. Breath was impossible, a knife slicing organs. She saw an orichalcum club lying on the floor and thought of the organs and blood and bones mined to build it. She thought of those ghosts trapped in the Filling. Adrenaline rushed through her. She crawled on her knees and reached a hand around the Devil's ankle.

The pain of the arrow wound tripled as the essence of Eureka's agony flowed into the girl and the girl's agony flowed into her. This time the vision was of a dappled silver horse, stolen from the girl's family by the gossipwitches.

Eureka got up slowly. Artemisia clouded her mind. She took limited, shallow breaths, hardly enough to sustain her as she moved through the tunnel, away from the castle, away from the fantasy of guilt.

Nothing was real but her pain. When she exited the coral tunnel on the sand dune, she didn't believe it. She watched her fingers unbutton her shirt, her hands tie it around her chest to stanch her wound.

The moon looked like her mother's face. The roiling ocean sounded like her father cooking in the kitchen. But her father never sang when he cooked. What did she hear? It was so familiar.

Music from Delphine's waveshop boomed in Eureka's ears. Her other mother. Mother murder.

Brooks was in there. She wanted to go to him. No. She spat on the sand, disgusted with herself. She turned toward the purple Gossipwitch Mountains. The only way to release Brooks was to win.

She remembered the gossipwitch salve that had healed her once before. One foot in front of the other. Up the slope. Tripping over rocks. Trail of blood behind her. Clouds over the moon. The tide of pain was high.

〤

At last, Eureka saw the fire. Three gossipwitches sat in a bright circle, turning spits over the flame. She smelled roasted meat. She thought they were wearing purple. She thought she heard bees buzzing. She stumbled and caught herself on a massive rock. "I'm looking for my—"

"Haven't seen them," one witch said. The others laughed.

"Esme," Eureka said breathlessly. "Do you know where Esme is?"

The witches gaped at her. "You are not one of us. How dare you spread the gossip of our names?"

Eureka let herself slide down the rock. She crawled on her stomach toward the fire. The heat was calming and the pressure of the earth felt good on her ribs. Her mouth was filled with dirt. She didn't have the strength to spit it out. "You know who I am. You know why I'm here. You're home now because of me. Where are my family and my friends?"

"You gave them up, remember?"

Eureka closed her eyes. Her fingers worried the earth, feeling for a switch to shut everything off.

31

NOSTALGIA

Fingers parted Eureka's lips and a warm liquid filled her mouth. She swallowed once reflexively, then tasted the soothing caramel-chocolate broth and began to gulp.

She opened her eyes slowly. Ander leaned over her, smelling like the ocean. They were rocking, and for a moment she wondered if they were on a boat. His warm hand was on her forehead.

"I didn't think the dead could dream," she heard herself say distantly, which made her think of Brooks trapped in the waterfall in the waveshop. She yearned to go to him. But in the moments when her eyelids fluttered, she yearned for Ander, too. It made her feel weak, like she needed too much.

Ander's eyes shone with a tenderness Eureka didn't

comprehend. His love was a language she had once known, but now it looked foreign, a sign in a station she didn't understand.

"She's awake?" William's footsteps announced his arrival at her side.

Eureka sat up. She was in a moth-wing bower suspended in a vast purple cave. Her brother flung his arms around her neck. Claire was there a moment later. She let the twins hug her and she knew she was hugging back, but it didn't feel like hugging. She saw it from another perspective, somewhere far away, as if she were sitting on the moon, watching the children embrace someone they loved.

"I told you she'd wake up," William said.

"We're witches now!" Claire said.

"You lost a lot of blood," Ander said. "Esme found you on the mountain and brought you here. Her salve closed your wound."

A translucent layer of amethyst lotion faded into Eureka's torso. The wound beneath it was frightening.

"What time is it?" she asked.

"Late," Ander said.

"The arrow broke two of your ribs." Esme appeared behind Ander. "You are bruised, but you can fight."

"Pain is power," Eureka said. The twins gave her puzzled looks.

The cave where she'd awoken was a grander version of the witches' lair in the Turkish mountains. The walls were a lovely glittering violet, lit by blazing amethyst fires. The furniture looked as though it had been lifted from an expensive boutique hotel. Witches dangled from purple swings suspended from the ceiling and danced around the fires smoking long twisted pipes.

"Where's Cat?" Eureka asked.

Ander offered Eureka another ladle of the chocolate broth. "Cat stayed behind."

"What?"

"The Celans are building arks for the survivors of the flood. She wanted to stay and help. She thought she could use her quirk and the gossipwitch ability to fly to store up food before they left. It's the Waking World's last hope."

"So naive," Eureka muttered. She imagined Cat in Turkey, bees swarming her head, using her loving quirk to hand out cherries and hazelnuts to the people boarding the arks. She hoped her friend would crack a dirty joke at the end of the world.

"What?" Ander leaned closer to her.

"How did the rest of you get here?"

"We took Ovid's flume." Ander seemed surprised to have to explain. "Like we were all supposed to do."

Eureka shifted miserably. "But why?"

"To help you." He took her hand. "Don't worry about what happened when you left. We're together now, that's what matters. You got away from Brooks."

"Atlas," she said darkly. "Remember? There's a difference?"

"You don't have to push me away because you made a mistake."

"I know that." She groaned and flung back the fox-fur covering. "I have plenty of reasons to push you away."

"Eureka!"

"Dad?" She spun toward his voice and saw Ovid, reclined on a low lounge chair, surrounded by three witches. Eureka was surprised to feel disappointed. She thought she was done with that sort of feeling. Ovid wore her father's face for an instant before it cycled to feature Filiz's grandmother.

"I have to talk to Solon," Eureka said.

Ander helped Eureka from the bower. His assistance was infuriating, and she needed it. The witches snickered at her intensity as she hobbled toward the robot.

The robot twisted gruesomely. She saw her father again, then Seyma's features sharpened and dissolved. Then came the glower of Albion, the head of the Seedbearers.

"You ruined everything!" he shouted as his features melted into those of his cousin Chora. Eureka wished she had Delphine's jellyfish-tipped whip so she could get from the robot only what she wanted.

"Solon," she said, taking the machine's shoulders in her hands. "I need you. You said you were stronger than the rest of these ghosts."

After a moment of vague, featureless struggle, the lost

Seedbearer's eyes, nose, and lips solidified on the silver plane of Ovid's face. "The fugitive returns. Kill the fatted calf." He frowned. "Has Atlas got Filiz?"

"Yes."

"Tell me some good news." The robot clapped its silver hands. "What have we learned from the outside?"

"Atlas tried to blackmail me into crying by hurting Filiz."

The robot squinted. "How exactly was that supposed to work?"

"It wasn't," she said. "He thought I cared for her. He doesn't know what love and devotion are."

"Typical male?"

Solon was testing her.

"You asked me once what would happen if I allowed myself to feel joy," Eureka said. "Now I know. Delphine's feelings possess the same power as mine. I saw her weep with happiness"—she lowered her voice—"and her tear brought Brooks back to life."

"Where's Brooks?" Claire asked.

"It can't be," Ander said.

Ovid closed its eyes. Solon's voice said, "I never knew if the rumor was true. Tearline joy is so rare. Out of curiosity, what was it that brightened that dark heart?"

Eureka's cheeks flushed. "I called her 'Mother.'"

"So simple." Ovid rubbed its jaw. "Love never ceases to amaze me. Well, all you have to do is . . ."

"I know, cry a joyful tear to resurrect each of the billions of people I've killed," she said glumly. "And I have until sunrise."

"Sounds like a busy night, even for a party animal like you." The robot squinted at her. "You know, before now I had never considered how insignificant your eyes are."

"Thanks."

"For a girl whose tears do what yours do, your eyes are really very ho-hum. One begins to wonder—does it even need to be your eyes that shed the tears?"

"What do you mean?"

"I'm about to say something important, something I can recognize only now that I'm liberated from my wretched mortal form. This body"—it rapped softly on Eureka's wounded chest—"doesn't matter. If I were you, I'd give it up."

"And where do you propose she finds another?" Ander asked.

The robot leaned back on the lounge and cradled its head in its hands. It crossed its feet and put them on Eureka's lap. "Where Atlas would feel it most."

"I told you, I don't think Atlas *can* feel." Eureka paused to consider what she'd just said. She touched her neck, which used to connect her to Diana and the most primal love Eureka had ever felt. It was bare now. "That's it."

"What?" Ander said.

"Delphine told me Atlas's heart wasn't tuned for love," Eureka said.

"That sounds like something you say when the person you love doesn't love you back," Ander said. His tone pleaded for her to meet his eyes, to deny that she didn't love him. But she wouldn't.

"She was speaking literally," Eureka said. "Atlas's heart is out of tune."

"Is Atlas a robot like Ovid?" William asked.

"I don't think so," Eureka said, "but his heart was another one of Delphine's experiments. She did something to remove love from his range. If I can possess Atlas the way he possessed Brooks, the way he tried to possess you"—she looked at Ander—"if I can make him feel joy, make him cry with love, it would destroy him."

Ander studied her closely. "You used to want to redeem yourself, to fix the world. Now all you care about is killing Atlas? Do you know what it would mean to go inside him?"

"Her redemption and his death are tantamount," Solon said. "If Eureka succeeds in making Atlas weep with joy—she is right—the tears would be formidable."

"Powerful enough to reverse the Filling," Esme said in a quiet voice that suggested even the intimidating gossipwitch was sickened by Atlas and Delphine's plan.

"But what about *her*?" Eureka murmured. If Delphine was the darkness inside Atlas's shadow, she was the true enemy. She always had been.

"That is the question I've been waiting for," Solon said.

Eureka thought back to her last game of Never-Ever, played lifetimes ago on the bayou, when Atlas had used Brooks to hurt her, and she knew what she would do.

"We never see betrayal coming from the ones we love most," she said, and pretended not to see Ander shiver. She reached for one of the gossipwitch pipes, twirled it between her fingers. "But how do I possess him?"

Ovid pointed at Ander. "Ask him."

"No," Ander said. "I won't do it."

"You came here to help me," Eureka said. "What does Solon mean?"

"You die in this plan. If you go into Atlas's body, there will be no way out."

"Don't die, Eureka," William whimpered, and climbed into her lap.

She rocked her brother wordlessly and glared over his head at Ander.

"There has to be another way," Ander said. "I'll go with you. We'll fight Atlas and Delphine together." He gestured at Ovid. "We'll use their weapon against them."

"They have eight more machines just like Ovid, filled with millions of ghosts," Eureka said. "It wouldn't even be a fight."

"You underestimate me," Ovid said, in a voice Eureka couldn't identify.

"You already tried to kill yourself once," Ander said. "I won't let you quit again."

"I don't belong in the world I have to save," Eureka said. "This is the only way."

Ander shook his head. "I meant it when I said I won't live in a world without you," he said. "Eureka, don't you—"

Don't you love me? She knew that was what he wanted to say. She took his hand. "If you weren't a sun and I weren't a black hole, I would."

Ander's eyes were damp. She had never seen him cry before. When he turned away, Eureka was relieved. She was consumed by what she had to do, by the thrill of her discovery about Atlas. She thought of Delphine, more in love with her dark powers than she could ever be with another soul. Maybe they had more in common than Eureka realized.

She felt pressure in the palm of her hand. When she looked down, Ander was pressing the coral arrowhead, the tool Atlas used to enter his possessions, into her palm. It was stained with Ander's blood.

She rested her forehead on Ander's chest. They stayed like that for a moment. The throb of his heartbeat made Eureka's own heart race. Her breath picked up and stabbed her broken ribs. She pulled away. She gazed into his eyes and wanted to ask what he would do after she left, so that she could carry an image of him being okay in her mind. But that was selfish, and there was no answer, because everything anyone might do after Eureka left this cave depended on whether she succeeded or failed.

"Thank you," she said instead.

Ander shrugged. "It's not like I wanted it as a souvenir."

"I mean thank you, for everything."

Ander answered by sweeping his arm around her. He was careful of her ribs as he lifted her off her feet and brought her lips to his. They were locked in a deep kiss before Eureka could pretend she didn't want it. She drank him in—

And felt his joy. It came at her in a deep, profound rush, rejuvenating her soul the way the Crimson Devils' pain had crippled her. She followed Ander's lips around past moments of his brightest happiness.

Within their kiss Eureka saw herself as Ander had seen her: Through the dirty windows of her favorite diner in Lafayette, the Pancake Barn, whirling whipped cream clouds onto a short stack. Jogging along the bayou behind her house, her green cross-country sweatshirt flashing in and out of view among the trunks of oak trees. At the mall with Cat, doubled over with laughter as they tried on a store's most hideous prom dresses. On the brink of tears on the dirt road after Ander rear-ended her. Her teardrop on his fingertip. His breath against her cheek. *There now, no more tears.*

This was Ander's happiness. All of it was her. Eureka's heart burned with the urge to stay forever, and forever run away.

Ander pulled back first. She expected him to say something, but he stared at her with such amazement she wondered what his experience of the kiss had been, whether it was something he could give words to if he tried.

It was the last time they would see each other. It was so hard to make it end.

"Get to it, Reka," Ovid said in the guise of Dad.

From the back of the cave, Esme brought forward the enormous winged white horse, who neighed at Eureka and flicked her tail. "Let Peggy speed your way."

"I'm going to owe you for this, aren't I?" Eureka asked.

"If you succeed, we are the ones who will owe you," Esme said. "But you will be beyond us by then and unable to collect, so indeed, the gossipwitches will still come out ahead."

Eureka took the shivering moth-wing reins. She kissed each twin on both cheeks, making them giggle because no one had ever done that to them before. They hadn't had Eureka's mothers.

"When will you come back?" William asked.

"She isn't," Claire said.

William started to cry. "Yes she is. She loves us."

"If she loved us, she would stay," Claire said.

All her life, Eureka had cycled through the same logic regarding Diana. She didn't have an answer for William. It was not lack of love but a surplus that was Eureka's problem.

Esme picked up the little boy. She reached for Claire's hand. The witches were their mothers now, and maybe that was best.

"Please," Eureka said to Esme. "I'm all they have. I'm not enough. I brought you home. The least you can do is—"

"They are bright and their magic is valuable," Esme said.

"A prophet might say someday these mountains will bear the children's names. But you and I both know prophecies can be a drag." She touched the tops of the twins' heads. "They will flourish here."

Eureka hoped so. She hoped they all lived to be nine hundred and fifty, like Noah and his family had in another story about another flood. She hoped when she was finished with Atlas enough would remain of the world to shelter the bright and the magical. She hoped Ander would love someone else who could love him back as beautifully as he had loved Eureka.

She didn't say goodbye. That would have been a lie that she was caring, that she was kind, that she was something other than a mission. She mounted the white horse and rode through the moth-wing doors. She felt Peggy's wings spread above her in the brightening sky.

32

SUNRISE

From a casement in the highest tower of his palace, Atlas watched a pink sliver of light rise from the sea.

After Eureka and Peggy left the Gossipwitch Mountains they'd lost crucial time searching for the king. His castle was vast, its towers numerous, his Crimson Devils stationed in unexpected eaves. Then there were the king's gaudy wax replicas featured in most of the castle windows: Atlas aiming a cannon out of the armory at an invisible enemy; Atlas studying the heavens through a telescope on his balcony; Atlas corrupting a wax sculpture of an Atlantean maid against the windowsill of his bedroom.

At last, they found a brooding Atlas leaning out the tallest tower toward the ocean. Wind rustled his wild red hair. Eureka steered Peggy toward him.

Crimson Devils stood guard behind the king in what appeared to be a strategy room. Behind the girls, old men with plaited golden hair and red velvet robes gathered around a water map.

Peggy's coat was camouflaged against the travertine palace. She flew close to the walls, beating her moth wings, staying out of Atlas's view, brushing Eureka's legs against the palace every now and then.

"The arks are ready, sir," a male voice called from the room. "The last survivors will board by first light. Perhaps it is time you let the ghostsmith know Eureka is at large?"

Atlas stared out at the sea. The pink sliver of sun in the east had grown into a copper band. "She will come back. We have unfinished business, and she knows it."

"That's right, Atlas," Eureka muttered. "Let's finish it."

She clicked her running shoes against the horse's sides. Peggy swooped before the casement, directly in front of Atlas. A look of exhilarated intrigue crossed his face.

"Wanna get out of here?" Eureka asked.

"You know what I want," Atlas said.

A dozen Crimson Devils drew crossbows.

"Hold your fire," Atlas said, then, to Eureka, "You killed six of my guards, you know?"

"Surprised?"

"I'm getting over it."

"Then come on," Eureka said.

A very old man with long white hair called from the back of the room, "Sir, we must advise you—"

"Nice to hear from you, Saxby," Atlas said. "I was about to check your pulse."

"I'm going to cry for you," Eureka said to Atlas. "I want to. And I want you with me when I do."

Atlas pressed a hand against his heart. "It will be an honor."

"She's lying." An elegant Devil angled her crossbow at Eureka.

"If you shoot her you will spend the rest of your life beneath the lightning cloak," Atlas said.

Slowly, the girl lowered her bow.

"My subjects don't believe you," Atlas said intimately.

Eureka found herself flirting back. "I swear."

"On what?"

She paused, unprepared to take emotional inventory. What principle other than Atlas's destruction could she pretend to honor now?

"Swear on his life," Atlas said. "Brooks. When I was part of him you used to look at us in this very particular way. Swear on what was inside you when you looked like that."

"I swear on my love for my friend that I will cry if you come with me."

Atlas's minions pushed forward, jockeying to be included.

"Just you," Eureka added.

"Yes. Cozier that way." Atlas smiled. When he climbed onto the windowsill, Peggy flattened one of her moth-wing wings like a ledge. Atlas walked across it to meet Eureka. She held out her hand and was surprised his fit hers as snugly as Ander's had.

He slid behind her on the horse, pressed his chest into her back. She felt his heat. His arms encircled her waist. Her heart raced—not with fear, but with a strange thrill, like she was sneaking out with a bad ex-boyfriend.

They lifted skyward, above the sleeping city, passing through an innocent golden cloud on their way to their last stop.

⋊

Peggy landed on the beach. Her wings spun whorls of sand before resting at her sides. In the distance, the Gossipwitch Mountains glowed in the rising sun. The waveshop hung suspended a mile down the shore.

"I assume Delphine isn't joining us, but still working feverishly on the final robot?" Atlas asked as he helped Eureka off the horse.

Eureka shrugged as if she didn't care about anyone but Atlas. "This will just be us."

"Most of my fantasies start like that."

Eureka faced the ocean with a racing heart. "I need to clear my mind, to let the sorrow in."

"Happiness always overstays its welcome." Atlas drew a lachrymatory from his pocket. "Water is therapeutic in ways your world doesn't comprehend. We have powerful water shamans in Atlantis. If you need help—"

"I'll do it on my own." Eureka walked to the water's edge. It licked her toes, warm and wonderful. Soon she had waded in up to her waist. She let her feet lift off the sandy floor. She treaded toward Atlas, who had followed her. Their knees brushed below the water. "Would you turn around?"

"I thought you wanted me to see."

"Just for a moment." She touched his hand under the water. Her other hand gripped the bleached coral arrowhead stained with Ander's blood. "I promise it will be worth it."

Atlas faced the shore. His gold and red tunic rippled with the waves. Eureka took the tunic's hem and slid the heavy fabric up his back, along his shoulders. "Lift your arms," she whispered in his ear.

Goose bumps rose on Atlas's back. "You know how much I want this, but—"

"Shhh. Lift your arms."

He raised his arms and let her slip his tunic off. It sank into the ocean. Eureka caressed his back. Her nails etched soft pink waves across his skin.

"What are you thinking about?" Atlas asked.

"Terrible things." She raised the coral arrowhead. The

dagger that could carve a gateway for Atlas to enter Waking World bodies . . . and now she hoped it would do the same for her.

"Good," Atlas said.

She plunged the dagger into Atlas's back, enjoying the feel of his flesh catching the blade, giving way. His scream rang out. He spun and lunged as Eureka darted underwater.

She had not swum without her thunderstone in a long time. Salt stung her eyes. Atlas's blood clouded the water. From below, she watched him thrash, then lost him in a pool of panicked splashing.

She twirled, anticipating his attack from all directions. Her lungs burned with the need for air, but surfacing would be surrendering. Atlas could swim like a shark.

She had more work to do. Ander had only one set of gill-like slashes—and had not been possessed. Brooks, who had housed this monster's mind inside him, bore two sets. If Eureka wanted to get inside Atlas, wherever he was, she had to cut him a second time.

A jet of hot blood spooled over her shoulder. Eureka turned as Atlas's arm closed around her neck. She tried to swivel free, but he held fast. Her dagger stabbed at the water, his body barely out of her reach. She bit his forearm. Her teeth touched bone. Atlas squeezed her neck until she gagged on bloody water.

His other elbow crushed her nose. She felt the heat inside

her head, tasted thick blood in the back of her throat. Her vision blurred. Blood was everywhere. She clasped her dagger tightly as Atlas pumped his legs to reach the surface.

When they broke through he released her neck, grabbed her wrists, and tried to wrest the dagger from her.

"I hope that felt good," Eureka said. "Because I'm about to do it again."

"I can take what I want for free—or you can pay to part with it." Atlas drove the hand holding the dagger toward her neck. "But I will have your tear."

Eureka laughed as the dagger sliced her skin and more blood flowed into the ocean. "Yes, you will."

She strained forward and snatched the coral dagger from her fingers with her teeth. When Atlas dropped her wrists to grab it, she slipped underwater. She swam toward him, a piranha with a single tooth. She found his back. With a nod of her head, she tore into his flesh.

The dagger plunged deeper than she'd expected. She still held it in her mouth, but Eureka's face now felt like it was a part of Atlas.

She felt something lift away, and then she felt nothing—at least, not in any way she was used to feeling. It had taken forever and happened so soon:

Eureka was inside the monster. Everything else was gone.

His interior was an ocean, barbed with reefs of dead coral, sharper than the dagger she'd used to cut her way inside, sharper than anything she'd ever conceived. What once she would have seen with her eyes and felt with her body, Eureka now sensed with her mind. All feeling had disappeared, replaced by a new *knowing*.

Then the coral slashed her thoughts—and Eureka could no longer . . . remember . . . her mission. She blacked out on a sharp shore inside him.

⋊⋉

"Aaughh!"

Her mind screamed, using someone else's voice. She struggled to recognize the sound: Atlas's lips. Eureka's emotion.

The dagger had worked.

She tried to keep her thoughts still. They were all she had left of herself and they were in peril. Slowly, she allowed one in. . . .

Face him. But as soon as Eureka thought it, she lost the ability to concentrate. Her mind had known deep pain before—shame, grief, desolation—all incomparable to this. The reef inside Atlas murdered thought, slicing it into unrecognizable shards the way a dead reef she'd once snorkeled over in Florida had sliced the flesh of her thighs. *Face him* had been removed from Eureka's consciousness, an urge she'd never considered.

Somehow she knew she had to ascend the bladelike reefs. Without a body, she would have to think her way up—but how? When thoughts died on this reef, she wouldn't get them back.

This was what trapped Brooks, she thought. Then that thought met the reef with a deadly, thunderous boom. It was mutilated, lost, and Eureka could remember nothing for a long while.

><

Slowly, painfully, an idea came into focus: for much of Eureka's life, she had loathed herself. No shrink had ever found the pill to change the fact that her heart was a tank full of hate. Finally, it might do her some good.

I can't, she thought with purpose—an experiment.

When that rush of negativity left her mind and was shredded upon the coral, Eureka forgot a portion of her heavy fear. She had sacrificed it to the reef. She sensed herself moving higher inside Atlas.

Selfish.

Hypersensitive.

Suicidal.

One by one she acknowledged her deepest doubts and hesitations. One by one they left her, crashed upon the reef, and were destroyed. The dark echo of *Suicidal*'s death rang in her mind as she rose toward the surface of Atlas's inner sea.

There is no way out. Someone she used to love had told her that. She couldn't remember who. Then the reefs slaughtered the sentiment, so it didn't matter anyway. Her mind climbed the last barbed branches of coral, amputating one last long-held fear like a useless limb.

Joy is impossible. . . .

Suddenly she saw through Atlas's eyes. It was like her mind had fired across the synapse that connected thought to sight. It reminded Eureka of looking through the peephole in a hotel room door. She saw the red inner rims of his eyes framing a world painted different colors than the ones she used to see. The greens were saturated, the blues profound, the reds pulsing and magnetic. Her new vision was strong. She saw every scale of each darting fish. She watched an elderly gossipwitch ascend a distant mountain peak, and admired every golden fold of her jowls.

She stood waist-deep in the water and took a moment to inspect her new body, her taut thighs and the foreign flesh between them. She touched the muscles on her smooth, bare chest, the stubble growing on her cheeks. She made both of her biceps bulge. She yearned for someone to fight. With Atlas's camouflage she was liberated in a new way. She could be as ruthless as she'd always needed to be.

She scanned the beach. A turquoise palm tree swayed in the wind. She felt an irresistible urge to unbuckle Atlas's belt and pee on that tree. She laughed at the dumb cockiness of the idea when she still had so much to accomplish, such important tears to make him shed. And then she did pee, right there in the ocean, because she was inside a boy's body and it was insane. She slipped her pants down, freeing the most thrilling part of Atlas, and let go. She lifted each of her legs. She swiveled her hips. She made an arch in the shape of a rainbow.

When she was finished, she probed her back, touching the wounds she'd dug. They were numb. The coral dagger still protruded from Atlas's flesh. She pulled it out. Her new mouth screamed, but that was Atlas's reflex, his suffering, not hers.

"You're out of your depth," the lips of her new body said. It was Atlas speaking.

Her eyes went blurry, then her view of the beach was torn from her as her mind flowed backward onto the sharp dead coral below.

"Still want my tears?" she tried to say, but the words slurred, incoherent, from Atlas's lips. Moving his limbs was easier; she didn't know how to make Atlas's body talk convincingly. Yet.

What if he's right? Eureka gave that anxiety to the reef, using it to thrust her mind forward, crowding Atlas's dark, furious thoughts—*destroy her . . . punish her . . . how?*—until she forced her mind behind his eyes, and sensed his desires falling beneath hers. She hoped they shattered on the reef.

A corpse floated before her.

It took a moment to recognize it as her own.

She used to be the girl who looked like that. Moments ago, she'd had long, ombré hair, a bloody nose, skinny arms, and muscular legs. She'd had a beating, aching heart even though she'd tried to deny it. She checked her old body's pulse with Atlas's fingers. Nothing.

She had done it. Eureka Boudreaux had discarded herself. Her old blue eyes were open. They were the color of her father's eyes and their point of view wasn't hers anymore.

Eureka realized that even at her most extremely suicidal, she had never wanted to die. She had really wanted *this*, escape from a fixed identity, the chance to be many things at once—a bitch, a nymph, an artist, an angel, a saint, a strip-mall security guard, a tyrant, a boy. She had wanted to be loosed from the narrow way her world defined "Eureka Boudreaux." She had wanted to be free.

Her vision blurred. Atlas's desperation layered over hers. The mind that had possessed a thousand other bodies didn't know how to rid itself of one possessing his. His hands grabbed her corpse. He took his fury out on it.

His fingers tore her throat, ripped her skin apart, tore into the cartilage of her neck. His fists rained down on her brittle ribs, cracking what the witches' salve had half mended. Eureka didn't stop him; she knew nothing would bring her body back. She relaxed into his rage, curious when and how he would exhaust himself.

She'd been wrong to think he had no feelings. When

Atlas's emotions erupted, they ruled him, the way falling in love with Ander had ruled Eureka. He knew rage but not its opposite. Eureka would guide him so deeply into joy that it would kill him—and, she hoped, raise the souls inside the Filling to a higher place.

But first she had to say one last goodbye.

33

WATERFALL

Eureka swam toward the waveshop as a king.

Every few seconds her vision blurred, and the ocean reeled with Atlas's rage. The only way she kept his thoughts at bay and her own thoughts above the reef was to focus on reaching Delphine. Soon Eureka could hold Atlas's mind off for a full minute. Then for three.

She came up for air, treaded water. She practiced making words coherent. "I'm almost through with you," she said.

She scanned the beach. The Gossipwitch Mountains loomed ahead. She thought she would have made it closer to Delphine, but she didn't see the suspended wave. She flung Atlas's foot over a sandbar and stood up, chest-deep in the ocean.

Lightning struck the water twenty feet ahead. But the sky above was clear. Something golden bobbed in the waves. Whatever it was had caused that lightning. Eureka swam toward it and discovered Delphine's loom.

She trained Atlas's remarkable vision on the beach. The naked body of a boy lay on the sand. Was it Brooks? No. The boy's skin was silver—a ghost robot. She waded forward, dragging Atlas's gaze across another robot, also sprawled upon the shore, perpendicular to the first. Soon she'd counted more robots. Seven of them were splayed, motionless, across the shore. Their bodies had been purposefully positioned, limbs extended at odd angles, to collectively create a design.

Or rather, each body had been stretched to form a letter. The ghost robots spelled a word.

Even if Eureka had never seen the labyrinthine written language of Atlantis on the pages of *The Book of Love,* her Tearline intuition would have decoded the message in the sand. The word was missing its last letter, but she was able to grasp its meaning.

The transliteration sounded something like *Eur-ee-ka.*

It was Atlantean for *joy.*

Atlas roared, and Eureka felt her consciousness shoved backward within him. She saw only white and knew she was soon bound again for the coral as Atlas screamed, "Delphine!"

Eureka willed her mind forward to the place from which she could manipulate Atlas's body. She focused on ramming his fist into the center of his face. When she succeeded, she felt no pain but knew he did from the way his thoughts faded and her vision of the beach returned.

"Don't make me hurt you again." Her words in his throat sounded clearer, expressing the perverse flirtation she'd intended.

Movement at the crest of a sand dune—near the palm grove Atlas's vision painted turquoise—caught Eureka's attention. One ghost robot chased another. Their bodies were identical, but the pursuing robot was special: Ovid wore Solon's features as it lunged to grab the legs of the other robot and brought it down upon the sand.

Solon was the inscriber of the message in the sand. He'd withheld the meaning of her namesake until now, when she could use it. Did it mean he still believed in her?

The other robot struggled, then straddled Ovid's chest and wrestled its arms into surrender. Its fingers searched the sand and found a heavy rock. Eureka held Atlas's breath as the robot bashed the boulder into Ovid's head.

Sparks flew. Eureka couldn't see Ovid's face crushed beneath the stone; it was wedged deep into wet sand. She didn't know if ghost robots died, but she could see that Ovid would never rise again.

As the victor rose from the orichalcum carnage, Ovid's arm glided toward its opponent's face and touched its cheek, a gentle caress. Then it jabbed two fingers under the robot's jaw and twisted them into the infinity-shaped keyhole Eureka knew marked its neck. The ghost robot keeled over onto Ovid's chest, as if in an embrace. Neither of them moved again.

"Delphine!" Atlas's mouth shouted. "She will betray you—"

To quiet him, Eureka slashed Atlas's cheek with the coral dagger.

At the far end of the beach, where the waveshop had once been, Delphine lay on her back. Waves lapped her long hair. Brooks straddled her, a shocking, erotic pose that sent jealousy surging through a fault between Eureka's and Atlas's minds.

But something separated Brooks's and Delphine's bodies. Eureka had to get closer to see what it was. She dove back into the ocean, drawing all of Atlas's speed as she swam.

"Delphine!" Atlas shouted as soon as Eureka surfaced.

Her dagger slashed his other cheek. Blood rained upon the water.

At the sound of Atlas's voice, Brooks lifted his gaze. His eyes darkened with a hatred Eureka reminded herself was not meant for her.

Brooks had pinned Delphine to the beach beneath the same waterfall that had once imprisoned him in her waveshop.

"Where is Eureka?" Brooks and Delphine asked in unison.

"She is dead," Eureka said about herself to her best friend.

"No," Brooks said. The waterfall fell from his hand. It smoked and boiled and disappeared into the ocean.

Delphine pushed him aside and splashed toward Atlas. Her skin was one great greenish-purple bruise. Her hair was a matted nest stuck to her cheeks, and her red lipstick had smeared to a bright pink smudge that reached her chin.

"I decide who is dead," she said.

In her new body, Eureka towered over Delphine. She was amazed by how delicate, how fragile the ghostsmith appeared. She grabbed the back of Delphine's head, drew her pink lips forward, and kissed her deeply on the mouth.

Eureka had no body to feel pain, but she could sense the rapturous ache explode in Atlas as his mind was blown back to the depths of his being. Then came the vision Eureka had feared since she decided to kiss Delphine to death:

A cave within a rainy mountain range. A fire bright in the hearth. Love thick as honey in the air. A baby cooing at her mother's breast. And then, in a flash of lightning, the baby was gone. Wrapped in a fox-fur blanket, tucked in a young man's arms. The man ran down the mountain, toward another world.

Leander . . . Come back . . . My baby . . .

Delphine's original misery flowed into the recesses of Eureka's mind. It was supposed to empower Eureka as she absorbed it, as it killed Delphine. That was what had happened when Eureka kissed the other girls. But this was different, deeply intimate, like losing Diana a second time.

Delphine was the origin of everything Eureka hated about herself. She was the source of Eureka's darkness and her flood. She was also Eureka's closest family, her Tearline and her blood. There was no choice to reject or embrace this connection—both were happening all the time. Eureka and Delphine belonged together. Both of them had to die.

She cradled the ghostsmith, kissed her harder, more passionately. She sensed Atlas's body grow faint. Delphine's eyelids twitched. Her veins lit up like lightning and her skin began to smoke. Charred flesh bubbled along her body like rivers of tar. Atlas screamed as his lips and hands felt the burns, but Eureka would not let him let go.

The ghostsmith fried from the inside. Eureka didn't stop kissing her until she slackened in Atlas's arms and, eventually, was still.

At last Eureka pulled Atlas's lips away and dropped the ghostsmith's sizzling, blackened body in the water. Pieces of her floated away. Eureka wondered briefly about the fate of Delphine's ghost.

"There is one death the ghostsmith doesn't get to decide," Eureka said, and wiped Delphine's kiss from her mouth.

Rough hands shoved her—shoved Atlas—so hard Eureka fell backward in the water. Brooks leapt on top of Atlas, wrapped his hands around the king's neck. Eureka's mind clouded from the lack of oxygen.

"Brooks!" she gasped. "It's me."

"I know who you are." He plunged her underwater.

"It's Eureka!" she spat when she surfaced. "I possessed Atlas like he possessed you. Stop! I'm about to—"

He plunged her down again. She didn't want to fight him, but she had to. He could not drown Atlas before she cried the tears that would release the wasted dead. She kneed him fiercely in the groin. He reeled away and Eureka came up for air to find him on his knees, wheezing.

"If I weren't me, would I know you were born at nine thirty-nine p.m. on the winter solstice after putting your mom through forty-one hours of labor?"

Brooks straightened, stared into Atlas's eyes.

"Would I know you used to want to be an astronaut, because you planned on sailing around the world after college and didn't want to reach an end to exploration? Would I know roller coasters scare you, though you'd never admit it, though you've sat next to me on every one I've ever ridden? Or that you kissed Maya Cayce at the Trejeans' party?" She wiped Atlas's wet face. "Cat told me. It doesn't matter."

"This is a trick." There were tears in Brooks's eyes. Not sadness, she sensed, but hope that it was *not* a trick, that Eureka was not actually gone.

"Would I know you took theater for three years because I had a crush on Mr. Montrose? Or that you're afraid your dad walked out because of you, but you never talk about it because you've always seen silver linings? Even when all I am is a rain cloud?" She paused to catch her breath. "If I were Atlas, would I know how much Eureka Boudreaux loves you?"

"Everyone knows that." Brooks cracked the briefest smile.

She clasped Atlas's hands to his heart. "Please don't kill him. If you do, I'll never have a chance to make things right."

Brooks waded closer. When they stood inches apart, he closed his eyes. He squeezed Atlas's hand, which was strong and muscular, a boy's. He let go and drew his hand near Atlas's face but didn't touch it. When he opened his eyes, Eureka watched him struggle to see her spirit.

"What now, bad girl?" he asked.

She laughed with unexpected relief. "You've been inside the Filling. . . ."

Brooks nodded, but seemed reluctant to elaborate, or to remember.

"Delphine brought you back with a special tear. If I can do the same from inside Atlas, I can mend some of what I broke. You were right, there's no way out for me, but maybe there's hope for the rest of the world."

Her vision blurred and she lost sight of Brooks. She thought it was Atlas surfacing, but quickly realized someone else now shared his body.

"Did you think I'd simply die and go away?" Delphine spoke through Atlas in a slow, terrifying voice. "I am the puppet master. I get the last word. This has always been my story to complete."

Eureka took control of Atlas's voice. "I know how your story ends." She fought Delphine for Atlas's eyesight. Brooks was a dim, distant throb of light at the end of a dark tunnel.

"You made an enemy of other people's joy because it threatens you. But I'm giving it back to Atlas. I'm going to make him feel so much it undoes the ghastly things you and I have done."

Atlas laughed with Delphine's icy viciousness. "You don't have it in you."

The ghostsmith resurrected the sharpest doubt, what Eureka thought she had shredded on the coral reef. Eureka's sadness had caused so much pain. How could anyone reach the level of joy needed to undo that? Fear sent Eureka's mind reeling toward the knife-edge of the dead white coral, but just before it cut her thoughts apart, her vision focused briefly. . . .

She thought she saw Brooks take the dagger from Atlas's hand.

Don't, she tried to tell him, but she'd lost control of Atlas's voice.

Then Atlas screamed, and something bright drew near Eureka's mind, something that hadn't been there before. It felt—even though she could not feel—as if someone had taken her hand. Brooks had discarded his own body and entered Atlas, too.

You're not supposed to be here, Brooks.

I'm supposed to be with you—she sensed him all around her—*until the end of the world and the ride home after.*

It *was* the end of the world, and maybe the beginning, too.

Brooks had found Eureka when she needed a lift more than anyone ever had.

Joy hatched at the back of Atlas's throat. Eureka sensed from his body's stiffening that the king had never cried before. When her tears sprang in the corners of his eyes, they were joyful—but they were also vulnerable and rueful, yearning and optimistic.

No emotion was pure. Joy was grief turned inside out, and grief was joy in different lighting, and no one could feel one thing at a time. The tears she'd cried when she flooded the world must have done some good somewhere, because they were tears born of love for Brooks. Those were the tears that brought Solon's wisdom into her life, the tears that had allowed Cat and the twins to discover their quirks. They were the tears that freed Ander from Seedbearer bonds.

Keep going. She felt Brooks urge her on, even as she knew he knew she couldn't stop. Her mind was a waterfall of memories: The twins sharing a swing under a powder-blue canopy of sky. Diana slinking behind Dad in their old kitchen, adding too much cayenne to his soup. Rhoda cleaning closets. Eureka running and running and running across bayous into sunsets. Climbing oak trees to meet Brooks at the top of the moon.

When her tears hit the ocean, they parted the water at Atlas's waist. A wave pulled back and crashed over his head. For a moment, all four minds inside Atlas swam as one to propel his body above the surface of the sea.

But the sea was no longer the sea. It was a field of blooming white narcissus, buds tangling higher every moment, stems growing wild along the shore, planting roots among the limbs of empty ghost robots.

Then the buds blossomed into people, who turned to one another, old souls in a new world bursting into bloom. The promise of a fresh beginning glittered in everyone's eyes like dew. Tears, Eureka realized, each one a maze of infinite emotions.

When a rainbow colored Eureka's vision, she realized she was witnessing her redemption bloom into the world from above. She was free. But if her joy had killed Atlas, where was his corpse? And what had become of the ghostly, disembodied minds of Brooks and Delphine?

The Gossipwitch Mountains stood below her. She saw the twins, rainbow-hued and running to the edge of the witches' lair. When they saw the endless garden of blossoming souls, Eureka felt their laughter buoy her.

A girl in a brilliant purple gown stepped from the cave to join the twins. Esme smiled and caressed the hollow of her neck where an iridescent black pearl sparkled on a silver chain. Smoke rose from the pearl, and Eureka grasped the darkness trapped inside. Delphine and Atlas had been returned to a new Woe, crystallized inside the gem. The Tearline prophecy was complete and would decorate no heart but Esme's ever again.

A little ways away from Esme and the twins, Ander stood alone. He gazed upon what Eureka had done and wiped away tears. She wished their love could have followed an alternate history, one where Eureka was still at his side, but sometimes pain was the aftershock of love. When Ander's foundation stilled, she hoped there would be space for joy in his memories of her.

Soon she saw the rings of Atlantis. Huge wooden arks fanned across a bright blue bay beyond the island. Eureka saw Cat at the helm of one, flirting with a sailor. And far beyond those boats, new worlds were rising, flowering into being, coastlines budding with souls Eureka didn't recognize and never would. Dad would be down there, though she couldn't see him, along with the rest of the souls once trapped by her tears. She wondered if Dad remembered all that had happened, how his dying message to Eureka made the difference in the world's salvation. She tried to let him go with love, just as he'd done with her.

Then Eureka was in the rainbow. She was a memory of something poignant reaching across the sky, crossing a flock of doves. She knew she was stretching toward Diana, and that they'd soon be reunited, excavating Heaven's pearly clouds.

Are you still with me? Brooks found her on the bars of color Eureka thought she'd been climbing alone. She thought about his first name, which she rarely did.

Until the end and the ride home after, Noah.

Acknowledgments

Eternal thanks to my readers: you have opened your hearts to Eureka and bravely shared your own love stories. I'm always here.

To Wendy Loggia, whose faith in this story nurtured my own. To Beverly Horowitz, whose insights are precious gems. To Laura Rennert, whose counsel makes the highest mountain a gently sloping hill. To those who touched this book at Random House and at Andrea Brown—I'm honored to work with the best.

To Blake Byrd, who took me on the sailing voyage that inspired Eureka's. To Maria Synodinou in Athens, for your conviction about Atlantis. To Filiz at Sea Song Tours in Ephesus, for a mystical afternoon. To Tess Hedlund and Lila Abramson, for connecting me to what matters. To Elida Cuellar, for an essential measure of tranquillity.

To my family, for knowing the drill and loving me despite the racket the drill makes. To Matilda, for new eyes. And to Jason, for exploring with me all the wondrous fruits of love.

About the Author

LAUREN KATE is the internationally bestselling author of the TEARDROP and FALLEN series. Her books have been translated into more than thirty languages. She lives in Los Angeles. Visit her online at laurenkatebooks.net.

Follow Lauren Kate on

FALLEN

LAUREN KATE

'Sexy, fascinating and scary'
P.C. Cast, author of the *House of Night* series

Some angels are destined to fall . . .

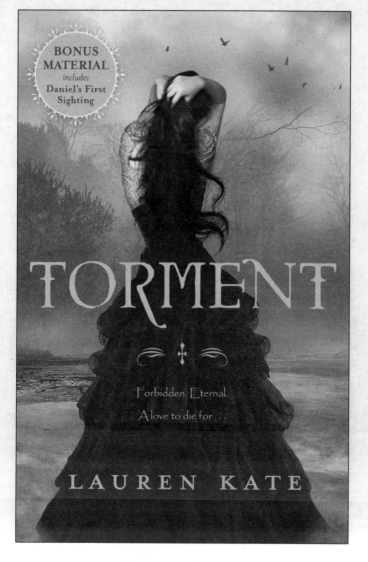

BONUS
MATERIAL
includes
**Daniel's First
Sighting**

TORMENT

Forbidden. Eternal.
A love to die for . . .

LAUREN KATE

Love never dies . . .

"*Every single lifetime, I'll choose you.*
Just as you have always chosen me. Forever."

ALSO BY LAUREN KATE

In the fight for Luce, and for love, who will win?

ALSO BY LAUREN KATE

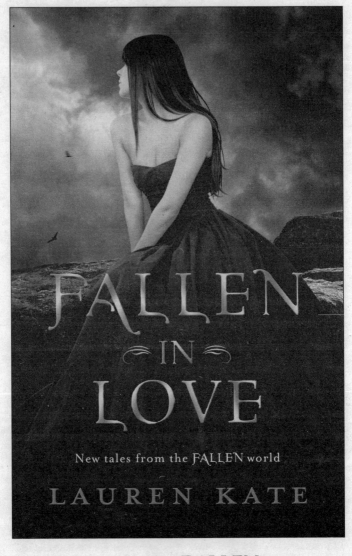

New tales from the *FALLEN world*